T0022480

'An ode to grief and sibling love from a great new voice writing about our messy and uncertain times.' Kit de Waal, author of *My Name Is Leon* and *Without Warning & Only Sometimes*

'A beautifully layered story about the complexity of relationships, political and sexual identity, loss, activism, familial love, being European, Brexit chaos and living in Brighton. Poignant, astute and hopeful.' Sharon Duggal, author of *Should We Fall Behind* (a BBC Two Between the Covers Book Club Choice)

'Bedford achieves a rare feat with this novel: he writes about disappointment in a way that is highly compelling. *A Bad Decade for Good People* is a fascinating exploration of political hope, friendship, difficulty, infatuation, and unrequited desire.' Naomi Booth, author of *Exit Management* and *Sealed*

'This captivating novel is a reminder that love, coupled with courage, just might conquer all.' Heidi James, author of *The Sound Mirror*

'Deeply, profoundly human, while at the same time precisely capturing the essence of a time and a place, *A Bad Decade for Good People* is one of those books which genuinely seems to fabricate a whole world. In prose that is subtle, deft and unobtrusive Joe Bedford's debut leaves the reader heartsore in exactly the right ways.' Will Burns, author of *The Paper Lantern* and *Country Music*

A BAD DECADE FOR GOOD PEOPLE

JOE BEDFORD

PARTHIAN

Parthian, Cardigan SA43 1ED
www.parthianbooks.com
© Joe Bedford
Paperback ISBN: 978-1-914595-55-4
Ebook ISBN: 978-1-914595-56-1
Editor: Robert Harries
Cover Design: Emily Courdelle / www.emilycourdelle.com
Typeset by Elaine Sharples
Printed by 4edge Ltd, Hockley
Published with the financial support of the Books Council of Wales
British Library Cataloguing in Publication Data
A cataloguing record for this book is available from the British Library.
Printed on paper that meets FSC standards

For Anna

A man that is born falls into a dream like a man who falls into the sea. If he tries to climb out into the air as inexperienced people endeavour to do, he drowns...

Joseph Conrad, *Lord Jim*

If the policeman's baton had found Laurie half an inch lower she would be blind in one eye. Instead it left her with a long, crescent-shaped scar, which she wore like a medal, never hiding it and never knowing how it made my stomach flip. Every time I saw it I had to shake off the memory of her blood running down over her eyelids and onto her jacket, and afterwards the stitching and the gooey rivets it left behind and the halo of yellow bruising that hung around the socket for weeks.

Her scar was all I could see while she pleaded with me by the side of the road, until we were lit in the headlights of Dad's car and then running, slipping, gripping each other's clothes in the ditch. I remember the sound of Dad's voice carrying over the hum of the engine, the faint warmth coming through Laurie's jacket as she held me, the smell of mud and silage. The hills opposite looked like the silhouette of a man sleeping on his side, cut against the stars – the kind of thing you notice at midnight in the countryside, with someone who makes you feel as though things could be better. That and the raw feeling that your failure isn't yet total but just another blip in time, waiting to pass.

We tried not to laugh aloud as Dad stumbled back into his car, slammed the door and sped away. After that Laurie was earnest again and pleading for me to pack it in at the pub and come away with her to Brighton, where she'd found the perfect place for us to *carve something out*, her words. Where Helena was waiting, whose name she couldn't mention without smiling.

'I just want to make it right,' I said, but she didn't recognise my guilt, never could.

She just pointed the torch up to her chin and pulled a face, which forced me to laugh. The stars above her head disappeared and I saw the long, moon-shaped line of damage illuminated above her eye. *Half an inch lower, that eye would be blind*, I thought. Then she'd be someone else and I'd be someone else. Though she'd always be my sister.

1
SOMEONE ELSE

2016

When summer arrives in Brighton, it bursts all over the city like a paint bomb. That year, summer came early and when it did the city seemed to breathe a deep collective sigh of relief. The pavements filled out with people blinking in the sunlight. I watched them on the promenade, stopping to take pictures of the white light skimming across the sea – the same people who'd bustled about under brollies all spring, now dry and warm, walking with free and easy steps. All different now the weather had changed, just as Helena had promised.

I watched them idly while the sun went down over the Lanes, shuffling along the queue for a cab on East Street. You could call it bacchanalia – the life of the place as its doors and windows begin to open. It's the feeling that this is how the city should be at all times, the city at its most natural, when the dusk no longer drives people indoors but draws them out.

Certainty, liveliness and comfort. And underneath, just the ghost of a feeling that at any minute one mighty gust of wind might blow all the colour from the streets.

Though not tonight.

The party was at Duncan's – a friend of Helena's who lived with a few others in a disused school building on the edge of town. The corridor looked almost identical to the one Laurie and I had marched down as teenagers – mottled carpet, scuffed blue walls skirted with white. A sign on the wall reminded guests THIS IS NOT A SQUAT, though that's what Laurie had led me to believe. There was a message about their landlords – a property company that rented out empty buildings to vetted tenants. Something I'd never heard of. EU flags led down to the assembly hall, along with calls to VOTE and DONATE.

It was Helena who invited me. The invitations normally came from her and then Laurie would follow up to insist. For two months Laurie had tried to sell me house parties as *underground get-togethers* and pub drinks as *action meetings*, and assured me that the marches and demos would pick up once the weather improved. She said our night at the school would be a chance to make plans for the referendum campaign. Though even as I followed the dizzy calypso music down the corridor I was relieved to see I was walking into just another party.

There were no crisps or balloons in the assembly hall but neither was there any daggering or smack. Just forty-odd people standing around drinking Jamaican lager under Remain campaign banners and Laurie, a head taller than most of them, polemicising under the climbing ropes. She stood with the same old over-wide posture, legs apart, elbows too far out, a slight stoop at the shoulders. Identical to the day she stood up to a PE teacher who was telling me off, physically stood up to him, eye to eye. Big-sister stuff. I tapped her on the shoulder and she turned and grabbed me so that the bottles in my carrier bag crashed together. She wore her jacket that night – one of a pair, hers and mine. I should have expected that.

'*George, George, George, George.*'

She gave my smile a gentle slap and waved Helena over. Helena had a semicircle of boys around her cawing with laughter, but when she saw me she bowed out quickly and skipped across. She gripped me harder than my sister had done, even ran her fingernails up the hair on the back of my neck. She told me while still holding me how nice it was to see me, and how she was so glad I could make it, as if there was any danger of me rejecting one of her invitations.

Laurie was excited to tell me she had a canvassing thing lined up for us the following week. She blabbered the whole thing but I got the gist.

Helena interrupted her with a kiss. 'Sorry, George. She's always on politics, whenever we come here. Help me out, won't you.'

I laughed. 'What can *I* do?' I'd hoped we could keep her off the referendum, at least to begin with. Slim chance.

'George understands,' said Laurie. 'And don't forget,' scrunching her face, scary monster, 'he's my *little* brother.' She squeezed my neck into a headlock, really squeezed. I wrestled free.

'So aggressive,' muttered Helena, and then hooked us by the elbows. 'Let's find Duncan.'

People parted for us as we walked – it made me feel like someone who was meant to be there. That feeling came from Helena, I knew that. She gave it to everyone.

A slate on the door of Duncan's room read HEADMASTER. Two plastic seats were bolted to the floor beside it, just like the ones Laurie and I had occupied so many times while waiting for a bollocking. I remember how she'd taken a hardback from the school library and ripped it in half, vertically down the spine, with one strained motion, and how the librarian had burst into tears. No one but me understood why she'd taken that particular book, with Tony Blair's face on the cover, after I'd made a short, impassioned speech on Iraq that she translated into instant physical violence. The spine tore in her hands like cotton.

Her voice was hot in my ear. 'We'll chat later,' though really I'd be happy if we could get through the night without talk of demos, protests, riots. Still, I nodded firmly – *oh, hrmph, yes, of course* – and Helena pushed open the door. The first time I ever entered a headmaster's office of my own accord.

Laurie had let me kip on her floor when I first moved down, and only after several weeks of double shifts at the bar did I manage to move into a bedsit of my own. I was happy to hold my own set of keys – the first set of keys I called mine since university, with no debts to anyone, even if the place was poky and overpriced and faintly damp. *Lower ground floor*, meaning *below the ground*. 'That's Brighton,' so I was told. I slept in a sleeping bag at first, then on a single mattress from the BHF on London Road. If I'd taken the job at LSE I might have had a studio in South London by now, but I tried not to think about that. Actually it was only when I walked into Duncan's bedroom that I realised just how frugally I'd been living for so many years.

His bookshelves overflowed with records and tatty orange paperbacks. Framed posters and postcards covered the walls – Votes for Women, Rock Against Racism '78, *Coal Not Dole*. I was immediately jealous of the desk at the far end of the room, a huge thing with decanters, papers and a green blotter.

That was about the only thing that looked like it belonged in a headmaster's office, and even that had a kind of Tony Benn feel to it. I didn't see Duncan until he was already marching towards us from the record player.

'Here he comes,' I said.

Duncan was an eyeful of a man at all times, a living billboard for that kind of lifestyle. He really did march across the carpet like a comrade-in-arms. He performed continental air kisses for Helena – *mwah, mwah, mwah* in the Russian style – and I thought for a second he was going to do the same with Laurie but they settled for a hug. Firm grips, white knuckles.

'Ah, George.' He saluted. 'Welcome to headquarters.'

'Thanks for having me.'

'Fair few *reds* floating around tonight,' winking, 'keep your wits about you.' He always underplayed the London N1 in his accent, but it was still there. Laurie didn't seem to mind and neither did I. He was charming and I liked it. 'What's in the tote?' he said.

'One red, one white.'

'Grand. Cava first though – we're keeping Lidl in business this year. Champagne socialists, aren't we just?'

He drank from an old-fashioned champagne coupe cupped in the palm of his hand. Behind him I recognised Marta at the desk, his new *fellow traveller* as he put it. She wore dungarees and a headscarf in Catalonian yellow and red. I didn't know the guys she was with.

She spotted us, scooped up three fresh glasses.

'Marta, *estimada meva*,' Duncan said, though by her sympathetic smile I guessed this was the only Catalan he knew and possibly incorrect.

She kissed him, then me, then turned to watch her friends stumble off towards the main room. One of them – a little guy in a leather jacket – held on to the other so tightly I thought they must be an item. Good-looking couple. Marta reassured us: 'He's fine. Antonio's getting him some water.'

And then it was the five of us, the core of the group, so it felt like, the ones who were always there – Laurie and Helena, Duncan and his latest *fellow traveller*, and me. Marta had a gentle way about her that I took for deep, instinctive kindness. She handed me a glass.

'Thank you,' I said. 'So decadent.'

When Helena took hers she eyed me and said *Designed after Marie Antoinette* and pushed it to her tit so that the skin around her cleavage was sucked into the glass. There was a brief moment of electricity, which I tried to dampen with laughter, but already Duncan was tugging his collar and shaking his head like *There goes the neighbourhood*. After he poured out the last dribble of cava for us he lifted his coupe for a toast and I met eyes with Laurie across the circle. The look on her face then, in the headmaster's office with her new friends who I think by then had already accepted me, was the same look of gratefulness she'd looked up at me with from her hospital bed at Whitechapel. Six years ago now. She looked at me like something had been achieved, like she was fulfilling a promise to me. Though up until I arrived in Brighton I had wanted it to be the other way around.

Duncan was following the referendum closely for his blog – *Left Nut*, silly title – and was always fired up enough about it to set my sister off. After that it was Helena's turn to step forward and keep everything together. She had a gift for that. I would watch her friendly, easy disposition get even friendlier and even easier, and notice how good she made people feel about themselves. She knew about socialism and Scottish independence and the names and voting records of all our shitty MPs. Laurie listened to her with such silent respect it was like watching her in front of Chomsky or Žižek, though without the spittle. Seeing her there, so unusually placid while Helena spoke, made it feel like the versions of ourselves we had left behind in the village were a million miles away. Until Duncan set her off again with his little rousing indictments.

'...a way for Tory backbenchers to manoeuvre themselves into power...'

And that kind of talk.

This party was no different – we rallied around the referendum for several hours while people came and went and the party slowly filled out, until around midnight when I found myself on the bed between Laurie and Helena. Laurie was reiterating the mantra she'd developed at school and never abandoned – *I want change, I want a revolution* – and Helena listened patiently.

'There's just so much stuff to organise. I know everybody is trying to play down the danger here, and yes, I'm sure everything is going to be fine, but...'

I had half an eye on Duncan who was spilling white powder onto his blotter. That was his scene as well, along with the politics. Marta sat on his lap, stroking his ear.

'...and honestly, now George is here we'll be able to do so much more. George has a real head for these things, don't you George? You should have seen us at school...'

As the powder disappeared up Duncan's nose, his face rose and his eyes locked on mine. Then he was coming over.

Laurie sat up straight and shuffled to the edge of the bed for him to sit. Duncan fell onto the mattress with a thump that jogged half the drink out of my glass. He lay there quiet and grinning, a loved-up moon face, and asked what we were talking about.

'London,' said Helena.

Duncan swooned. 'Old London town. *Viva la* revolution.'

'Oh, yes,' I said. 'I forgot you two lived together. Where was that?'

'Islington,' said Duncan. Which was, I thought, where his dad worked as a councillor for the Greens. 'This wench made it half bearable.'

'Forget about London.' Laurie gripped my arm. 'It's grim. Brighton is much more committed, I think. Much less cynicism.'

Duncan laughed. 'Well, you're bound to dislike London if you only ever go up when they're rioting.'

Laurie had told Helena the story of her scar more than once when I was there and probably again when I wasn't. She'd told others as well – Helena's friends, friends of friends, strangers at parties. I wanted to escape but I was squished between them on the bed and I could feel the booze flushing in my face.

'That was in 2010,' she said. 'I've been a few times since then.'

'George was there too, weren't you, darling?' Helena stared at Laurie's scar, and then her eyes fell on Marta, the new girl. I knew I'd have to take my punishment.

'I didn't know that was your cup of tea,' said Marta.

'Well, actually,' said Laurie, 'it was George who saved me from getting more fucked up than I did.'

I squirmed to show I wanted to leave. Nobody moved.

'Come on.' Duncan seemed happy to listen too, though he'd already heard it. 'Tell all.'

'Never mind that,' I said. 'Marta, I want to meet your—'

But Laurie was ready to spill. 'That was my first time in London – I think it was probably the first big protest we ever went to together, wasn't it?'

And so I was picturing it too, whether I wanted to or not.

I had run for the train that morning, even though it was me who suggested we join the march, and sat wheezing on the floor of the carriage while Laurie bought my ticket. I was supposed to be at sixth form – seventeen years old – and she was ecstatic that I'd suggested I bunk off so we could go together. We wore our denim jackets that day, the matching ones.

The crowd felt like a mosh pit, with all the middle fingers and the shoving. It was me who was curious to get to the front, Laurie who pushed us through to where the crowd was thickest. There were placards about tuition fees and austerity, and the red smoke of a flare blew over the heads of the students and anarchists and all the normal people who felt betrayed by the Lib Dems jumping into bed with the Tories. Same way Laurie felt. Behind the demonstrators I could see the riot police in their shields and helmets, and behind them the horses and vans and more journalists. The cameras made the whole thing feel like a film set.

We'd been side by side, Laurie and I, until the first baton cracked against the skull of the boy beside us in a clear, lone sound that never left me. The boy fell back against me – I let him fall – and the crowd tried to scatter. I felt the panic of being pushed towards the police, with their stern eyes behind the glass, like being herded off a cliff. Screams, blood and my hands raising above my head. And then my sister was lost.

'Anyway…' Laurie spun the yarn for the group on the bed. By now Marta was all ears and I was wriggling, writhing, praying for an excuse to leave. 'I don't remember much after that. Whitechapel Hospital was where I woke up. I woke up and this lovely bastard was already there. Watching over me.'

'Well, I—' But the shame of it caught in my throat.

'That's so inspiring,' said Duncan. 'Ken Loach could have written that.'

I stuttered. 'She's making it sound more dramatic than it really was.'

'I am not.' Laurie gripped her jacket. 'George dragged me right through the line after I got my head bashed in, right through to where the paramedics were.'

'Laurie, please.' I tried to sound light. 'You're embarrassing me.'

'What? No! You're a bloody hero.'

'A bloody hero,' Helena smiled.

What Laurie didn't know was that I'd thrown my jacket into the conifers at the end of our driveway after finding a spot of her blood on it. I pictured the mulch of it decaying into the clayey West Sussex soil, its denim threads passing slowly through the earthworms, beetles, bacteria. It made me want to throw up. Duncan squinted as though he'd finally picked up on the ill look on my face, just as a blonde girl in a beret fell onto the bed, hissing something very urgent and garbled. The rest of us clambered up awkwardly, tipping each other off balance with the movement of the mattress. The blood rushed to my head.

Duncan turned to Laurie directly and gestured towards the door. He said discreetly: 'I think something's going down in the main room.'

Laurie took me by the elbow and pulled me with her. The exodus from the headmaster's office was total.

'Thriller' played in the assembly hall, months off-season, and as the music cut out we pushed through the crowd under the sound of Vincent Price's laughter and nothing else. Everyone was staring at something going on by the opposite entrance. An opening formed in front of us, with Laurie physically moving people aside. Duncan held Marta's hand. I followed behind. In the silence the disco lights blinked epileptically.

A semicircle had formed under the climbing ropes. Clinging on about ten feet up was Marta's friend, the boy in the leather jacket. He was shouting in a language I couldn't understand, and laughing and hiccupping. I looked around for his friend, the one Marta had called Antonio, but he'd disappeared.

The boy slipped, people gasped, my nerves leapt. He didn't fall. That sobered him up, I think, because then he came down slowly, hand over hand. When he reached the ground, he picked out Duncan and stepped right up into his face. The force of it knocked Marta back – she fell into Laurie's arms. Marta wriggled free, wouldn't let Laurie hold her. Something must have caught her septum piercing because blood splashed down over her lip. It compounded the spin in my stomach. I noticed the pins and badges on the front of the boy's jacket – CND, PLO, ANL. He looked Duncan in the eye and said *Fucking fakes* in a deep, wet slur. Duncan faltered, Helena pulled him back. And then the circle was empty, except for me, at the front, and the boy in the leather jacket. He looked me in the eye. I looked for somewhere to vomit.

I heard my sister's voice behind me. 'Don't worry, George.' I glanced back and she looked like she was itching to get involved but Helena was holding her hand now. Beside them, Marta wept in Duncan's arms. The boy took no interest in them, only in me. I was tipsy, more than tipsy. My brain tried to focus on the chipped paint on the wall of the assembly hall but my body remained in the moment. People were shouting *Just leave!* but the boy wasn't listening. No one was touching me now; I was in limbo. The centre of the circle. The boy with the badges walked forwards and the nerves ran through my mind like *Christ what's happening I thought Brighton was supposed to be a lovely place* and then we were touching nose to nose.

I just stood there, head spinning, waiting for the violence. I felt like I'd already been punched in the stomach. The only inclination I had – the only thing my body was telling me to do – made no sense at all, but it was rising in me and it was strong and loud and I could feel it taking over. Where it came from, I had no idea – maybe from the booze or my panic or wherever – but I rose onto my tiptoes, just for a second, and kissed him gently, mindlessly, quite sweetly, on the nose. After that the silence was very real, except for his little flurry of fingers, rubbing his face like he'd been stung by a bee. I jerked back, slipped and fell. Then there was a hand reaching down to me, its palm hot and wet, dragging me up. I blinked the blotches from my eyes.

The man named Antonio stood in front of me in a heavy cloud of aftershave, so strong it crinkled my nose. His eyes found mine and held me there – steady and open and his face still and purposeful. He looked at me so intently it was as if everyone else around us were actors rehearsing an awkward drama and a firm, competent director had appeared to readjust the scene. Like the only one of us without a costume.

He put a firm hand on his friend's shoulder. '*Amigo, puedo ver que eres una buena persona, pero incluso debes…*' He spoke directly to him, extraordinarily fast, punctuating his words with his free hand while he gripped the boy's sleeve. He whispered and jabbered and sighed. The boy looked confused but Antonio kept talking, faster even, laughing at points. We all just watched.

The boy turned as red and shiny as a strawberry. He tried to turn away but Antonio lightly twisted his leather lapel so that a badge tinkled to the floor. '*Nunca, nunca, nunca debes tratar a las mujeres de esta manera.*'

Then he clicked his fingers and the boy lowered his head and walked away towards the corridor. We stood waiting and everything was quiet except for the sound of Marta heaving in Duncan's arms.

Before anyone moved, the man named Antonio turned towards us and said in firm but broken English: 'I am a-sorry.' He was quietly proud and I hoped and expected he might say something more, but he didn't. He simply bowed, turned and followed his friend towards the exit, stage left.

Duncan was the first to move, shouting something like *Good riddance*, and then Marta, who hugged him even tighter, and then Helena, who threw her arms around Laurie and kissed her fiercely — something so passionate I thought I shouldn't have seen it. I could see then what Laurie meant to her, how they kept each other safe. And then Helena was off again and laughing and making things well. We looked together then, the group, with everyone huddling around me and congratulating me for my kiss as if after some kind of victory. My heart rushed a little, being in the centre of the circle, just by being surrounded by my sister and these people who I liked and who knew how to be exciting. It felt like the way things were supposed to be.

At the back of them Laurie simply stood there, her eyes moving between me and the gently swaying ropes, holding my eye for just a moment.

'I was there, okay? I would have sorted him.'

The adrenaline ran through to my fingers. 'I know.'

'No, I mean it. I'm always here for you, George.' She grabbed my head. 'I love you. I'm so happy you're here.'

I nodded and wondered, only briefly while fingers ruffled my hair and the rest of the assembly hall erupted into joyful gossip, whether this was all part and parcel of the bacchanalia, the life of the place and the bubble of its politics. A continuation of the party.

I kissed my sister on the cheek. 'I love you too.'

Laurie was always protective of me, and it made no difference to her that she was a girl and I was a boy. If any of the kids at school brought that up, it got even worse for them, and she knew how to dish it out. She didn't let Dad get away with that either, even though since Mum left she had been the only girl in the house. The only *woman*, I mean, after she turned about eleven.

Dad never laid a finger on either of us, never even raged at his most sloppy drunk. I don't believe he had it in him. And for all his grunting skinhead manliness he wasn't angry when Laurie came out to him, same evening I told him I wanted to study in Wales. He only laughed and said he was *glad one of us is getting some pussy*, and Laurie took me by the hand and we stormed out to the conifers at the end of our cul-de-sac – the place we always talked things over. She was sorry she hadn't told me first, though I knew. The boys at school had already started teasing me over it – crude words that struck hairy images in my mind. I knew Laurie had slept with a couple of girls already, and she knew I'd never got more than a snog off one. Later at Bangor I only lost my virginity because I knew how late I was losing it, and after that I felt relieved and a little sick. I rang Laurie about it and she congratulated me, though she also told me she hadn't slept with anyone since school. Not until Helena. They met at a human rights thing in London and after that they'd stayed in touch and Helena had moved down to Brighton and Laurie had decided to follow her.

It was Laurie who walked in on Mum that time, with someone other than Dad, just a few weeks before she flew off to the South of France. I was too young to remember.

Summer in Brighton, a few weeks since Duncan's party. I still had the image of that guy, Antonio – his calm face, which had floated between me and the violence – sitting at the back of my mind. Under one of the Dutch elms that line the Level park, I opened a can of posh lemonade, Laurie opened an energy drink, and we looked out over the naked bodies in the sunlight.

There were two hundred of them at least, mounted on bicycles or standing casually beside them, chatting away like it was any other day. It was a sea of body paint and banners, flab and saddles, spokes and ribs. Everywhere I saw penises of all sizes and shapes, and breasts and vaginas and pubes. There were young people who might never have been naked in public before, and old hippies with bags of skin. Over them hung dozens of flags, all limp in the still air, and banners with the words VOTE REMAIN. They weren't linked, the Naked Bike Ride and the campaign, but something about them seemed to intersect, at least in Brighton, where spirits were high. Eleven days until the vote, and still it was only Laurie who seemed worried about it.

She stood with her hands on her hips, clothed – *Thank God* – taking it all in. Inside me, the novelty of the day and the nerves of being in a crowd fought for control. I looked over the bodies for anyone we recognised, though I didn't want to catch anybody's eye directly. More cyclists edged towards the start line, due to set off shortly.

'Over there.'

Laurie barged through the crowds – not maliciously, just carelessly. The same way she'd charged through the playground at lunchtime with me in her wake. I could see it bothering people, their eyes turning on us. I manoeuvred carefully through the bodies but contact was inevitable. I felt a patch of someone else's sweat wet my T-shirt.

'There they are.'

We found our friends at the opposite edge of the park, close to the start line. Helena wore a sports bra, Marta a white T-shirt that made her summer melanin pop. She'd finally got a flat, just that week, and already she looked more well rested. After however many weeks living sixteen to a room in a backpacker's hostel, I was unsurprised she didn't want to get naked in public.

Helena kissed Laurie on the neck. She must have tried to convince her to join – she'd certainly tried to convince me – and now Laurie was saying how happy everyone looked and maybe she should have gone for it after all. Which was bullshit. The crowds surrounded us on all sides, swelling slightly as they had at the riot in London, at the beginning.

Marta asked if I was alright.

'Me? I'm fine. Where does the bike ride go, exactly?'

'All through town. Then we join the beach at Black Rock and have a dip in the sea.'

Helena added: 'There's a club night afterwards.'

'Sounds squishy,' I said.

As my eyes wandered over the cyclists preparing to set off, I did a double take and froze in place. Laurie was already staring.

Emerging from a lull in the procession, Duncan strode across the grass pushing his bike by the seat, lifting his free hand to tweak his workman's cap at somebody in the crowd. His body was pale and patchy with dark hair. The line of a long tattoo snaked out from one of his wellies. He walked proudly, defiantly, as if knowing that everybody would notice the length and heft of his penis. I stepped back with my tepid lemonade in my hand and he passed to give Helena a hug, her bike in between them. From the way she looked at him I guessed that she'd already seen him naked, that they'd already got past any of that in those *London years* when she slept with men. She was always open about that, though she'd never mentioned Duncan specifically. At least not to me – it was none of my business. Laurie put her energy drink on the grass to applaud.

I joined her. 'Duncan. Good to see you. Well, all of you, apparently. Bravo.'

He offered me his hand and as our palms squelched together I thought *God what else has this hand touched?* I made a conscious effort – desperately conscious – to maintain eye contact throughout and then, when he wasn't looking, wiped my hand on my shorts.

He breathed the sweaty air. 'Lovely day for it. Shame I'm the only one who's gone full Godiva.' He whispered something in Marta's ear and she nodded and smiled. By then everyone was saying how he was *serious about this one*, though I didn't know him well enough to tell. He looked disparagingly at mine and Laurie's clothes. 'When will you two get your kit off?'

I swallowed a big gulp of lemonade a little too vigorously, felt the cold of it sitting in my stomach.

'Sorry,' I said. 'Other plans.'

Laurie had arranged for us to post Remain leaflets through the letterboxes in Whitehawk. I think she was put out that no one else offered to help – if anyone had I might have been able to skip it myself. Even Helena said she needed the day off. So it was just me and Laurie, and the others apologised and made plans that in eleven days' time we'd all get up early and go down to the polling station together, draped in blue flags, to cast our votes. The next day, after the results were in, we would celebrate.

Helena pouted. 'So serious.'

'Shame,' said Duncan as he straddled his seat with a lunge.

But it really wasn't.

Helena had told me she'd be going nude for the bike ride but I guess she'd changed her mind. Which was fine by me. Being naked in public – sober and during the daytime – is beyond me, and I was relieved when an air horn sounded and the riders at the front edged away.

We applauded the elderly especially and I was embarrassed to catch eyes with an old man in a military beret. A gap appeared behind a happy family all cycling together. Across the line I had a clear view of the spectators opposite, also clapping and cheering. Among them, standing at the front in reflective sunglasses, I saw someone I recognised – a tall dark man with a smile on his face.

If I'd come across him somewhere else he might have been lost forever. In fact, if the city had remained as it is in winter, with the whole population hiding indoors, that might have been the case. But in Brighton, in summer, it's impossible to walk around for long before bumping into someone whether you're trying to or not. I knew already by then that Brighton is in so many ways just another village, where the same people make the same circles, revolving around each other like horses on a carousel.

Antonio was fully clothed, drinking cider, apparently by himself. His black hair looked sleek in the sunlight. I waved at him but I couldn't see where he was looking through his sunglasses. No one had seen him since the party in May – he and the drunk guy had checked out of Marta's hostel the day after.

I nudged Laurie. 'Look, it's him.'

'Who?'

'Him. The guy from the party.'

Laurie didn't understand. I watched Antonio applauding with his can under his arm.

'Wait here,' I said, and then slipped in between the moving bicycles.

He stood still as I approached. I saw myself reflected in his sunglasses, peering at his face. I felt the nerves of the day melt into a little flush of curiosity. 'Remember me?' I said.

He pulled off his glasses and narrowed his eyes. Dark and direct, severe even. The man without a costume. His aftershave stung my nostrils as it had before. The smell of it seemed to fit with his crow's feet, the grey in his hair. Older than I'd noticed in the dim light of the assembly hall. For a moment I thought he was going to turn me away. Then he pointed his finger in my face.

'Yes.' He pronounced it *Jess* with an absurdly hard J. 'To the party. You was on the floor!'

I laughed. 'I was at the school when your friend – well,

when your friend had one too many. You were there with Marta and Duncan, I think.'

He smiled but evidently he had no idea what I was saying. I'd forgotten completely that he'd broken up the fight without a word of English. I glanced back at Laurie but she and Helena were falling over each other at some private joke.

'Sorry, I didn't give my name. I'm George.'

'Antonio.' His hand was rough and firm.

'Antonio, nice to meet you. Where are you staying now?' I wasn't sure whether he was still at the hostel, or had left because of the fight or for some other reason. But he didn't understand my question.

I asked again: 'Do you have a flat now?'

Still blank.

'Apartment?' I tried.

'Ah, *no*. One other hostel. Hostelpoint.'

Which meant he must have been living in hostels for several weeks at least. Duncan had done a *Left Nut* piece on long-time hostel guests, migrants looking for jobs, saving money, living day to day. I'd been in any number of hostels and guesthouses for the six months I'd been abroad after university, moving from place to place, and had found it hard enough. I couldn't imagine living indefinitely in a hostel, trying to eke out a normal life as Marta had done in Brighton. It would suffocate you.

'Are you here alone?'

He didn't answer.

'*¿Solo?*' I tried.

'*Ah si, estoy solo. ¿Hablas español? Todos mis amigos están en el trabajo pero yo aún no tengo trabajo. En realidad, he estado buscando algo…*'

'Come,' I said. 'Come with me. Marta and Duncan are here, and the rest of our friends. *Amigos.*'

He thanked me and then walked directly out in front of the naked cyclists, stopping them with a wave of his hand. They skidded and wobbled and struggled to avoid him. I followed behind him laughing and apologising and tripping up.

The sun was still rising and the morning was getting hotter. I found Marta dabbing a spot of chain oil onto Duncan's nose while he laughed, sent off a tweet, slipped his phone into his wellie. He had ten thousand Twitter followers apparently, not that I spent much time on there.

'Do you remember this guy?' I said.

He bowed to Marta and greeted her in Spanish – she was genuinely pleased to see him. When Duncan spoke his friendly patter came out with forced charm. I'd seen this happen before, when he wanted to impress people. I wondered if he felt any self-consciousness about his exposed penis now. If he did he showed no signs of it.

'Pleasure to see you again, brother.' He doffed his cap. 'Forgive the formal attire, won't you?'

I wanted to introduce Antonio to Laurie but she and Helena were still laughing together and staring into each other's eyes. When they finally turned, they looked at him just as Duncan had done – like his presence required a quick gathering of thoughts. Maybe because he was good-looking, maybe because he was older.

'This is my sister Laurie and her girlfriend Helena,' I said.

He shook their hands, looked Helena and her bicycle up and down.

'You…' Again the hard J as in *Jew*. '…cycle… in the race…'

She laughed. 'Yes.'

'*¡Pero!*' His arms flailed in mock indignation. 'Why so much clothe?'

'Yes, Helena,' Duncan chided. 'Why so many rags?'

Laurie tensed up beside me but even she must have been able to tell by Antonio's tone that he was only joking.

Helena laughed. 'And why yourself?'

'*¿Yo?*' Antonio presented himself with a bow. '*No tengo bicicleta. Pero, pero, pero…*' He wedged his cider between his knees, crossed his arms to the hem of his shirt and pulled it with one deft stroke over his head. 'This is Brighton?'

The girls applauded and Duncan hollered *Respect*. Antonio's skin was rich and rough with several wide scars across his chest. He stood proudly with his hands on his hips, chin pointed in profile. He glanced at me like I might follow, and then Laurie, but neither of us moved. That was when I regretted we had things to do.

Helena toyed with the lip of her bra.

'This is Brighton,' I suggested.

With the same fluid movement she pulled off her sports bra and swung it above her head. Duncan made a deep bow of worship. Antonio and Marta cheered and I did too, seeing how happy and comfortable she was, until I noticed that Laurie wasn't making any sound at all. Helena came up to her, pecked her on the cheek and offered her her bra without a word. Laurie placed it in her bag with the leaflets and turned away to check her phone – or pretend to.

Helena winked at me before turning back to *ding-ding* the bell on her bike.

*

We waited while more of the riders set off. Flab, saddles, hair, paint. An old man in budgie smugglers passed close to us, dragging a trailer with heavy speakers behind his back wheel. Hard techno music came between us briefly — one solid clattering rhythm like someone banging on sheet metal — and then receded into the parade.

Helena asked Antonio where he was from.

'*¿Yo? Soy español*, yes.'

'Whereabouts in Spain?'

'*¿Dónde?*' Antonio clutched his heart. 'Guadalupe, *en* Extremadura.'

Guadalupe. I picked out the sound of it. I thought Guadalupe was an island somewhere, or maybe a Mexican woman's name. I was going to ask but someone jostled between us — a fully clothed, middle-aged man in sandals and socks. His camera had an expensive-looking lens attached, and after clicking repeatedly at a female cyclist he looked down at the pictures, pushed a few buttons and waited for the next young woman. I saw a few men across the park doing the same thing — all middle-aged, all fully clothed. Laurie squinted — it took her a minute to process. Then the photographer stepped out from the crowd as our friends moved to depart and openly took a picture of Helena and her bare breasts.

'*Oi*,' said Laurie.

The photographer ignored her. I recognised the look on Laurie's face. Helena just laughed.

'*Oi*,' my sister said again, her chest inflating.

'Hold on, Laurie,' I said. 'Excuse me.' The photographer ignored me too, and that got my own anger up. '*Excuse me.*'

I couldn't contain Laurie much longer, but before anything happened Antonio stepped forward, cupped the photographer's lens in his hands and shook his head.

'No. You cannot.'

The photographer tried to pull away but Antonio kept touching his camera.

'You cannot. Not to *fotografía*.'

Laurie seemed to have no idea whether to take it further – neither did I – while Antonio spoke Spanish quite calmly to the photographer, who couldn't understand and just kept saying *Be careful, that's very expensive.*

Helena laughed. 'Our friend has a very pronounced sense of right and wrong.'

Duncan sniffed in approval. 'Well, if you're going to take pictures, why don't you take your own clothes off?' He gave him a pose of sarcastic smut, quite lithe.

A few people around us joined in with the heckling until the photographer was surrounded by the noise of *Off! Off! Off! Off! Off!*, with Antonio still trying to extract the camera from him. Laurie lurched forward with her fist raised but I stopped her. We watched Antonio hold the photographer's eye and then slowly take the camera into his hands. He held it out for Helena.

'*¿Borrar?*'

Laurie asked me what he was saying. I shrugged.

'*Borrar. ¿Lo borraremos, vale? Borrar.*'

'He's asking if you want to delete it,' said Marta.

The photographer made a weak grab for the camera but

Laurie held him back at arm's length. I felt a bubble of courage in my stomach. I had no idea what to do with it.

Helena spoke calmly. 'Give it to me.'

She took the camera, pressed a button and gave it back to Antonio. Before Antonio handed it on he turned it towards the photographer, drew a big excited smile and took the man's picture. Then he gave back the camera and the photographer slinked off into the crowd.

The people around us were laughing and a few of the other men with cameras were edging away. Helena thanked Antonio, so did Marta – none of them seemed upset by the incident. They would have ridden off quite happily with the photographer snapping away, but since Antonio had chosen to intervene it seemed like an unidentified wrong had been righted. He took his accolades silently, almost disinterestedly.

Laurie thanked him but there was no slap on the back, no handshake. Antonio simply lifted his cider and the two of them turned away from each other. I opened my mouth to invite Antonio to help us with the leafleting. But for whatever reason, perhaps because the fact that Laurie hadn't touched him was stuck in my mind, I told him to take my number instead and offered to meet up with him soon. Already, feeling it without thinking it, I knew I wanted us to be friends.

Antonio took the number. '*Jess*,' he said. 'Very, very, very good,' with a soft B sound on every single V.

We left him there watching the cyclists depart, and walked slowly up the hill towards Whitehawk. The sun beat on my head and my lemonade was spit-warm, but I was happy. The anxiety of the crowd had vanished.

'Nice guy,' I said to Laurie. I could still smell his aftershave.

'Yes. Nice guy.'

'How many leaflets do we have?'

'Two hundred.'

'We're a shoo-in.'

The noise of the cyclists followed us up Edward Street. Horns and bells and music.

I said: 'Duncan has a very large penis, doesn't he?'

Laurie shook her head and laughed. 'Fucking monster.'

I thought about Antonio on and off, just in brief moments while I helped Laurie and the others make preparations for the celebration on Friday. That face was still stuck in my mind – that drawn, old-world face that I'm sure had a story to tell.

There was a group chat about the party that someone had named *Remain Party Victory Party*. It pinged off so often I had to mute it. Marta posted a picture of herself with her big Spanish guitar – she was preparing a special performance with a few other acts. Helena planned to make a speech, Duncan said he'd bring bunting. I wanted to contribute myself but I had no idea what to do except turn up wearing blue.

Antonio's message came a few days before the vote. The surprise of it jogged me awake at six in the morning. Half asleep, I read and reread the muddled syntax of Google-translated text.

It was nice to meeting you last week at the nude bicycle event.

Perhaps we can take a beer on the beach and I can improve my English. I will buy you beer, Hove Lawns beach on Thursday 23 midday. That will be good.

Then a separate message several hours later.

I am Antonio

Thursday was the day of the vote. I'd already told Laurie I'd follow them all down to the polling station so we could cast our ballot together. But now the sheen to that idea had faded. They'd be talking politics all day, and Laurie would be especially fired up, and the rest of them would be overly excited about something that for whatever reason didn't really grip me. I knew it was important and knowing it was important made me feel guilty about not being invested in it like Laurie was, but a part of me wanted to skip straight to Friday's celebrations. Then again, I'd already promised Laurie I'd be there.

I only made my mind up that morning, Thursday 23 June, when Antonio sent me a picture of his long fingers around the neck of an open beer bottle and his bare brown legs stretching out towards the sea. Even then I didn't make my mind up so much as follow the unexpected feeling in my chest.

I messaged Laurie.

Go on ahead

I'll swing by later x

I found Antonio laid out in the exact position of the picture he sent, staring at the burnt-out skeleton of the West Pier. He was on the stretch of shingle opposite Hove Lawns, where the tourist barbecues peter out and the sound of the waves is stronger and clearer. Though the sea was quite calm that day, and all I could hear was the faint sound of traffic from the main road and the splashing of an old woman in a Union Jack swimming cap. Otherwise we were alone.

'Antonio?' I said it as if I didn't recognise him.

He clambered to his feet. His shirt was unbuttoned and I could see the thick black hair in a wet diamond across his chest. I flinched when he hugged me, and felt awkward when he held on to me too long. I could smell the sea on him and underneath that the aftershave lingering on his clothes. Yes, I was pleased to see him, but I was also English. When he let me go I saw his broad, open smile. He sat back down without a word.

At first he said nothing at all and I thought *Maybe we aren't actually going to talk, maybe we're just going to sit here*, which went against every bone in my body. I was ready to ask him a question, any question, when his phone rang and he spoke quickly in Spanish and then hung up.

He sat up and said with genuine sincerity: 'I am a-sorry.'

'That's fine.'

He held out a beer bottle for me.

'Are you sure?' I said. 'Is it too early?'

'Take.'

So I took it. With the heat on my back and the condensation dripping over my fingers, I felt suddenly like I was in an advert.

'Look this.' He scrolled through his phone and found a picture of a teenage girl standing with her arms outstretched under a goalmouth. Gloves, shin pads, the full kit. A dusty pitch. He held it in front of me for several seconds. I thought *God, if this is his girlfriend I'm leaving*. He kissed it with the full force of his lips.

'My *sisser*.'

'Oh, right, your sister was calling?'

'My sister.'

'Let me see.'

The girl's knees were bent and her face was completely determined, as if the photographer was actually about to kick a penalty. I guessed by the pigtails and curtains on the spectators that it was an old photograph, but the young girl, who must now have been a grown woman, still looked very much like Antonio. The same sharp eyes and Roman nose.

'I love very much,' he said.

'That's sweet.'

He scrolled on. 'And this my mother.'

An old lady in a wicker chair. Dyed black hair. A recent photograph. I told him she was very beautiful.

'She is dead.'

'Oh. I'm so sorry.'

'She is dead *marzo*. March.'

'She died in March? I'm so sorry.'

I didn't know what else to say. He was still staring at the picture – I thought he might cry. I'd never seen a grown man cry, except once when I'd walked in on one of the alcoholics in the Shoulder of Mutton toilets – his girlfriend had ditched him or something like that. I'd told the guy everything was going to be okay. I wondered if I should do the same now.

'Is okay.' Antonio kissed the screen again. 'She was very hard woman. Is still my mother.'

'Yes. Yes, of course.'

There were many pictures of his mother as he scrolled through, along with a house, a garden, an old grey dog, a yellow sports car. He kissed the phone several more times, even the picture of the car, and then caught me by the arm. I flinched again. His fingers were rough against my skin.

'And you? You family?'

'Oh, right.' I pulled out my phone and held it there. There was a message from Laurie, unread. 'Actually, I don't have any pictures of my family. Wait, no. I've got one.'

I scrolled through for it but he didn't understand.

'You family is dead?'

'No! God, no. No, my family live about fifty miles away. On the border between Sussex and Surrey. My dad runs a pub. Here.'

It was the only picture I had of me, Laurie and Dad together. Mum is there too, holding me as a baby, while Laurie stands in front of Dad reaching up to grasp my little cotton shoe. Behind us, the Shoulder of Mutton looks worn and scruffy in the previous owner's paint. That was the first picture Dad hung apparently, after he'd done the place up.

'Ah, yes! I forget. You have one *sisser*, like me. His name is?'

'Her name is Laurie.'

'Laurie, *si*. She is good *sisser*?'

'Yes, she's the best.'

'And you mother? She is in Suss-sex?'

I shook my head. 'No, she lives in France.'

'So is just you your father sister?'

I smiled. 'It's just us.'

We looked out at the waves for a long time, and only after a great pause where he seemed very eager to tell me something did he suddenly say *¡Salud!* and clink my bottle.

I never missed Mum. She didn't want to stay in touch but there was no real pain there, only when I saw Laurie suffering for it, which she sometimes did, usually around Christmas. I'd never really thought it odd not to have a mother at the Christmas dinner table but maybe it was. It had always been just the three of us – Dad and Laurie at either end of the table and me in the middle facing the empty fourth chair. Antonio came from the opposite end of life – long dining tables with uncles and aunts and cousins and people from the village. He showed me pictures where every meal looked like a party, every day a birthday, a saint's day, an occasion of some kind. A whole calendar's worth of dinners and drinks and family discussions. And never an empty seat.

Down on the beach, the shingle warmed underneath us. When we finished our beers, he pulled out another two, and after that another two, and another two, until more people were setting up with towels and Frisbees and our conversation accelerated even in spite of the language barrier, which I didn't mind at all. We made trips to the public toilet one at a time, and only when I was walking there alone did I check my phone. I didn't open the several messages that had since come in from Laurie but I could guess the gist. I decided to wait until either me or Antonio got fed up or bored, which surely wouldn't be too long, and then I would go and meet Laurie and the others, whatever they were doing.

After the beach had filled up with people leaving work, I returned from the toilet to find Antonio reading through a piece of paper, mouthing the words to himself. I arrived without him noticing.

'Busy?' I said.

Antonio laughed. 'Is for work. *Mira este.*'

I sat down and pushed my fingers under the warm pebbles to where it's cooler. Antonio showed me the paper. *Curriculum*

Vitae: Antonio Javier Gutiérrez Jimenez. Thirty-nine — older than I thought. He pulled a Spanish-English dictionary from his bag and spent some time finding the words *naval engineer*, before throwing his thumb over his shoulder, rubbing his fingers together in the universal sign for money and shaking his head definitively. He didn't need to explain — Duncan's blog had already done that. The guests at the hostel were well educated, intelligent and willing to work. Some of them were graduates, professionals, high earners. But Spain had nothing to offer them. So they came to the UK to tend bars and mop floors.

Antonio sighed. 'Many Spanish want for work here.'

I realised that since he'd been talking about his job search the trace of nerves I'd brought with me that morning had calmed and my head wasn't swimming. Everyone around me seemed to be stuck in a cycle of getting work, losing work, looking for flats, finding flats. And here was Antonio doing it in a country where he could barely speak the language, without a single sign of panic. It was as if he moved through the whole thing gracefully, as I wish I could myself.

'Well, I can help you,' I said offhand.

He sat up straight. 'You want help me?'

'Sure.'

His face dropped. He wrung his hands and for the first time that day he looked anxious. It was like I'd passed it from me to him. I wanted to put a hand on his shoulder but my Englishness prevented me.

'What's the matter?' I asked.

'Don't want say.'

'Oh, come on. Don't be shy.'

'Ah, *hostia puta*.' He sent a stone skittering towards the water. 'I'm sorry. I lie. I invite you not for this.'

'For what?'

'I invite you… I want ask you help me but not with a job.'

'Then with what?'

My nerves tightened again. My imagination started to spin. He said: 'You seem a-kind.'

'A kind of what?'

He checked his dictionary. 'Kind. Good.'

'Oh, kind.' It took me by surprise. I had no idea what he was going to say, and 'kind' wasn't a word I immediately associated with myself. 'I'm not really.'

But he was already rifling through his bag. Eventually he pulled out an old photograph and passed it to me without looking up. I took it – the thing was falling apart – and looked it over. It showed a young man in an open jacket standing in front of the sea, hands on hips, his face turned in profile, his trousers pulled up high above his waist. There was a medal on his chest, attached with a ribbon. He looked very much like Antonio, even more than his sister and mother did, especially with the big nose that stuck out in front of the pier behind him. He looked very proud, like he belonged to a proud age.

'This the father my mother father.'

I squinted. He started flicking through the dictionary but couldn't find the word.

'Is *mi bisabuelo*. My mother father father.'

'Bis-ab-wello?' I took the dictionary and looked it up.

'*Bisabuelo, si.*'

'*Bisa*— oh, I see. Your great-grandfather.'

'My *grey gran-father*. Yes.' He mimed holding a rifle. '*Un soldado*.' Pulled the trigger.

'He was a soldier?'

'*¿La guerra civil?*'

'Oh, the Civil War? He fought in the Spanish Civil War?'

'Yes.'

I was surprised to see his eyes fill with water when he said this. There was what I took for passionate loyalty and love in his voice. Straight away, I wanted to be around that.

'What was his name?' I asked.

'His name. I *no segurro*.'

He turned my hand to reveal the back of the picture. In faint pencil were the words *Art, 1939*.

'Is this his name, Art?'

'I think yes.'

'Short for Arthur?'

He didn't understand. '*¿Qué dijiste?*'

'Art is short for Arthur.'

Again he looked like he was going to cry. In anyone else I might have taken that as insincere, the emotion brought on by a simple piece of information. As simple as an Englishman's name.

'Didn't you know your great-grandfather was called Arthur?'

'Art, Arthur. Very, very good.'

He was thrilled by this and I looked at the photograph again but still I didn't understand.

'My mother... This *fotografía* – it was inside...' He mimed the opening and closing of a drawer. 'She give me... before... Ah, *por el amor de Dios, no tengo el inglés suficiente para esto...*'

He was struggling. I picked up the dictionary and handed it to him.

'Nice and slow,' I said.

I didn't know too much about the Spanish Civil War, except for the words of a Clash song me and Laurie used to sing while cross-legged on the floor of her bedroom, something Spanglishy. I knew that on one side there'd been the anarchists and communists and journalists like George Orwell and Martha Gellhorn – people Laurie and I looked up to as teenagers – and on the other side those who supported General Franco, the fascist dictator. *Good guys and bad guys*, how I thought of it back then. It took most of the afternoon on the beach to get through Antonio's explanation of the photograph, with the dictionary passing back and forth between us as the beach filled out with people finishing work. It got hotter and drier and louder and I didn't even think of drinking water. Antonio pointed out details on the photograph – the medal, the line of his nose – and nodded emotionally and excitedly when I understood something. There was genuine longing in his eyes and I was swept along by it.

'So you're looking for him? Your great-grandfather?'

'Yes.'

I could picture the kitchen in the house Antonio's mother had left him, where she'd given Antonio the photograph of a man the family had never discussed, not even once. The house now empty, the kitchen quiet.

He said: 'My *grey gran-father* is dead, yes?'

'Oh.' I looked at the date. 'Yes, probably.'

The man in the photograph – a volunteer who'd served in

Spain during the Civil War – had olive skin and thick black hair just like Antonio's. It was hard to believe he was English at all.

'And why Brighton?' I asked.

He took the picture and held it up to the sea so I could see the image of the West Pier, all intact and fresh-looking, against the remains of scorched black timber that has stood in its place since 2003. The picture must have been taken almost exactly where we were sitting.

He said: '*Impressionate*, no?', though I think he meant *impressive*. He held his fist to his chest. 'I want understand.'

And the words ran through my mind in a clear, explicit voice: *Yes, so do I.*

'I'll help you,' I said. 'To find him. Absolutely. And to find a job, of course.'

He had wanted me to say it that plainly and I had wanted to and now he was shaking my head and hugging me like he'd hugged me when I first arrived. He held me so tightly I couldn't breathe and when he let me go he started taking his shirt off. I laughed nervously – people were looking. He pulled his shorts up high and reached for my T-shirt. I pulled back. He pointed me towards the water.

'Oh.' I laughed. 'Are you swimming?'

'*Nadando*, yes.'

He reached again for my T-shirt but I pulled back.

'Sorry, I don't.' It had been twelve years – I'd almost drowned during a swimming lesson at school. I probably should have said *can't*.

'Come, you swim.'

I pushed him away and picked up a beer. 'You go ahead.'

I expected him to keep pushing but he suddenly softened as

if he understood completely, and then stepped back and saluted. I saluted back and then he stopped, struck with a sudden thought, and hustled his phone into my hands.

'*Toma mi foto.*'

He stood with his hands on his hips as he'd stood at the Naked Bike Ride, face turned in profile, proud and serious and sucking up lungfuls of air through his nose. I laughed and looked at him there in the rectangle of the screen. He looked like a classical statue, masculine and faintly silly. Someone with a history that I wanted to be a part of. *Click.*

Then his hands came together in a firm clap and he ran towards the sea, right past the people relaxing on the shingle, and leapt into the still water with a splash. He emerged from under the surface shivering theatrically and swearing in Spanish, yelped, dipped back under. I looked at him there in the sea with the skeleton of the West Pier behind him, and then down at the photograph.

Art, 1939. His medal on his chest. Pride and passion and loyalty.

We drank into the evening, just the two of us, under the noise of the waves and the gulls. Then after the sun disappeared he tapped me idly on the shoulder.

'You friends, Marta and other, they like the... *como se dice, activismo político...*' He searched for a word in the dictionary and then mangled the word *activity*, though I think he meant *activism.*

'They do.'

'And you?'

'I don't know,' I said, and then for the first time that day I was thinking about the riot in London, except that now it was moving in slow motion, quietly and harmlessly, as if it'd happened to someone else. 'I used to be very fired up about that kind of thing. Me and Laurie used to do lots of protests and stuff like that. At school, I mean.'

'You *sisser* has...' He didn't have the word but he drew his finger slowly over his eyebrow.

'A scar, yes. It was a bad injury.'

I hoped Antonio would say something but he didn't. He just looked at me, waiting.

I rose onto my elbows and looked out at the sea. Drunker than I thought. 'You see, I let her down once, and she doesn't even know it. We were at a march a few years ago, before I left school...' But I stopped there. Something in me, more than just the beer, wanted to tell him all about what happened when we were separated, about how I was knocked with a shield that broke bones in two fingers, and how I fell and the boots stamped around me and I covered my head until someone lifted me to my feet. I even wanted to tell him how when I'd stood up my arms had risen above my head without me telling them to, in surrender. An automatic response. And I wanted to tell him about what happened at the hospital in Whitechapel, the bit I tried not to think about.

The memory slammed shut. I told myself I wasn't ready.

'You feel bad,' he said. 'Is family. Every person feel bad.' And in his voice that sounded natural and true, like there was nothing to feel guilty about. I shrugged and smiled and my nerves washed out again with the slow sibilance of the tide. Maybe another day.

'*Entiendo*...' Antonio laid back. 'Boat?'

'Hm?' I looked for a boat but saw only the strips of light on the dark water.

'You boat?'

I laughed. 'U-boat?'

He flicked through the dictionary and pointed out the word.

'Oh, shit. Did I vote, you mean?'

He gasped. 'You did not?'

'No. God, I completely lost track of time.'

'You must. For me, yes – big thing. *¡Por los trabajadores de tu pueblo, vamos!*'

'Yes, I suppose so.'

He pulled at my shirt. 'You must, you must.' He was laughing but he meant it. I hadn't even thought about what the referendum might mean to him.

'It's okay,' I said, 'they're open till ten.'

I checked my phone. Half nine. A few more messages from Laurie, the group. I think they were at the pub hanging the bunting for tomorrow. A message from Laurie at 21.01: Where the fuck are you. I'd forgotten all about them.

'Christ, I'd better go.'

'*Vamos.*'

My polling station was at the Baptist church at the end of my street. I already had my card with me. We ran through the streets, where people with EU flags were already celebrating and others were smoking outside the pubs, enjoying the warm summer night. Crossing Western Road I was almost knocked down by a number 25. When we arrived at the polling station my chest was tight, unbearably so. The woman at the desk asked me if I was alright and I said *Hunky dory* through hoarse wheezes that made Antonio very concerned.

'It's fine,' I told him. I didn't want to use my inhaler in front of him. 'Shit lungs.'

I took a slip and entered the booth. My head was spinning and the blood was rushing around my ears and now, having gone over that moment in my mind many times, I can't remember if I put my cross in the place I wanted to.

My hands were shaking when I left the booth.

I took out my phone and messaged Laurie:

Apologise

*apologies

Sorry got caught up

Just made it ha ha

See you at the party x

Antonio slapped my back and I thought maybe I should invite him to the celebrations the next day, but something within me, something selfish, told me not to. So we hugged and I said goodbye and he held me seriously and in the blur of my nausea and adrenaline I thought of his *bisabuelo* in front of the pier.

'I see you,' said Antonio, before he walked back towards the sea, slowly and purposefully, like a sober man.

I remember the first time Laurie voted. It was in the 2010 general election, just a few months before the student riots in London. Laurie and I weren't the only kids excited about it – actually it felt like young people all over the country were getting ready for something different. We went down to the polling station together, and after she had cast her ballot we hugged and I felt excited for her and for me, who'd be able to vote in another year. We even did a little jig on the church hall steps, happy and full of meaning and with no real knowledge of the terms *hung parliament* or *coalition government*. That had been a Thursday too.

This time the result came to me while I was still in bed, with the booze of my day with Antonio hanging over me like a storm cloud. 51.9% to 48.1%, with a map of the United Kingdom wearing a significant suit of Leavers blue. I checked the numbers for Brighton and Hove – overwhelmingly Remain, of course. I checked our old villages, grouped within Horsham though really we were nearer Crawley, not a liberal place. Remain had taken Horsham by a squeak, probably tipped over by the hippies from Balcombe. If that mattered now. I wondered what kind of celebrations would be going on at the Shoulder of Mutton tonight, with Dad and his St George's flags. I checked *Left Nut* for the inevitable early-morning breakdown. There was nothing.

A message pinged in the *Remain Party Victory Party* chat, just a brief message from Helena, before I dragged myself out of bed.

Still meeting pub 8pm

and after a couple of minutes,

Love you all x

The pub was quiet and the lights were dim. Duncan's bunting had been strung up the night before – blue triangles with yellow stars – and someone had blown up a dozen blue balloons that slunk along the floor. A roving light lit the faces of the few people who had turned up, half a dozen performers from Marta's circle. I recognised some of them – they sat solemnly with their guitar cases, not saying much. In front of the empty fireplace, Marta struggled to arrange a mic stand in front of a high stool, her eyes cast down. Even from the back of the room I could see she had been crying. Fairy lights hung from the mantle behind her, casting a blinking light onto the worn rug under her feet. Beside her, at the front by the mini sound desk, sat Helena and Duncan. I waved and looked around for Laurie. Helena pointed to the bar.

I found her slumped over a full pint, cheek squished against the palm of her hand, eyes half closed. I took her for drunk – wasted drunk, not just jolly as she was at parties. But when she saw me she straightened out and I could see by the sharp cynical glint in her eyes that she was completely sober.

She didn't smile when I hugged her. She just said: 'Where were you yesterday?'

'I was helping someone out with something.'

'Did you even vote?'

'Yes, I did. Jesus, Laurie, what's the matter?'

She looked me in the eye for several seconds and then took a sip from her pint. I put a hand on her shoulder and she softened. Really she looked more exhausted than anything.

'I'm sorry,' she said. 'It's those fuckers. I don't want to take it out on you.'

'That's fine,' I said. 'I'm as shook up as you are.' Though I wasn't. Actually I was distracted by thoughts of my afternoon with Antonio and his great-grandfather and all we'd spoken about. I remembered then I hadn't messaged to ask him what he thought of the result.

A sigh left Laurie's body. She looked like that so rarely I knew she must really be hurting – even more than I'd expected. She must have felt the same as we did back then, in those few months leading up to the riot. Bitter and sick and wanting to break. When she led us to the table, I noticed that her feet shuffled across the floor. She walked as she walked after the few times Mum called Dad at the Shoulder of Mutton, to sort out money and such, and if she was grieving like that I knew what would come next.

Our friends at the table were pleased to see me but their voices never got above a sad burr. Helena greeted me over the papers she was reading through. Duncan was tweeting like mad, knee bopping up and down, teeth faintly grinding. I sat down beside him, the only free chair. He was the only one to touch me – he put his phone down and crossed his hand over mine on the table, as if to comfort me. I was relieved when he released it.

'It's a fucking joke,' he said. 'Doesn't surprise me a bit.'

Though it must have done. He was just as sceptical about

the British public as Laurie was, but he hadn't said a word about what might happen if they actually voted to leave.

'It does me,' I said, and I wanted to show that the disappointment was more powerful than the surprise, but this wasn't true. 'I'm shocked.'

'It won't go through,' Laurie huffed. 'The thing about Article 51 is...'

She spoke and I listened. Duncan explained how holding the vote during Glastonbury was a deliberate move to exclude people of our age. Of course he was going to write about it. Laurie kept looking at me like she was waiting for me to join in. Then there were a few taps on the microphone and Marta began to speak. She was quiet and she stuttered – her usual grace was gone. The room winced at a moan of feedback.

'Thank you all for coming,' she said. 'To start us off I'd like to ask my good friend Helena to come speak.'

We clapped for Helena as she manoeuvred around the table and took her place in front of the microphone. The fairy lights behind her flickered mutely.

'Thank you.' Helena spoke clearly and evenly as she always did. 'It's tough to know where to begin. Obviously, it's been a bad year so far.'

There was no bitterness in her voice and no pity. She mentioned David Bowie and Alan Rickman and Harper Lee. Her voice went down a key when she spoke about the Labour MP Jo Cox, who had been murdered outside a library in West Yorkshire eight days previous. She spoke about the US election campaigns where the reality TV star Donald Trump had just won several Republican primaries. I hadn't paid attention to much of that. It all seemed so far away, just stories on my social media feed that rolled on and on like the random shapes of clouds across the sky. But now, when Helena spoke, the problems of the world suddenly seemed very real and specific in a way I'd never felt when I looked down at my phone or when Laurie told me about a revolution somewhere on the other side of the world. Helena made it sound like it was happening to me. I think that's how Laurie felt all the time.

She finished by saying: 'Whatever has happened and whatever happens next, we're still alive and we're still strong and we're not going anywhere.'

I clapped, everyone clapped, and a couple of the musicians got teary and Duncan filmed for Facebook Live. Helena's face softened when she said: 'Let's enjoy some music.'

She returned to the table and Laurie put her arm round her. Laurie looked proud and serious, like a bodyguard, and I was proud of Helena too, for her grace.

I smiled at my sister but still she didn't smile back.

I'd seen a few of the musicians before – they were all fairly good. A man in scruffy jeans sang about a collapsing relationship. A woman with tattooed sleeves sang a song with a line I still remember: *Cast in concrete by the higher powers / Like the gutters that circle the ivory towers*, which Duncan and the others clapped wildly for. A punk-folk duo in matching leathers asked *Why do we call it Great Britain?* which made Laurie thump the table in agreement. Helena covered her fist with her hand and whispered *Please*.

I wanted to give the music my full attention but my mind kept wandering back to Antonio and his great-grandfather and other things. In between acts the conversation was all politics and it tired me out. By the time Marta's turn came I was back at the bar, alone. Our applause clattered hollowly around the pub. A fair few of the performers had already excused themselves.

'Hi, everybody.' The guitar around her neck looked as big and cumbersome as a cello. 'Wish I could be singing for you in better circumstances.'

She wasn't nervous but when she sang it wasn't with the voice I'd heard on her home recordings. It was flat and breathless like a deflated balloon. She sang plainly and quietly – a song that should have been vivid and bright. I hadn't even thought that of all of us, it was Marta who might be most directly affected by the result of the vote. It wasn't even that she was a migrant from the EU, who might be asked for all new kinds of visas and papers and proofs – not invitations but *proofs* that she had the right to be here. It was that the country she lived in had looked at her – a smart, gentle, talented woman from Barcelona – and said quite clearly: *you are not us*.

I thought of Antonio then, and wondered if he felt the same.

At the climax of the song, Marta simply stopped playing. Her sobs came quietly through the speakers. I moved to help her but one of her musician friends was already leading her offstage. There was a concerned silence where the applause should have been. I thought Helena might take the microphone again, but her seat was empty and so was Duncan's. It seemed like someone needed to say something, anything at all, and for whatever reason I thought *Antonio would definitely say something*. So I breathed deeply and moved towards the stage with an impulse to speak but no idea what I was going to say. Before I got there, Laurie was up and holding the microphone. I stopped in the centre of the room. It was like being lit with a spotlight.

'Listen, everybody.' Her voice was so loud it distorted in the speakers.

I looked again for Helena.

'We've got to remember that we can't let those bastards win,' she spat. 'We've got to keep fighting...' She said something about *fucking Tories* and class war, and something else about the bus with the *shit numbers* on it. It reminded me of a morning in Year 11 when she'd stood up in assembly to shout down a policeman who was giving a talk about safety for girls. I'd laughed about it then, quite openly, while still hoping she wouldn't take it too far.

She spoke for several minutes and finished with: 'This referendum was won by liars and racists so fuck them, we'll fight them right to the end. Intolerant *scum*.'

It was supposed to be inspiring and a male voice shouted *Fuck 'em* but no one clapped. She ignored Marta and her musician friend who'd been watching from the side, looked briefly around the pub and marched right up to me. Shaking with anger.

'Where's Helena?' she said.

'I don't know.'

'I'm so worked up.'

'I know.'

'I just want to break something.'

Her eyes found an empty water jug sweating on the counter. She didn't touch it.

'I know, Laurie.'

'This country makes me furious. I had to say something...'

I wasn't sure what to say, since the word *scum* is something

I've never quite been able to square myself with, in any context. So I let her talk, since she needed me. I led her to the bar and ordered two Spanish lagers and accepted her frustration with a silent ear.

'You know the people who voted…'

She poured it into me, and though I wanted to help it went straight to my nerves and sat there. My nerves that up until then had receded behind thoughts of my new friend.

'I know Dad voted that way,' she said. 'He even texted me to gloat about it. Look, I'll show you…'

I thought about that time she'd torn Tony Blair's book in half in the school library, and the librarian's face as the two tattered halves fell onto her desk, poor woman. I imagined her going home after work and telling her husband about it. I don't know why it came to me then.

Eventually Laurie ran out of steam. 'Sorry, George. I'm speaking like it's your fault.'

'Not at all,' I said, but I could feel her anger inside me now and it had my blood up. 'I'm always here to listen.'

I don't think that's what she wanted to hear. She thanked me curtly and then got angry again. She was so wound up, I couldn't take it.

'One moment,' I said. Her words were on me like a weight across my chest. 'I'll be back in one moment.'

I rushed over to Marta and tried to hug her but she backed away. I asked if she was okay and did she want to come outside – that would give me the excuse to leave. Laurie followed me and immediately started ranting – at the barman this time, poor guy – and I knew I had to get out right that second, just for a moment.

'Let's get some air,' I said to Marta, and she walked ahead of me towards the door, wiping the tears from her eyes.

The air outside was heavy with summer, as if an invisible storm hung over us, ready to break.

'Are you okay?' I asked her, but she didn't answer.

She'd stopped crying and her eyes were fixed down the street, just past the pub's benches, where two people stood on the corner by the off-licence. It was Duncan and Helena, lit by the white light from the shop door. I thought nothing of it and moved to call them, but then Duncan reached out and slowly pulled Helena's hand to his chest. She let him hold it there for a moment – he was begging her, I think. She pulled away and he put his hands on her waist but she took them off gently. Then she dragged the back of her fingers softly across his cheek and stepped into the white light.

I watched Duncan, hopping from one foot to the other and wringing his hands, before he turned his head and saw us standing there. His hands dropped and the agitated movement left his body, but his expression was blank. The shrewd, lively mask he always wore slipped off.

'Marta,' I said, but she was already running down the street away from him.

He ran towards me and I put out a hand which he idly folded into his before he passed. 'Don't worry, George,' he said, barely slowing, 'everything's fine.'

I watched him jog on down the street, calling Marta's name at speaking volume, and then skip around the corner and disappear. A hand gripped my shoulder. Helena, offering me a drink of her little canned coffee.

'What's going on?' I said, but she simply drew a sip, which stained her smile.

'He doesn't mean anything by it,' she said. 'He just gets carried away.'

I held her eye then and she seemed happy to hold it. I knew that maybe something had happened when they lived together in Islington, something to do with her past straight life, which she was otherwise so honest about, but I couldn't believe anything was happening now. I never believed Helena would hurt my sister in any way, but even so I knew I wouldn't be able to tell Laurie what I'd just seen, and that made the feeling of gutlessness rise up within me and clutch at my windpipe.

Helena must have known what I was feeling. 'Don't tell Laurie, eh,' she said. 'You know how worked up she gets and she just wouldn't understand. She's so principled.'

'Helena, how am I not supposed to tell her? It looked like he was grabbing you.'

'He wasn't grabbing me. I promise you, George, it was just Duncan being Duncan.'

I looked down at the pavement. It was covered in the grey blotches of discarded chewing gum, blotches everywhere. Once you've seen them, you can't unsee them.

'Let's find the others,' she said.

I followed her back in, back to the table where Laurie sat by herself. Maybe she saw how bothered I looked, maybe not. She asked where the other two were and Helena said *They've taken off* and sighed. An easy emission of non-truth.

'Poor girl,' said Laurie, meaning with the referendum, I guess.

I sat there too hot and anxious to speak. I took out my phone for something to look at.

Laurie sniffed. 'There'll be trouble after this... Big trouble...'

I looked up and she was running her finger over her scar and my nerves were bringing images to my mind. The line of policemen, my hands raised above my head, the tears forming in my eyes, the sight of her limp body being dragged through the line by a stranger in a denim jacket just like mine.

'If people think the British people will just—'

I opened the thread of mine and Antonio's messages and saw the photograph of his long fingers twisted around the beer bottles, but it wasn't enough to distract me. My head was swimming in memory and the air in the pub was so thick it felt like drowning.

'It's just fucking exploiting people's fears—'

There was blood in Laurie's eyes when she was dragged to the ambulance, so she says – she's adamant she couldn't see or hear or think. But I watched the stranger in the denim jacket haul her across the concrete towards the waiting paramedics. The stranger in a jacket just like mine. While I stood there with my hands raised and watched.

'I swear we can't stand for this—'

The phone shook in my hand while I drafted and redrafted a simple message to distract myself and eventually sent the words Hot tonight, which I immediately regretted. I looked out of the window where a drunk couple argued in the street.

'Same as when they busted my head open—'

A picture appeared onscreen. Antonio at arm's length, all

wet in the white light of the flash with the black sea just visible behind him.

Laurie's hand landed on my shoulder. 'Everything alright?'

I looked at her in the dim light of the pub and saw Laurie's face as it was that afternoon, when she'd woken up at Whitechapel, so tired and weak but still with that glint of violent energy, to find me watching over her. I remembered how she pulled me in close by my jacket and thanked me for dragging her through the line to the ambulance. She looked up at me through her one uncovered eye, and I said something but I can't remember what it was – just that it wasn't, absolutely wasn't the truth. I had seen the man who dragged her through the line, an average-looking guy with an average-looking jacket. But when Laurie woke, I just froze up and let her mistake dissipate uncorrected into the quiet hum of the hospital room. The moment to tell her that *That was not me* simply passed. Then she'd kissed me on the forehead and that was how it ended. Quite gently, with a kiss.

'George.' Her voice soft and loyal as it was back then, her rant apparently over. 'George, are you alright?'

She was staring and Helena was staring, their hands folded together on the table as if over a secret.

'Yes,' I said, eyes fixed on the door, trying to picture Antonio, the night swimmer, bounding through the black waves at the seashore. 'Everything's fine.'

2
THE MAN WITHOUT
A COSTUME

The day Antonio got the keys to his bedsit I thought he'd want to stay in there alone and enjoy the privacy he'd missed out on for so many weeks in his hostel. Instead he coaxed me to the beach with a bottle of cachaça. Over everything, even above the relief of finding a place to live, he was mostly just grateful for the help I'd given him. Sincerely grateful and not afraid to show it.

Getting him a National Insurance number had been easy enough, despite his fears around the referendum. His CV was a nightmare of impressive-sounding qualifications impossible to properly translate. I couldn't imagine what the HR departments of supermarkets and cleaning firms thought when they saw *Naval Engineer* on their applications, but perhaps they were used to it. He had no references from the Spanish Navy, so he said, and never really seemed to want to talk about it. So I asked my manager Carlos if there was room for him at the bar, and when there wasn't, I put myself down as a reference instead.

We sent off applications to dozens of the lowest paid jobs available in the city. We went into agencies where young men in suits spoke to us all pally-pally and then never called us back. For Antonio it was a new world. All he saw was a city covered in vacancies, where a single search threw up dozens of adverts, all for positions he was sure he could fill. He didn't acknowledge once that he might be overqualified, or that businesses might turn him down because of his lack of English. He didn't even acknowledge that taking an entry-level job might be a knock to his pride. He just polished his shoes and kept his shirt buttoned to the top. Eventually he took a job as a cleaner for a firm with two dozen foreign workers and a supermarket contract. They gave him a uniform, which he was immensely proud of – it carried an insignia of a little yellow castle that sat where a medal might. I thought it looked vaguely Spanish.

Walking down the promenade, watching him twirl the keys to a pokey little flat with no garden, he looked completely content. There were couples strolling all over the prom, pushing prams, walking dogs, eating chips – normal people doing normal things. I bought us ice creams. He'd never had a 99.

'Did you have fun last night?' I asked him.

'*Si*, of course,' he said with a lick, '*me gustó mucho.*'

I'd been there with him for his last night at Hostelpoint. He'd gathered all the young people for a toast and then gone round the circle and pressed a condom into each of their hands, boy or girl. He made a speech about *responsabilidad*, and tried to lead a chorus of his favourite song – something from the Spanish Civil War called '¡Ay Carmela!', which no one knew, not even the Spanish kids. When he'd finished he took the stairs up to the bedrooms with his chin lifted high and one hand on the banister, as if to say *my work here is done*.

'Will you miss it?' I asked him on the prom.

'Ha! Miss the hostel? Sixteen people one room? Ah, no!'

But his voice rang false. He was liked in the hostels, and the young people seemed especially endeared to him, like he was some kind of benevolent uncle from the countryside, someone from back home. They laughed when they said he was *craaazy*.

'Not even the kids?' I said.

'The kids is just kids.'

They found his little moral crusades entertaining and so did I, though I could tell they didn't really understand the relationship between us. He had a little more English by then but mostly we gestured, mimed – it was like charades. I enjoyed the fact that small talk was so laborious we didn't bother with it at all. I liked being around someone who could only paint with the broadest brush and only say things he really meant.

We stopped to watch the basketball players on the seafront – men of all different ages, shouting in different languages, and behind them children who practised their jump shots while the game was down the other end. A stray ball rolled towards us and a woman with a crying baby bent down to pick it up. Antonio stopped her with a wave of his hand and said *No* quite firmly. She laughed at his grandiosity but he didn't respond. He just picked up the ball himself and returned it deftly to the court.

I drew the end of my Flake from the ice cream. 'I'm sure she could have managed.'

But he didn't understand.

We stopped at the carousel to watch the horses bobbing up and down, up and down. The speakers mangled an old English song I vaguely recognised, something you might hear at a barn dance. Antonio asked me what the thing was called in English.

'Merry-go-round.' But I was getting distracted. 'Do you have these in Spain?'

'Yes, we have.'

I'd been perfectly relaxed until we got nearer to the pier and the crowds got thicker. I think he noticed my nerves quicken – I could feel him watching me as we walked. On the other side of the pier, Madeira Drive was closed off for a rally. The whole mile-long street was lined with Vespas laden with multiple mirrors and men in Parkas and women with Chelsea cuts – the mod crowd, *Quadropheniacs*. These were Dad's people – he'd often boasted about growing up with the skinheads in Crystal Palace, getting the train down to Brighton for scraps on the beach. Dad was part of the second generation, the *This is England* crowd. That was before Laurie and I were born, before he and Mum bought the Shoulder of Mutton and moved to Sussex to settle him down. Though it didn't seem like that had worked. All they'd really done was buy him a social club.

Antonio tried to lead us into the crowds but I held back.

'What?' he said, but all I could think about was Dad and his Palace tattoo, the old newsreel footage and the old-fashioned bobbies who came down and clubbed them. Club after club after club.

Antonio came in front of me so all I could see was him. 'Come.'

I tried to look away but he wouldn't let me. He spoke softly, just loud enough that I could pick out a melody in his words.

'*Viiiiii-vaaaaaa la Quince Brigada…*' And then pouring the rhythm into my ear: '*Rumba la, rumba la, rumba la…*'

I laughed and tried to look away but he still wouldn't let me.

'*Viva la Quince Brigada – rumba la, rumba la, rumba la…*'

'Antonio.'

His voice got louder. '*Que te ha cubierto de gloria…*'

Three old couples in studded denim watched us – the punk end of Mod, not the Carnaby end – which made me think of me stuffing my old denim jacket into the conifers, the spot of Laurie's blood on it. *Club after club after –*

Antonio's voice burst out of him: '*¡Ay Carmela! ¡Ay Carmelaaaa!*' Fingers clicking above his head, stance lengthening out into a long flamenco curve. It was impossible not to laugh. Before I knew how to deal with it he was dancing and circling around me and a few of the mods were clapping and a skinhead cheered *Go on, son* until Antonio grabbed my hands and I was dancing with him, in the middle of the street, with his singing getting faster and faster.

'*Luchamos contra los moros, rumba la, rumba la, rumba la... Legionario y fascista – ¡Ay Carmela! ¡Ay Carmelaaaa!*'

Eventually he stopped to push the cachaça bottle into my chest, and bowed for the peroxide boys clapping for us. He put his arm round me and led me into the crowds. I drank happily with the liquid burning around my lips, sputtering on the thrill of safety and something like brotherhood. Like brotherhood, yes. But not quite.

Why he took it upon himself to look after me I'm not sure. The only thing I knew was that it was instinctive and unforced, because I could see already how he wore his conscience as a badge of honour. The language he borrowed from his books on the Spanish Civil War applied to everything in the world. Every spilt drink, every nudged shoulder, every pinch, wolf whistle and catcall. The world was a battleground and he carried that vision with him everywhere. He was on a mission and he never let me forget it for long.

'Look this.' He stopped us where the high shingle obscures the nudist beach and the male prostitutes sunbathe on the benches at Dukes Mound. He took out his phone and zoomed in on a stock picture of a medal, and then held the phone up against the tattered photograph of his *bisabuelo*.

'Is same.'

It was a red medal with a circular medallion mounted on a triangle and three protruding sword hilts. It looked a bit like a sheriff's badge. On the plate were the words REPUBLICA ESPANOL circled around an image of a soldier's head in profile. The soldier wore a helmet and looked proud of his achievements.

Antonio read aloud: 'The medal was instituted on twenty October 1938 for volunteers in the *Brigadas Internacionales* for their contribution to the fight against Franco...'

Through library books and internet searches we'd already found out that 2,500 British people – men and women – had volunteered to fight against Franco in the International Brigades. We found the names of three Brighton men but all of them had died at the battle of Brunete, none of them named Arthur. These men, along with most of the British and Irish volunteers, were part of the XV International Brigade alongside the Americans and other nationalities that made up their companies and battalions. This was all new language to me. It felt like history but Antonio spoke about it as if it were his own life.

'Very interesting,' I said.

'I found in library. Very good.'

A message came through from Laurie, something about a People's Vote protest outside town. The thought of her waiting for my reply brought some of my nerves back and when I looked up Antonio was walking to the shingle. He slumped down and I slumped down beside him. Then he asked me seriously and quietly why I was here.

'Pardon me?'

He pointed firmly down to the shingle more than once, as if meaning *right here*, but I understood.

'Do you mean, why am I here in Brighton?'

'You, *listo*.' He jabbed at his temple. 'You say me, "I have job in university London". *Pero* why? Why – are – you – a-here?'

When I'd told him about my interview at LSE, two years ago now, I did it in the same way I told everyone. That I'd looked down at myself in my smart borrowed suit and funeral tie, and 'freaked out'. It wasn't the life I wanted. Simple. I didn't mention how on my way to the interview I'd crossed the square where the riot had taken place and that only then did I 'freak out'. And I didn't mention how I'd felt when I got back after travelling and asked Dad for shifts at the Shoulder of Mutton. The frustration of my failure.

I put the fact that Antonio didn't understand me down to our language barrier, but only to help me push the truth out of my mind. I knew my story didn't make sense.

'I used to come down as a kid,' I said. 'And Laurie said it was a good place to live. Lots of culture, lots of good people.'

'Laurie came before.' He always pronounced it funny, more *lorey* than *lorry*.

'Yes. She moved down here first. She told me it was a good place to live.'

He shook his head as I suspected he would. He asked again

in that same emphatic, broken-up voice. '*Why – are – you – a-here?*'

'Well, Antonio, I...' but I hadn't really prepared myself for if someone didn't believe me. English people never pushed. 'I suppose I feel a bit lost.'

It wasn't a burden to say, it was a relief. I felt like that was what Antonio wanted me to say, just to say out loud for my own benefit. Or perhaps he wanted me to talk about Laurie, who I'd kept at a distance from him for the past few weeks, for reasons I was also pushing out of my mind. Antonio put a hand on my shoulder and that was enough. I asked what he thought of the city, now he had a flat, now it was home.

'I think this is very great city. For one person like you, it is very good.'

'For someone like me?'

'Yes. I am not the same. Different. But also someone like me.'

I wondered, as I often did, exactly what kind of person he took me for. He had said I was *kind*. But I didn't quite believe that. I wasn't sure what I was.

'You sister Laurie. What is she like?'

On the water I could see the tour boat making its run from the marina towards the West Pier. Antonio had asked me about it once, on one of the few occasions he mentioned his time in the navy. I didn't tell him but I'd never once been on a boat.

'She's great, really great. They all are. They're just very English.'

'I want meet,' he said carnivorously.

He'd asked before, several times actually, but I'd always fobbed him off. There was still something about converging those two worlds that made me uneasy. Or perhaps I just wanted to keep this one friend for myself.

'Well, you already know Marta and Duncan. And you met Helena and Laurie at the bike ride.'

A part of me wanted to tell him about what had happened outside the pub the day after the vote. He stopped me with a hand on my elbow. '*Venga*. I want meet.'

The second time he said it his voice was serious and even a little frail. I hadn't really considered that despite having lived sixteen to a room for several weeks he might be lonely.

'Of course. Well, we'll see them at Pride,' which was just a week or two off but which Helena and Duncan and the rest had been talking about for months. There was a party at Marta's new flat on Preston Circus, up by the viaduct. She had a roof terrace. I had no idea what to expect.

Antonio nodded contemplatively in the failing light, unsure, and we walked on.

I could feel the cachaça now – it sloshed around in my empty stomach. A fair few of the mods were chugging off on their scooters and people were sweeping the crap off the street so we turned back to the prom. When we reached the fishing museum Antonio climbed up into one of the old boats outside the entrance and pulled me up with him. There was water in the bottom and a few cans and the debris of a Grubbs meal. We sat by the edges pretending to row and saying *¡España! ¡España!* in the direction of the sea. We laughed and passed the bottle between us and slumped down against the wood of the hull. My tiredness washed into the bottom of the boat with the burger wrappers and I was feeling that *great day* feeling, that holiday feeling, looking at the lights of the wind farm out to sea.

Then Antonio started to cry.

I'd rarely seen Laurie cry, not since we were children, and never seen Dad cry. I didn't know exactly what to do. It made me feel something unfamiliar – something that made it obvious he wanted to be cared for, that the pride of him being older and all the rest of it didn't get in the way. I shuffled across and took him under my arm. He wiped his eyes and explained as best he could. He made the shape of a mountain with his hands, the symbol of Guadalupe – his village. He missed his mother, his family, his sister the goalkeeper. But there was something else, too. He pulled out the picture of his great-grandfather again. Arthur's face, turned in profile, proud nose sticking out. We still didn't know his surname.

'*Mi bisabuelo* was hero Republican. When he much young than me…'

'You shouldn't compare yourself to him.'

He looked me in the eye. 'All is thinking is. I am born nineteen seventy-six. He was *nineteen* when he fight. He was nineteen and already a very brave man. Already he was hero. Don't worry you. It doesn't matter.'

I took the cachaça, threw some back, handed him the bottle. I thought he was a kind of hero himself then, when he cried in front of me in the hull of the boat. That was when I realised it. 'Well, Antonio. Brave Antonio. *Bienvenido a Inglaterra*.'

'*Gracias*, Jorge.' His name for me, in place of George, which he couldn't pronounce, which made me happy every time he said it. 'Best man.'

*

We walked to his bedsit in silence. The flat was around Oriental Place, the area that was once the red-light district. My mind wandered to all the things that must have happened behind the curtains of the buildings opposite – posh Regency places with sash windows and black railings. Antonio's flat wasn't one of those. It was a new-build tucked off the main road. From the steps you could see the viewing platform of the i360 going up and down. It had just been erected and already people considered it an eyesore. I never minded the thing.

I slipped looking up at it and had to steady myself before we reached the door. He took out his keys and led us up the stairs. His bedsit was bigger than mine but cut into an L-shape wrapped around a useless inner porch. He had a window, a kitchenette and four white walls. And that was it. We stood in the middle of the empty room with Antonio marvelling at the space around us, lit only by the cold street light coming through the window. He walked over to the corner, pulled out his sleeping bag and spread it out on the carpet. As he did, a goalkeeper's glove slipped out – his sister's. He'd shown it to me before in the kitchen at Hostelpoint. He laid it out against the corner of the room like a bunch of flowers and smoothed out his sleeping bag. He slumped onto it, groaning, and even in the emptiness of the flat he looked every bit at home.

I stared out the window with the cachaça bottle warm in my hands, and as he dragged the sleeping bag over his body I heard him faintly singing.

'*Legionarios y fascistas… ¡Ay Carmela!… ¡Ay Carmela!…*'

I thought his eyes would be closed but they weren't. They

were wide open and searching mine. Too intense for me to hold.

'See you soon, mate.'

I don't know why I said *mate*. I never said *mate*. I turned away with the tired, flushed feeling heavy in my muscles.

A summer breeze from the window crossed my face and ran underneath my shirtsleeves. With just a hint of chill.

I had no idea what to expect from Pride, after all the hype that Brighton builds around it throughout the year, but in the end I felt nothing but excitement as we walked into the Pavilion Gardens and saw them completely obscured by the crowds. They covered the grass, the pavements, the short walls broad enough to sit on, even the bushes and flowerbeds. They chattered excitedly in the bright sunlight – large groups with crates and drums, smaller groups with shopping bags full of warm cans, mingling with strangers, inviting each other to sit. In an open circle, grown men skipped rope. Everybody – almost everybody – was splashed with rainbow colours, even the two policemen walking slowly through a cloud of potent, nettle-smelling smoke they seemed happy to ignore. Bare nipples appeared ubiquitously. Glitter prevailed. Underneath the wigs and whistles I saw the faces of normal, deserving people – office workers, shopkeepers, baristas, binmen. A just relief for the average weekend drinker, allowed a box of wine on a Saturday morning, on the pavement, in full view of their colleagues. I was happy not to find a glimmer of nerves in me.

Antonio was surprised I wasn't working behind the bar that day. I told him I'd won my freedom from Carlos in a card game. I'd had to put up my next four free Saturdays as collateral, but I'd cheated and won. Carlos knew I cheated, I think, but he let me go.

We ran around to meet the parade passing on the other side of the Pavilion and found more people tightly packed together. I kept an eye on Antonio as the floats passed, wondering how he'd respond to it all. He'd arrived in a buttoned shirt with the sleeves rolled up and jeans with smart shoes and a belt – not exactly festival wear. Since then, someone had smeared a sparkly rainbow on his cheek, which he pointed to repeatedly, and his shirt had lost some buttons. He cheered at the floats, especially those with fetish burlesque, inflatable penises or drag acts. When a pair of mounted police passed with tinsel on their helmets, he looked awestruck. We followed behind them in a wake of colourful debris and crushed plastic. The space closed in around us until we were part of the parade itself, watched by the people still waving flags from the pavement.

The parade stopped and started, on past the pubs and shops broadcasting camp music, past the cafes barricaded at the door with tables selling punch, past the ambulances and circles of drunk teenagers handing out balloons. We joined the queue for an off-licence – it snaked all the way around the aisles of beans and tampons, out the door, down the street. Antonio raved about the day. Quick, excited Spanish – an absolute torrent of it. Something he did when he got overexcited, until I calmed him down.

A message came through from Laurie.

On route?

She knew I was with Antonio and we'd already had the conversation about how much time we were spending together. I told her he was a good guy, a solid guy, and she just warned me to make sure he wasn't a weirdo. Maybe just because he was an older man. *Don't end up getting Rohypnoled* were her actual words. I told her not to worry about it, he was straight, but she just laughed and we left it at that. I knew if she was really concerned, she would have knocked his lights out and dragged me away.

I had to clamp my hand over Antonio's mouth to remind him about the party. A few shirtless boys tried to get him to dance with them in the off-licence. They were laughing and so was I but when they put their hands on him he drew back, firmly but politely, and bowed with his palm to his chest.

'*Está bien mirar, amigos, pero por favor no me toquéis*, thank you.'

After that they seemed bored with him and danced off down the aisle. He took a bottle of Buckfast and cradled it in the crook of his arm as if it were a child in his care.

'Antonio—'

'Yes, yes,' tapping his temple seriously, 'I remember. We go now?'

A girl in the shop told me it was four o'clock.

I sent a message to Laurie:

Running all the way x

I led Antonio out of the shop – the boys from the queue followed us and then danced down the street ahead of us. He passed me the first genuinely cold drink of the day, G&T in a can. I kissed it. Then we were both downing our drinks in one, and spluttering over the cold of them, and cheering at an old man with a perfect white thong of untanned skin creeping up from his naked arse.

*

Marta's new flat looked directly onto the main road from the ground floor. Music from the party faced out into the streets and the steps were covered in people dancing. A few people in frills and feathers looked down at us from the roof, waving at the crowds like performers from a stationary float. I pointed them out to Antonio, gripping his arm, showing him with a proud nod that these were our people, his people. His eyes drew narrow and his chest puffed out.

'Very good, Jorge,' was all he said.

We shimmied through the people on the steps, through the corridor, which was so full we had to tuck in our bellies, and into the living room. Except for the sunlight, it could have been any party past midnight. A few people had cracked their glowsticks prematurely. A framed portrait of Joan Baez tilted under the weight of silly spray. The furniture had been pushed against the walls and the living room floor was filled with moving bodies. The first person I recognised was Duncan.

He danced on a dining chair with a girl who had her hands around his waist. She flicked her green highlights. It wasn't Marta. They weren't grinding on each other, not exactly – just dancing to a song from my schooldays I'd forgotten all about, something sweaty. The look in Duncan's eyes was vacant-drunk. I'd seen him a couple of times like that over the summer and I knew Marta didn't like it. I waved to him but he didn't see me.

Antonio shouted over the music. 'Where is you sister?' He was beaming now.

'Let's see.'

People danced with us instinctively as we moved through but I was excited to find Laurie and Helena. It was only on the stairs, trying not to knock a snogging couple with my dirty feet, that I realised I had at some happy moment relieved myself of my shoes and socks.

We met Marta on the landing. I guessed by the look on her face that she'd already seen Duncan and the girl and wondered if I'd seen it too. She twiddled her septum piercing, eyes tracing the coving over our heads. I could see she wanted to talk, but maybe not in front of Antonio, who I guess she barely knew.

'*¡Buenas tardes, Marta!*' He mimed strumming a guitar. '*¿Estás tocando música para nosotros esta noche?*'

She smiled politely. 'English, please.'

'*Oh sí. Eres de Barcelona, ¿no? ¿No te gusta hablar español a veces?*'

'No. Anyway, my native tongue is Catalan.' Still she smiled, though with no joy in her eyes. 'Do you have a drink?'

Antonio presented the Buckfast like it was a key to the city.

'Oh,' she said, and seemed to relax. 'Monk sauce. Well, that won't do.'

I recognised it, the same kindness we'd spoken about together once while dishing out veggie sausages at a barbecue in Hove. The kindness that takes you out of yourself, which guaranteed no one would ask how she was or where she'd been or why she was quieter, typically, than everyone else. She told us graciously to wait, and after a few minutes she emerged from the bathroom with two glasses made of actual glass, filled with an actual drink. They dripped with cool water from the bathtub. I rubbed mine on my face. *Heaven.* Antonio was so bowled over by her generosity that he seemed to sober up for just long enough to give her a firm, military *¡Salud!*. She laughed softly, her good nature shining through.

There was a buffet on the sideboard in the nearest bedroom – tapas, breadsticks, bowls of untouched crisps. Through the window that opened out onto the roof, I could see bright colours and glitter and dancing. Antonio lifted up a cocktail stick for Marta to inspect.

'This is *tapa* – particular to my town.'

'You don't say?' she said.

'*The same!* Yes…' He twirled the stick. 'Is the same.'

She asked where in Spain his town was. He was proud to explain, making a map of Spain on his palm and pressing the entrée onto Guadalupe. While he spoke I watched the dancers on the roof, all mixing and swirling and spinning each other round. Then a few dancers parted and in the gap I saw Laurie and Helena, away from the dancing, alone by the mess of aerials. They were speaking seriously, it looked like, and trying not to be heard. Helena saw me watching them from inside and pointed me out. I shot them down with double revolvers on my thumbs and forefingers. Helena feigned a hit, let some blood spurt onto Laurie. They beckoned me outside. If I was interrupting something they both seemed glad of it.

I slapped Antonio's open palm with mine. He looked shocked, as if I'd squashed Spain.

'Let's go onto the roof.'

Marta ushered us on and I watched the confidence recede again from her face while the kindness remained. 'Go ahead,' she said. 'I'm afraid of heights.'

'So am I,' I said, Antonio pushing me with his heavy hands. 'I think.'

*

There were a dozen people on the flat rooftop – some dancing, some talking idly. From there I could see the streets below beginning to empty out, the litter of drunk teenagers stumbling over the kerbs. Above them, painted people hung out of windows, waved at us from other parties on other rooftops. And beyond them were the chimneys and the last purpling light of the sky, still full of noise.

Antonio ignored Laurie completely until he'd made a full bow to Helena and again offered up our Buckfast, which had now lost its cap. She refused and he bowed again, taking her hand and thanking her and telling her she had a beautiful home. He was in a bowing mood, it seemed.

'Thank you so much but I don't live here. This is Marta's house.'

'Is very beautiful,' Antonio reiterated. 'Very English.'

Which I suppose it was, like all the houses on that street. The sash windows, the cornices, the roof. Very Brighton even. By then Marta had a steady job at the university but she'd already told me the only way she could afford this flat was because she shared it with seven other people, all Spanish migrants who'd come through the hostel. A familiar situation.

Antonio took out his phone and held up a picture of a small white villa for Helena. She pulled his outstretched hand towards her. 'Is this your house in Spain?'

'This is my family house. In Extremadura. It has swimming pool, garage, there is olive here…'

Without his eyes leaving the phone, Antonio squeezed Laurie's arm and told her: 'I must make him to go with me there.' He meant me. 'He was in all world, but he never was in Spain!'

Laurie stared down at her arm where he'd touched her, said nothing. From all that I'd told her about Antonio and the very few times they'd seen each other, she couldn't have been surprised by his familiarity, if that's what it was. *He's a traditional kind of man*, I told her, though I think she took that as shorthand for *dinosaur*. She looked at me through the corner of her eye, serious and on guard. I wanted to get her alone to ask her what was wrong. Helena asked Antonio if he missed home.

'Yes,' he nodded. 'But Brighton...' He always said the word with a heavy emphasis on the second syllable – *Brightón*, as if it had a missing G on the end. 'The people is so...' but he just scrunched up his face and growled.

I flinched when he pinched my arm, and then hit him back. Laurie continued to watch us from the corner of her eye.

'Tell them about your sister,' I said. I thought that would bring her in.

Antonio's face turned to deep emotion, a feigned lack of breath, a clutch of the heart. 'My sister coming here. For my birthday.'

'That's wonderful,' said Helena.

'You meet,' he said. 'All you meet.'

'Well, naturally!' she said, and she seemed to mean it even if Laurie, running her finger over the lip of her plastic cup, looked unconvinced.

I whispered in her ear. 'You alright?'

'Sorry. Yes, I'm fine.'

Antonio poured Buckfast into all our cups, whether we already had drink in them or not, and made us clink.

'*Salud, salud, salud.*'

I was smiling and Antonio was smiling, and Helena and Laurie seemed happy to clink, and I recognised the music as something scrappy and melodic from the late 70s. Whatever it was it reminded me of the hours we spent sat cross-legged on the carpet of Laurie's bedroom. Those safe, gangly years.

Antonio gave a Spanish trill as the dancers closed in around us, the smoke and laughter, kicking legs. Someone passed me a shot of something green. *Andalusia, Federico Lorca, the Guardia Civil* – yes, that was it, Joe Strummer's jutting voice, that song from our teenage years, 'Spanish Bombs'. I grabbed Antonio and tried to point out the Spanglish to him but he didn't understand. He was saying something and his lips looked red and eager but whatever it was got lost in the spitty voices of the few people singing along and swinging each other round as the sun disappeared. I held on to Antonio and shouted in his ear *Listen! Listen!* and then he pulled Laurie and Helena in so it was the four of us together under the music.

Again I caught a sense that this was how things were supposed to be, though even then – perhaps because of the tiredness creeping up on me – a voice in my head said, quite clearly, as if coming through the music itself or perhaps through the hum of noise rising off the city at dusk: *sunsets don't last forever, Jorge*. But what could I do about that?

The green shot swirled in my hand like a perfect little universe.

Heave-ho, down the hatch.

From here there are only flashes of memory. A girl with a fluorescent hula hoop. A fag burn on my forearm. The choking smell of Antonio's cologne. I was far beyond the appropriate level of drunkenness for a rooftop, but I felt like everybody was. *That's one of the functions of Pride,* one of them said, a woman perhaps, *on top of the – hic – politics of it. That's what we're supposed to do.*

My sobriety rejoined me sometime after I'd lost my drink, when I realised I was holding a bottle of water and a cigarette, neither of which I could imagine having asked for. The sense of where I was came fast, like waking up suddenly on public transport. I may have actually slept, since it was now night-time and the music had become more charged and driving and there were twice as many people on the roof. I was alarmingly near the edge – I think that's what woke me up. I had to yank myself away from it. The people moved their bodies around me quite happily, completely focused on the music and each other.

The first people I recognised were Laurie and Helena. Thank God. I headed straight for the crook of Helena's arm. I think I was interrupting a tiff because Laurie growled the word *Trummmp* before they both fell silent.

She was sober, I think. She stood up idly onto the ledge of the roof. Helena snapped at her to step back down. She did.

'I'm going to get a drink,' she said.

Helena took my arm. Her hair was tousled and there were dark bags under her eyes but she was fine – she could always hold her drink. She was in better shape than I was at least, though now my mind was clearing. She asked if I was enjoying the party.

'Wow. Yes, it's fantastic. The roof is fantastic.'

I was swaying a little too broadly. She steadied me.

'I was just looking for Antonio,' I said.

She pointed him out. He was by the window that brought us onto the roof, gesticulating wildly for Marta. The mascara was running under her eyes.

'Poor girl,' I said, and considered going over, though it looked like Antonio was handling it.

I hadn't expected Duncan to go for somebody else, in front of everyone, if that's what was happening. But then it didn't surprise me either. Still, it was none of my business, not really.

'She'll be fine,' said Helena. 'Laurie's a little disappointed, I think.'

'What do you mean?'

'She thought Duncan was different, that's all. I told you he just gets carried away.'

He just gets carried away – yes, that's what she'd said before. Maybe that night outside the off-licence had been the same kind of thing. It bothered me that they'd put me in that position, having to keep it a secret, however innocent it might have been. I'd had to carry that around since June, knowing that Laurie was the only one of us who hadn't seen what had happened. Whatever had happened. I could have told her – I thought of telling her, so many times – and maybe then they all could have cleared the air early and moved on. But no, that wouldn't have worked out. Not with Laurie.

'And how is Antonio?' Helena asked. 'Is he enjoying himself?'

'Oh, yes. Yes, he's loving it.'

She squeezed me tighter. 'He's quite enamoured with you, isn't he?'

'He's grateful, I think. To have someone around.' But I

didn't sound convincing, even to myself. I'd been lucky to put off having this conversation even for the few weeks I'd known him.

'He doesn't have a girlfriend, does he?'

'No.'

'I didn't think so.'

Antonio was still comforting Marta, though she didn't seem to be following what he was saying. Her eyes were cast down like they'd been at the pub that night. Struggling for the strength to lift.

'And you?' said Helena. 'What do you think of him?'

'Antonio? What do you mean?'

'George, darling. Don't be obtuse.'

The lights and the music were swirling around us then.

'Honestly, I don't know what I think. Most of the time I think he's straight, like he makes out to be, and then occasionally I get the sense that he might be attracted to me physically.' It was more than I'd articulated even to myself. 'I don't know.'

'And what about you?'

I laughed. It didn't come off. 'I'm straight. I mean, I've got off with men in the past but I'm straight. He's exciting. He makes me feel...' But I didn't have the words. 'I don't know. He makes me feel safe. He's like Laurie, he's like a big brother.'

Helena kissed me on the cheek. 'He's nothing like Laurie, darling. Just try to work out what you want, and what he wants.'

Then, lunging through the open window, Duncan came up with the girl from downstairs. I could see her properly now –

dyed blonde hair with green highlights and pale freckled skin. She looked a lot like Marta, even down to the beauty spots on her arms. Duncan saw who was on the roof, turned the girl around, and went straight back through the window.

Marta burst into tears.

Helena rushed over. Through the crowd I could see Antonio holding Marta by both arms, rubbing his hand on her elbow and through her hair and talking in her ear. I could see he was consoling her and for a moment I failed to process what was happening when I saw her wriggle, and heard the scream. She screamed at the top of her voice, a scream that clattered around the rooftops, far above the music – an ugly sound, impossible to mistake. Helena pulled Antonio away, forcefully enough, then let him go. He backed off with his palms raised.

One of Marta's housemates bustled her inside the house. The people all around stared at Antonio. A girl in white denim filmed on her phone. I reached him in a daze.

'Good God,' I said. 'What did you say to her?'

'*No dije nada, solo quería...*'

I saw Laurie clambering back onto the roof in a hurry. She rushed over to us, looked me up and down. 'What's happening?' She held Helena back by the waist but there was no danger. Helena said *Laurie, please* and she let go of her. She asked Antonio firmly what had happened.

'*Todo lo que quería decirle era que había estado en la misma posición que ella antes y...*'

Before we could fix it, Marta's housemate reappeared on the rooftop. I could see by her face she meant business. 'I've put her in the bathroom.' Her accent thickly Spanish. 'She's really upset.'

'Listen to me,' I began. 'I really don't think—'

'I think it would be best if you two fucked off.'

Antonio didn't understand. I took his elbow. 'Come on.'

He stared at Marta's housemate as if wanting to challenge her, even just to challenge her for an explanation, but he lost his words.

'I'm serious,' she said. Her face was full of righteous anger. 'I really am.'

I slurred: 'I really don't think it's how it looks. If you—'

'Please, just fuck off.'

I looked back to see a boy in carnival costume biting the paint off his nails and the girl in white denim with her phone, still filming. My head span. Awful awkwardness and injustice and the need to escape. I looked at Laurie – I was sure she would try to insist we stay, or that she'd offer to come with us. She stood there looking like she was making up her mind about something.

'Laurie?' I said.

But she said nothing and she didn't follow us.

'Fine.' I led Antonio through the bedroom, the landing, the stairs, and in the corridor we passed Duncan and the girl with the green highlights who were arguing and never noticed us.

After we were spat out onto the street I could see half a dozen faces peering at us from the rooftop – Laurie and Helena among them. I led Antonio under the bridge where the drunken crowds were thinner.

'I'm so sorry, Antonio. God, that was awful. Are you okay? What happened?'

He explained at passionate length in his own language, rambling on as if I understood. Overexcited. I squinted at my bare dirty feet on the pigeon-shit pavement and listened while the drinkers on the street stumbled, cackled, retched. The final transition from day-Pride to night-Pride.

After ten minutes I said once, just once: 'I'm sorry, Antonio. I don't understand.' That made all the confusion drain from Antonio's face and pool into a neat, helpless smile.

For all the music and shouting around us, it felt like we were alone when I looked into his eyes. I smiled back, struggling with something within myself and noticing it, and he reached out to put a hand on my shoulder. A firework burst above the bridge and someone barged through, right through the middle of us, on their way to the park.

'Thank you, Jorge,' he said, returning his hand to my shoulder.

'*De nada*,' I said.

'You are very especial to me.'

I wanted to tell myself that the look in his eyes was brotherly, as I'd taken that look all summer, but it wasn't. I was just trying to make it easier on myself.

'Yes,' I said. 'I mean, your friendship is very special to me.'

He hugged me tight, like a brother, like he understood. Then his hands moved down to the small of my back before we parted. And I knew he didn't understand.

He leant in as if to kiss me and I leant back. 'I'm sorry, Antonio.' Not knowing if he was aiming for my cheek, like a Spanish man might, or for my lips.

He breathed deeply, nodded, stepped back. Then he smiled. 'Yes, Jorge. Of course, Jorge.'

As if all I'd asked for was a little more time.

I never got the full truth about what happened at Pride. Antonio spoke about Marta and the rest of them as if they were his friends – not even old friends he'd temporarily fallen out with but a friendly crowd who were looking forward to bumping into him soon. He insisted I invite them to his birthday celebrations, even stopped to watch me message them, but the replies were scarce and vague. When I asked Laurie in person, she told me that she and Helena would be at the March for Europe in London, and then I knew there was no hope of getting a crowd together. Without Helena we wouldn't see Duncan or the others, though maybe that was for the best. All I really wanted was for Laurie to be there, especially since Antonio's sister would be there too. I even asked if she would change her plans, skip the march. *Already committed*, she said, though I knew it was because she didn't really have time for Antonio. Pride didn't help, even if she did know he wasn't hitting on Marta. So I went alone to Antonio's flat on the day he turned forty.

He met me at the door in his work shirt with the insignia of the yellow castle. He held on to me by my backpack as we hugged and I wished him *Feliz cumpleanos* in my terrible accent. I don't know if he picked up on it but the anxiety was turning my stomach – not for the potential awkwardness of having to tell him I'd come alone, or even for meeting his sister who was due to arrive that afternoon, but because of the secret I carried in my backpack. Something I'd been working on for several weeks, that neither Antonio nor Laurie nor anybody else knew about. I just had to give it to him before his sister arrived.

'*Venga*,' he said on the stairs. 'I cook.'

It was almost exactly a month since he'd laid out his sleeping bag in the empty room. In that time the place had been transformed. The Brighton tradition of leaving unwanted domestic goods out on the street – regardless of how broken they are, how difficult to move or how degradingly stained – amazed Antonio from the day he arrived. He never got over the fact that people would simply abandon working televisions, chests-of-drawers, cracked mirrors, chairs with split wicker seats, dusty decanters, misshapen woks. Now the stuff filled his flat to bursting. I moved aside a pile of his Spanish Civil War books to sit.

'This is *salmorejo*,' he said, pointing to the blender. He dropped in pieces of onion, garlic, pepper, tomatoes.

'Oh, you've got a blender now.' I reached for my backpack. I had to get it done, now or never. 'Listen, I must give you your presen—'

He interrupted me with the blender. I thought I could get a word in after he'd blitzed the vegetables, but before I could he reached into the sink and pulled out a whole baguette dripping with cold water, then stuffed the mush into the machine and shouted *¡Morir!* – a death wish. The mixture beat violently for several minutes before settling to a calm pinkish grey. It looked like the paint on an English cottage, or brain soup. He halved another baguette – unsoaked – and poured the mix over it with pieces of boiled egg and Serrano. As he added the oil and I made one last attempt to interrupt, a woman's voice came through the window.

His face lit up. 'Is her!'

He shot out and I sat there with my backpack at my feet, thinking about the present inside. I'd have to give it to him in front of his sister now, no choice. I wish I'd rehearsed it in my mind. A dollop of the pinkish grey pulp dripped from the plate to the counter. I was still holding my breath from a puff on my inhaler when she came through the door.

Antonio had always described her as a vulnerable young woman who he took pride in looking after. But this woman had a sharp look in her eye and taut lips that looked like they never smiled. Her pantsuit looked expensive and professional and brought out the breadth of her shoulders. She looked less like the teenage girl in the goalkeeper's uniform than like the pictures of Antonio's mother. Actually, in the line of her nose and the square cut of her jaw, she looked a lot like Antonio himself, only nearer my age than his.

I rose and exhaled loudly and stuck out my hand which she failed to notice. Antonio came in behind her with her suitcase. He hugged her and then me and then her again. I made some room for her on the sofa while he fussed with his phone.

Music started. *¡Ay Carmela! ¡Ay Carmela!*

'I'm George.'

'Yes, I know. I'm Alejandra.' Her voice was hoarse and even. '*Antonio, no esa mierda, por favor.*'

The music died.

'I'm so pleased to meet you,' I said.

'Likewise.'

Antonio ground some pepper over the food. I thought *Maybe I should offer her a drink* though it wasn't my flat. 'Your English is very good, by the way. Your accent is superb.'

'I know. I teach English in Madrid.' She reminded me of Laurie, just faintly. That severe way she could be with strangers.

Antonio passed around the plates and I followed their lead on how to eat it. After a few silent bites he asked her in English: 'What you think my home?' and she wiped a little of the sauce from her mouth.

'George, we're going to speak in Spanish from now on.'

'Oh,' I said, 'yes, of course,' though she wasn't asking permission.

They spoke rapidly and seriously. I ate the *salmorejo* in silence – it was starchy and plain but well flavoured by the ham. Occasionally I got a gist of what they were arguing about – the word *trabajo*, 'work', was repeated often. I took it from the way she gestured around the room that she was unimpressed with the bedsit or perhaps just with the accumulated junk. At one point Antonio got up to show her the goalkeeper's glove waving at us from the bedpost, which seemed to soften her. But after that they were arguing again and I just sat there chewing and trying to look like I wasn't listening. I felt even worse when I considered that they might be talking about me. I thought maybe I should leave. But how would that work?

Before their argument came to a head a message came through from Laurie. A photograph of her and Helena and a few hundred flags and banners flapping in the wind, with the words *You would love this* underneath. Her face smiling but purposeful.

Alejandra pushed her plate away in frustration. Antonio hustled the dirty dishes into the sink.

'Sorry, Jorge,' he said. 'We have family talk.'

'That's okay. The food was delicious by the way.'

Alejandra lit a cigarette. I subdued a cough.

'Okay, *venga*,' said Antonio, spritzing himself with aftershave though he must already have been wearing a gallon. 'We go out now.'

Which was fine but I hadn't planned on giving him his present outside the flat. And now I had no idea whether everything was alright between him and his sister and me, though those two seemed ready to put the argument behind them. I guessed that was their way.

Antonio asked me when we'd meet the others. I could feel Alejandra watching my answer.

'They're all in London,' I said, and Alejandra blew a long line of smoke. It was almost sarcastic.

'Hm, London…' Antonio weighed this up for a second, and then threw his concern over his shoulder with a flourish. 'Then boat is for us.'

'The vote? What vote?'

'No the boat.' He rolled his eyes. 'The *boat*.'

Alejandra stubbed out her cigarette on the dinner plate. 'Come on or we'll miss it.'

Antonio handed me a bottle of Bacardi for my backpack and turned away. As I drew down the zip, Alejandra came between us, slipped the bottle from my hand and placed it gently behind a rusty cocktail shaker on the floor. I met her eye but she said nothing, just reached down and zipped up my bag for me.

'*Vamos*,' said Antonio, and I stood there with the backpack. I thought maybe I should hang on to his present until another time. *I could even leave the backpack here, as if by mistake… and then come back—*

Alejandra held the door open. 'Let's go.'

I'd already told Antonio the story about me nearly drowning during a swimming lesson, though I'm not sure he understood it. It had happened sometime near the end of primary school – my hair got caught in a vent while retrieving a rubber brick and the teacher had to yank me out and give me mouth-to-mouth. After that I had to watch the classes from the balcony above the pool, clothed and dry with the shame of having snogged a male PE teacher hanging over me for the rest of my school life.

Perhaps just because of that I never swam again, and because I couldn't swim the water became another thing that brought the nerves up in me. I hadn't explained that to Antonio, not clearly at least, so I couldn't really blame him when he pulled me by the wrist onto the tour boat that leaves hourly from Brighton Marina, having refused to let me wait in the West Quay or even to pay for my own ticket. Though Alejandra understood. I could see by the way she looked at me as I shuffled across the gangplank. I could feel it as she watched me checking under my seat for a lifejacket – not panicking, just checking. I wanted to tell her I was more nervous about the thing in my backpack than by the open water but instead I sat there and tried to listen to her brother who was jabbering excitedly in broken English. At least he was happy. It was his birthday after all.

As the boat chugged away from the jetty and out along the high walls of the marina, I felt Antonio's arm pass around me and slap me warmly on the opposite shoulder. He left it there, as he sometimes did when we were drunk, and beside me Alejandra crossed her legs and stared out at the boats. Only after we passed through the gap in the marina barrier did the engine begin to roar as we sped up across the open water.

From the sea, Brighton's shore stretches out in one long continuous line, unnaturally straight and unbroken but for the stone groynes that reach out from the shingle. It looks almost fake in its seamless straightness, like a Potemkin village for invaders from off-coast. Antonio loved every inch of it, leaning right across me to point out curiosities to his sister. He got especially animated when we passed the fisherman's enclosure east of the Palace Pier, though even squinting I could barely make it out. I don't think he noticed how I gripped my seat at each bump of the boat and said nothing to either of them while I held in my stomach. Or perhaps he could see from my face that even with the white water splashing up around us, a part of me was as thrilled by it as he was.

I was just finding my stride when Antonio called *Un momento* above the roar of the engine, and then, craning his head around: 'I want speak with the *capitán*.'

Over the heads of the passengers behind us I could see the captain's face laughing in the broad window of the cabin, a ruddy kind of face like you might expect. Alejandra called after her brother in Spanish but he dismissed her with a wave. I didn't know if he was allowed in there or not, but in a moment his face appeared in the captain's window, looking serious and comradely and overtly masculine. Alejandra lit a cigarette, which she hid in the palm of her hand as she smoked. The cold look that had been on her face all day remained, directed now only at me.

'My brother loves boats,' she called into my ear.

I couldn't hear, she had to say it again.

'Oh,' I said. 'Yes, he loves the water, doesn't he?'

'It reminds him of the navy.'

She stared at me then, quite openly, as if what she said had been a challenge.

'Yes,' I said.

She leant in again. 'He told me you helped him to find the job at the supermarket.'

'No, not really.' The boat rocked awkwardly at the crest of a wave. 'Anyway, he'll get something better when his English improves.'

'Yes, well.' She blew smoke over her shoulder. 'Perhaps *if* it improves.'

I didn't know what she meant but the way she stared at me did nothing to ease my nerves. The white foam splashed up violently around the boat.

'Look,' she said, but what she said next was taken by the crash of the waves.

'What was that?' I called.

'Are you a homosexual?'

I thought I must have misheard her but I hadn't. Ahead of us, the skeleton of the West Pier loomed out of the water, black and menacing.

I had to shout. 'What are you talking about?'

Another bump.

'You heard what I said. Are you a homosexual?'

I paused. I could have told her that I'd never slept with a man but why was she asking me at all? What did it have to do with her? Obviously she wanted to know what kind of relationship I had with her brother, but even if it was like that, even if we had slept together, what right had she to ask me like that? If she was that keen to know, why didn't she just ask her brother?

'I don't mind,' she called. 'Just tell me so I know.'

But before I could think of anything to say, Antonio stumbled across her lap and wriggled back into his chair.

'*Impressionate, impressionate,*' he said. 'Next time we bring Laurie, yes.'

I was thrust towards him by the tilt of the boat turning back to the marina.

He leant into my ear. 'Jorge,' so his sister couldn't hear, 'the rum.'

Alejandra got up and walked to the edge. Standing there in her suit jacket, looking over the railings towards the shore with her chin lifted, she looked like their *bisabuelo*. My nerves were in my throat then so that it felt like the boat might tip any second and hurl me into the water. I glanced down at my bag. On top of everything I'd forgotten about my secret.

'I'm sorry,' I told Antonio. 'Must have left it in the flat.'

His palm found the back of my neck, rubbed it warmly and carefully. '*Idiota.*'

Antonio marched us back down the seafront and straight to the off-licence at East Street where he came out with a bottle of Cane Trader and a single can of Coke, which he gave sarcastically to his sister. He wanted to show her the Lanes and we followed him dutifully through the cobbled alleys and around Ship Street and Middle Street till we were flushed back out onto Kingsway as the sun went down. We wandered down the Potemkin promenade, which had looked so quiet from the sea, past the nightclubs and the queues of young people and the shuttered arcades. I heard a couple of teenagers arguing about Trump, who I still hadn't paid a whole lot of attention to, despite Laurie's efforts. It's true – I was falling out of touch. Antonio led us to the fishing boat he'd wept in on the day he got his flat, explained something about it to Alejandra that took a full half-hour. He tried to get through the fence that shut off the sleeping carousel but failed. When we got to the pier he wrung his groin and said: 'Come, Jorge, we piss.'

I laughed. 'No, thanks. There's rivers of piss under there already.' His sister was watching me. 'I'll stay with Alejandra.'

A few lads with plastic pint glasses stumbled past.

'I'm fine,' she said. 'Go ahead, "Jorge".'

When Antonio said it, it sounded like a mark of endearment and respect. When she said it, it sounded like a grubby fetish.

He dragged me by the wrist and the movement of my feet sent pebbles skittering ahead of me under the pier. Nobody was there. He stood facing me, without pissing, and put both hands on my shoulders. Other than the unsettling sound of dripping water, it was horribly quiet, as in a cold, dank basement where anything might happen.

'Come,' he said, and tilted my head back to pour a little Cane Trader down my throat. 'I want tell you something.'

His voice was low and flat and the rum had made his face flush. I tried to move but his eyes were on me. 'Please don't worry my sister.' He meant worry about her.

'I don't think she likes me very much.'

'She is. She is just sad because she is in love with married man. He is in Madrid.'

'Oh. I see.'

'Listen me.' He lifted one stiff finger to my face so that I knew that his own secret, whatever it was he wanted from me, was coming. He breathed. 'I want you come to Spain. With me.'

'Oh.' I caught a breath. 'You want to go to Spain.'

'Yes.' He was triumphant. 'Together. My home...'

He reeled off a string of details about his house, his garden, his swimming pool, his car. He said it would cost practically nothing and that I'd only have to pay for my own wine. I nodded along carefully to his excitement.

'Well, I'd have to see about work,' I said, 'and about money in general—'

But he didn't listen. 'When I have found my *grey granfather*... We go to statue memorial in London.'

'Where?'

'The statue *monumento a las Brigadas Internacionales*. Is in London.' He was beaming then but I wasn't sure what he was talking about. 'And then we go to Spain.'

I tried to speak about my money issues again but he just threw his arms around me and the warmth of his body came between me and the cool, wet air under the pier. I could feel his love for me then, the deep value I had for him, and his joy that I was there, with him and his sister, on his fortieth birthday.

'Listen, Antonio...' I'd decided to save his present until Alejandra wasn't around but now the excitement in his voice was bringing it all out of me. 'This is your present. Your birthday present, I mean.'

He laughed. 'Is it beer?' His laughter echoed around the underside of the pier, a few birds flew out and a figure in a sleeping bag, laid out on cardboard by a steel post, sat up slowly in the dark.

'No, it's not beer.' I pulled out the plastic folder.

Antonio looked at it without touching it. 'What is?'

'Take a look,' I said.

He opened it and pulled out the single piece of paper inside. He read it carefully, with no emotion on his face, for at least a minute. I watched his eyes scan the page, line after line. Eventually he lowered the paper and dropped his head.

His voice was quiet. 'What is this?'

I stumbled over the words. 'It's a family tree. Actually, your family tree.'

He looked again but said nothing. I pointed out at the name at the bottom.

'This,' I said, 'is your great-grandfather, from the photograph. His name was Arthur John Martín.'

His eye moved from the name at the bottom to the names above, none of which were English. In fact they reverted immediately to Spanish. I pointed out Arthur's father and grandfather.

'It seems as though your great-great-grandfather Javier came over from Spain just before the First World War, to work at a dockyard. Arthur was the first one born in the UK.' Something I'd been amazed to find through my weeks of pouring through local history files, searching through archives – the Spanish inflection waving at me from his surname. Arthur John Martín.

Antonio looked up at me with the tears glistening on his face.

'So it seems like you're Spanish after all,' I joked.

He went quiet, wouldn't let me look away. I could see the water welling up in his eyes, and his lips were also wet and unsmiling. He shut his eyes and leant forward and must have thought I was doing the same. His lips came towards mine so I could smell the rum coming off him. I almost leant forward and kissed him. But I didn't.

'I'm sorry,' I said. 'This isn't what I want.'

He didn't look upset, just overwhelmed. I don't know if it was the shock of my present or of me pushing him away.

'Okay,' he said, though I had no idea whether it was. He smiled weakly, held up the paper. 'Thank you for this.' And then turned and marched out from under the pier.

I watched him jog across the stones towards his sister, watched her crush her cigarette under her shoe. Antonio took her by the arm and walked on with her and I followed and listened to him jabbering in Spanish. From behind and with the rum slurring his voice I could only understand one word, repeated over and over with increasing power and volume.

Jorge, Jorge, Jorge.

By the end of September nothing of summer was left. The blue sky that had hung almost uninterrupted over the sea was covered now in ubiquitous cloud. The flow of tourists that sustains the season petered out slowly until the streets were half empty. Walking along the prom I remembered how Laurie had described the place in winter, when the cold wind chases you up into town from the seafront and the pubs are steamed up and crowded. I knew it would be like this again, with the whole city hunkering down for the long, cold stretch ahead.

All through October, while the leaves fell and were turned to mulch by the rain, Antonio said nothing about his attempt to kiss me and I didn't have the courage to bring it up. Instead he talked about Spain and ignored any indication I gave him that I didn't currently have the money for any kind of holiday at all. The colder it got the more he spoke about it, looking up the temperature on his phone, showing me the flight prices falling off-season. His sister's question rang in my mind at odd times but Antonio never seemed to notice me drifting, just kept on and on about our trip when I would see his *pueblo*, meet his family. When I finally sent him a message one morning in November saying *Ha Antonio I need to save $$$*, he offered to take me to a pub to talk it over. I told him I was already halfway up Clifton Hill on my way to Laurie's house – she was taking me down to some march of hers, a regular thing I'd been putting off for weeks that I couldn't excuse myself from any longer. I got a message back within a few seconds:

Get me on way.

I found Laurie on the corner of her street with her boots set wide. She wore her denim jacket that day, maybe just because we were heading to a protest. I was softened by the sight of her jabbing away at her phone in frustration. Laurie the Luddite. Above us the sky was full of rainclouds, ready to burst.

I chided her. 'What are you doing?'

'Trying to check the polls.'

Everybody was talking about the US election — at least Laurie and the rest of them were, and the news, which seemed to be nothing else. Antonio never mentioned it once.

'When's the vote?'

She looked at me like I'd been in a coma. 'Tuesday night. Come round if you like. We're watching it at Marta's.'

We had stayed up all night for the general election in 2010, eating Kettle Chips in Laurie's room, and then sleepwalked through school the next day trying to work out how a hung parliament might turn out. I had no idea how things in the US might go, though Duncan had written repeatedly in *Left Nut* that Hilary was a 'dead cert' and that Trump's defeat would be a well-earned humiliation for the Right. Laurie didn't seem so sure.

'Tuesday night?' I said. 'Yes, maybe.'

Her screen was frozen on an image of Trump's face, smug and froggy. 'Come on, then,' she said.

'We've got to pick up Antonio on the way.'

She sniffed. 'Did you invite him?'

'Not exactly.'

'He does creep me out sometimes.'

'Don't be ridiculous.' I wanted her to be joking. I hadn't mentioned the kiss at all.

'He's a nice guy,' she said. 'I'm not saying he's not a nice guy. He's just different.'

'I know,' I said. 'That's what I like about him.'

'He's forty, for a start. Why is he hanging around with guys half his age?'

'Christ, Laurie. You're starting to sound like Dad.'

She paused on the pavement. 'Don't say that, George.' Though she knew what I meant, whether she liked it or not.

After that she only really wanted to talk about Trump and the swing states but I managed to keep her off it for most of the walk. I asked if she'd heard of a place called Rojava where the Kurds had built some kind of autonomous region that fought for democracy and equal rights and other good, progressive things. In reality I knew nothing more than I'd got off Duncan's blog, but Laurie seemed pleased I'd taken an interest. We found Antonio outside the supermarket in his uniform. He'd been on a ten-hour shift that only finished an hour ago but already he looked half drunk. He sauntered towards us with two full shopping bags in his hands. The walk of the liberated.

'*Buenas dias*, my friends!'

Antonio hugged Laurie as if he'd come across an old friend in a foreign country, and I realised they hadn't seen each other for several weeks, maybe a month. I expected a hug too. Actually I was worried as I always was that he'd be over-affectionate with me in front of my sister – something she might not understand. Instead I was surprised when he extended a very firm, very formal handshake to me. Though he winked at me while he did it.

Inevitably, he had beers for us. Laurie refused but he opened three anyway so she had to take one, though I knew she'd nurse it so she didn't have to take another. Antonio raised his and I raised mine, and Laurie was forced to join.

'*Los tres mosqueteros* – bah!' he said.

Laurie squinted. I had no idea what he was talking about either.

'*¿Uno para todos y todos para uno, no?*' He laughed sloppily. Drunker than I thought. '*Athos, Aremis, Porthos.*'

Laurie folded her arms. 'What does he mean?'

'The three musketeers.'

Antonio lifted his bottle for us once again. '*¡Salud!*'

I lifted mine. '*¡Salud!*'

Laurie took a moment, and only eventually lifted hers. '*Salud.*'

She set off first and Antonio put a gentle hand on me before we followed. He wore a proud, knowing smile, as if he was pleased that he'd gone out of his way to include Laurie, or as if there were a secret between us, some kind of pact. I recognised that look – the expression that must, for hundreds of years, have accompanied the words *knight errant*.

New Road was busy with shoppers and people in suits and the street homeless who were chatting in a large circle by the old telephone box. Like any other day. I didn't know who'd organised the protest but it was a good spot for it. People had to manoeuvre around the two groups of people facing each other down outside the theatre bar, and some inevitably stopped to talk or take pictures. Antonio wandered instinctively towards them – he was always curious about that kind of thing – and Laurie and I followed behind.

One group handed out leaflets under a large Israeli flag fluttering wildly in the wind. Another much larger group stood opposite with a long banner reading END THE OCCUPATION in black, white and green. A few of their leaflets had blown up against the benches. The two protest groups seemed in no mood for reconciliations of their own, and instead stared at each other and gave out the occasional insult. I recognised our friends on the Palestinian side.

Helena spoke calmly but firmly through her megaphone. Marta was there too – she was into Catalan independence and Palestinian liberation and that kind of thing, though she never preached about it. Duncan had a *keffiyeh* around his neck and a cold, narrow look in his eye for the opposition. That's what I took it for at first, before I smelt the weed on him. He and Marta watched us from the side – no longer a couple but still sleeping with each other, so I understood. I'd already spoken with Marta about how Antonio was just trying to help that time. She seemed to understand. But still she let herself be moved away from us by Duncan. As if we were dangerous.

Helena handed on her megaphone and came to see us. She kissed Laurie, then me, and then gave Antonio a continental peck on each cheek. I asked if the protest was *her thing*. *Her things* were always benign – I'd feel more relaxed if it was.

'Not exactly,' she said. 'We're part of the action group, we meet at the Cowley Club.' A kind of activist's social hub – a place Laurie enjoyed. I'd never been inside. 'We hoped to get a few more people...'

She told me they were competing with some kind of all-day fundraiser for climate change. She handed Laurie a stack of leaflets – the top one had a picture of an olive grove being smashed by a bulldozer. Laurie passed on half the leaflets to me and just one to Antonio.

'You for *Palestina*?' Antonio asked.

Laurie was proud. 'I'm always for the rebels.'

Antonio tutted. 'Don't forget. Franco was rebel. Trump is rebel.'

Before Laurie got the chance to answer, Antonio seemed to spot something of interest over by the benches where the alcoholics sat, and wandered off. Laurie looked at me but I just shrugged. She turned towards the people on the street. Shoppers and businessmen and the street homeless by the telephone box, getting on with things.

END APARTHEID, my leaflets said.

'Ready?'

She left me no option to refuse.

Around Laurie's GCSEs, some men from the army came to recruit at our school and I made up some leaflets telling kids not to speak to them. I remember Laurie and I ducking from the teachers and dinner ladies to pin them up all over the corridors, laughing together when we were caught by the headmaster and given detention. I felt proud all that day, until we left school and Laurie spat on the ground in front of a young soldier who passed us in the car park. I expected trouble but the boy's face just turned down towards the pavement. Walking to the bus, Laurie joked about our victory with the leaflets but I stayed quiet.

I knew that part of her was still alive and even getting stronger, but she didn't always have chance to show it. No one on New Road seemed especially interested in her spiel or in the flyers – people in Brighton have seen and heard it all before. I handed out my lot but I was relieved when we ran out. When I rejoined the group, and Laurie lingered back to lecture somebody about Gaza, the only person who seemed keen to talk with me was Helena. The rest simply protested.

She tugged my sleeve. That old conspiratorial manner. 'Guess what.'

'What.'

She beamed. 'I'm coming up to Sussex.' As if Sussex was another world altogether. 'For Christmas.'

This surprised me, though I tried not to show it. Laurie had mentioned nothing to me and I thought it strange that she chose to invite Helena then, when at the time I knew they were having problems. Actually, they'd been arguing ever since Pride, before that even, though keeping their tensions to hushed voices spoken in the corners of parties.

'That's wonderful,' I said.

'Maybe you should invite someone.'

'What do you mean?'

'For Christmas. To make a four.'

'Are we playing tennis then?'

She knocked my arm. 'I mean Antonio.'

I looked around for him but I couldn't see him. It was lunch hour now and the crowds on New Road were getting thicker and noisier.

'To the village? No, I don't think so.'

'Why not?'

'I don't know. Not this year.'

Not this year. In truth, I'd never once overlaid the image of Antonio onto the setting of our Sussex roots. He'd even given me the opportunity to invite him by telling me explicitly he had no plans for Christmas. But still I couldn't picture it. When Helena suggested it there on New Road, as if it would be the most natural invitation in the world, the first thing I thought was that I'd be embarrassed to show him the villages – my dull, flat countryside. The thought was forceful enough to push that other thought away, the one I didn't want to deal with, not just yet. Anyway. Laurie and Helena needed me, too.

'I can't see him,' I said, looking over the banners. 'Can you see him?'

Laurie appeared beside us and I noticed Helena refuse, with just a subtle twist of her wrist, to take her hand.

'Helena says she's joining us for Christmas,' I said, over-chipper.

Laurie grasped for her hand again and this time she took it, though the fit of their fingers looked awkward.

'That's right,' said Laurie. She tried to sound chipper too. 'Poor soul.'

I asked if she'd seen Antonio. She pointed to the other side of the protest, the blue-and-white half. Antonio was there, with a great doped smile on his face, taking a bagel from a woman in a MAGA hat. *Jesus Christ.*

'Excuse me,' I said.

They watched me as I wandered over to the other side – I could feel their eyes on me, Duncan's in particular, though maybe it was just my imagination. Antonio was trying to ask the protestor for a word he was missing but she didn't understand.

'It's called cream cheese,' I told him.

'*¡Jorge, mira! Ella es mi casera. Y estos son deliciosos…*'

The protestor smiled though evidently she couldn't understand. Antonio repeated slowly in English: 'This is my *lan-lady*.'

His landlady, an American woman he'd mentioned a few times for her kindness. I'd expected to meet her anywhere but here, at least not on that side. In that hat. She held out a bagel for me.

'No,' I said, a little too strongly. 'Thank you.'

'I'm trying to ask Antonio whether he's Jewish.'

I suppose he could have passed for Sephardic quite convincingly.

'Me?' he said with a mouthful of bagel. 'No. I'm a Spanish.'

His landlady laughed and I told her abruptly I was pleased to meet her and pushed Antonio back to the Palestinian side with cream cheese falling from his face. The action group watched us coldly as we crossed sides and I jumped at a moan of feedback from the megaphone. Helena spoke again, something about the West Bank. Further down the road, two community support officers paced slowly towards us. Laurie had already noticed them – I watched her shoulders broaden out. I found myself noticing the scar above her eye and being unable to look at it. For the first time in a long time.

Duncan was explaining something to Marta. '…that you can't always go by the polls. There's no way the electorate will swing by so many points overnight. As for his support from the Zionist lobby, I don't…'

By the red in his eyes and the overwhelming smell coming

from his mackintosh, I guessed that Duncan was higher than usual. He spoke automatically, drifting in between clouds of raw information and his own wit, dulled by the weed. Antonio listened intently, watching Duncan's lips through a squint. He nodded in the right places, made cooing sounds, winced when a joke was made and then laughed too late. It was possible that Duncan used enough proper nouns and swear words for Antonio to follow but I couldn't tell. It only became clear that he'd understood nothing when Duncan ran out of steam and Antonio, speaking as if a light had finally come on in his head, asked: '¿*Pacifismo?* Pacifism?'

Duncan zipped up his coat. '*No war.*'

'*Si, pero* – sometime you must have war.'

The CSOs arrived beside us. They looked over the whole thing without judgement, just looked. Helena went across to be friendly with them and Laurie stood behind her trying to look big. I thought about pulling her back but Antonio was struggling to make his views clear to Duncan and Duncan was struggling to control his temper. That's when I felt the faint flush of nausea run through me.

'War is wrong,' said Duncan, staring him in the eye. There was something desperate about him, almost helpless.

'Yes, yes. War is no good. But sometime it is *obligatorio.*'

'Not true. There is always a peaceful solution to be found, even if that means—'

'No. Sometime you must fight.' Antonio's voice rose. 'For example, if—' He gave a Roman salute indicating fascism. Several people on both sides glanced in our direction. 'Then *you*,' the hard J prefixed to his *you* again drawing heads, '*you* must make organise to remove.'

'Listen. I know the argument. But if Gandhi can bring down the British Empire without…'

Antonio huffed. The booze was glazing him over. 'My *grey gran-father* was hero *guerra civil…*'

I stepped in and tried to explain to Duncan about Arthur John Martín while Antonio dug clumsily through his pockets, I guess for the photograph. The CSOs were still talking to Helena but they looked us over with more interest now. Laurie was standing up straight with her arms crossed, more than ready. I caught an image of her face at Whitechapel. The blood curling into her mouth.

Duncan stiffened. 'It doesn't matter what the cause is. Violence against other human beings is categorically wrong, no matter what. It doesn't matter what you're fighting for.'

Antonio forgot about the photograph. '*Cuando uno tiene problemas con los fascistas, no le queda más remedio que…*'

He'd been even more fired up about Franco and all that stuff since I'd given him the family tree, but there was nothing I could do about it now. I tried to calm him with a hand on his shoulder but he ignored it and that made me bristle. The CSOs were making their way towards us now. Laurie refused to move and the two of them had to walk around her.

I was taken aback when Duncan leant in with a look of real disdain and said to Antonio with slow, over-pronounced bluntness approaching pidgin: 'No. No war. Never.' I'd never seen his face that red. He was visibly panting.

I watched Marta walk off – she must have had enough. Helena took her place, put one hand on Duncan's chest, like a girlfriend might do. Antonio squinted at them both and I saw a little thought run across his face. He lifted his finger right up to Duncan's nose. 'You – don't – know.'

The two CSOs challenged him first. *What's going on, what's the problem, is there a problem here* – a bubble of English noise. I rushed out something like *Nothing's wrong, just a misunderstanding* and someone else said *All good, all good, nothing to worry about* but they weren't happy with it. One of them suggested it'd be best for us three to move along. Me, Antonio, Duncan. Her voice made it sound like we didn't have much choice.

Laurie appeared in front of us. The big sister. 'It's a peaceful protest.' Her voice far too loud. 'Why don't you find someone else to bother?'

Helena hissed in her ear. She shrugged her off.

'No need to be impolite, madam,' one of them said. 'We're just asking.'

'Well, madam someone else. Fuck's sake.'

I pulled her by the elbow but she turned and eyeballed me like I was taking their side. She looked at me in that way she sometimes did, like she was showing off her scar to me. 'Fucking toy policemen,' she said. 'They do my head in.'

I told her not to worry about it but she was getting redder and redder.

She shrugged me off. 'They can't do anything anyway.'

One said: 'We have the power to arrest anyone who...'

'Fuck off,' said Laurie and then Helena was dragging her away, and she was shouting about why no one else seemed to care. The CSOs considered following her, I think, but Helena was leading her off quickly enough. I caught eyes with her before she turned away and I could see the disappointment in her face. Not with me, I think. With everything. So many of her protests ended up with her walking off or being led away and nothing in the world having changed.

Duncan joined Marta and a few of her friends and the lot of them were pointing at me and Antonio and talking about us openly.

'Come on, Antonio.'

As I took his arm, I noticed he was shaking. We walked off arm in arm with the CSOs watching us and the sounds of his landlady and the other protestors insulting each other ringing in my ears.

'*¡No Pasarán!*' he shouted over his shoulder. An old slogan from the Civil War he was always proud to declare.

Shamefully, although I walked away with him quite willingly, I felt a knot in my stomach. It wasn't just that I couldn't take this man home for Christmas. For the first time, I was embarrassed of him. And not just the embarrassment of his behaviour underneath the pier, which really I didn't blame him for.

It just seemed like his crusade never rested.

The Shoulder of Mutton was as it always had been, dark and coarse and with a feeling that it was still falling apart, bit by bit. I walked in alone with my backpack full of wrapped presents, feeling like a stranger, and looked over the rough black beams and the sag of the ceiling and the frosted light that cast shadows over the crude doodles scratched into the tables. The same flaccid Union flag still hung between the pictures of ploughs in frames screwed to the wall – all of it preserved like exhibits in a museum. Dad's pub. Once it had felt like our living room.

It was Christmas Eve but I'd had to work and didn't arrive until the evening. A Christmas tree shed needles by the fireplace, and beside it the old knackered pool table was strung with paper snowflakes cut from motoring magazines. One spun just above my head in the doorway, the wheel of a tractor dangling in place of mistletoe. I was amazed that Laurie told me to meet them in the pub, amazed she was willing to take Helena anywhere near it, until I found out it had been Helena's idea – *of course it had* – and that she was intent on seeing the site of our teenage dramas, our old battleground. Laurie must have told her about the perennial St George's Day banners and about the people we'd left behind in the villages – all in various stages of decay, broader, paler, mangled from work, or else happily settled with families. I expected to see Dad when I walked in – all three of them maybe, together at the bar, a little uneasy picture postcard. *Meeting your daughter's girlfriend.*

Dad wasn't there. Someone else was serving, a kid from the villages who must have been school-aged – Dad was always employing kids like that. Laurie was arguing with him. Helena stood there with her arms crossed and a pained look on her face, like a mother waiting for a tantrum to pass. One of the old men at the bar tapped on her shoulder and asked her something. Her face became gentle again and I heard her say *She's always like this* as I approached.

'Helena?'

I wanted to greet her with something jovial – maybe a *Howdy* – but I was already turning all gauche and asthmatic as I had been as a teenager. Stepping across the sticky carpet felt awkward – it was just like stepping back into my former gangly self. So I just said *Merry Christmas* with a ripple of tiredness. Behind the bar I noticed the old photograph I kept on my phone. Me, Laurie, Dad, Mum. I'd seen it countless times, but seeing it then made me think of Antonio's face when I showed it to him on the beach. His face in my mind again. Waiting its turn.

Helena clung to me as if to the lip of a life raft. 'Oh, George.' So tightly it choked me. 'Merry Christmas.'

I couldn't imagine she wasn't getting on with Dad – she got on with everyone, so did he, mostly – but Laurie could be difficult around him. I could picture Helena sitting there while the two of them argued, trying to lighten the mood as she always did when Laurie got like that. Trying and perhaps failing. As she let me go she said: 'Oh, I'm getting on just fine,' though I hadn't asked. Laurie turned with three pint glasses in her fingers, tutting playfully. I was glad to see she was chipper, even if she had just been arguing.

'He ID'ed me for fuck's sake. No idea who we are.'

The locals were watching us now. We were recognised. Helena wanted to sit in the corner so she could watch the pub. We settled just off from the heat of the fire with the needles from the Christmas tree under our feet.

'So.' I tried to sound light, like Helena. 'What do you think?'

She hummed. 'I love the beams. And the ceilings are so low.'

In a room of Sussex accents her voice rang clearly – it was almost posh, certainly cultured. Against the dark wood, the worn carpet and the framed photographs of farm machinery, everything about her, right down to the way she held her pint glass, looked suddenly so cosmopolitan.

'I can picture you two in here as teenagers,' she said.

'Can you?' I said. 'At least we're not on the snakebite-and-black anymore. We were both a bit more charged up back then.' But *back then* didn't really apply to Laurie, who was now staring around the pub as if waiting for an argument, same way she used to.

Helena winked at me. 'I bet you fitted right in.'

A roar of laughter rose up from the boys at the pool table, a flurry of coarse masculine sounds and the plain low drawl of their voices – the way they speak in that part of Sussex. If I'd had any of that I was keen to lose it. Everybody who left the villages has lost it. You hand it in on the way out.

'They all sound like you,' Helena said to Laurie.

But she denied it.

I hadn't spent a lot of time with the two of them together, not since the march in November. I never made it to Marta's flat to watch the US election results as they came in, and instead met Helena and Laurie for a quiet, awkward coffee the next morning. Laurie was devastated and wouldn't let me or Helena comfort her. Since then I'd only seen them together a few times and could never keep Laurie off the topic of Trump or Theresa May or the scourge of the Leavers, no matter how much it seemed like Helena didn't want to discuss it. That was when the frost really came over them, just as the temperature in Brighton nosedived into winter, and it was obvious now that the frost still hung over them because they barely looked at each other, barely touched. I felt like I was sitting in on a make-or-break holiday.

Helena asked me all about growing up in the village – about school discos and house parties and bunking off – and I told her about our japes and kept us off Trump and his neo-Nazis for as long as I could. I described the fetes and flower shows and how all of that probably made Sussex quite a nice place to retire. All small talk. Whatever was going on, Helena seemed keen to keep things light. She was musing on the carriage clock above the fireplace when my phone pinged.

'Is it Antonio?' she asked.

Laurie rolled her eyes, didn't bother to hide it.

'Yes,' I said. 'He's asking if I'm going to the New Year's party.' Fancy dress at Duncan's. 'Did you invite him?'

'I didn't, no.'

Which surprised me, because I'd mentioned nothing about it. It wasn't that I didn't want him there, but I definitely didn't feel able to invite him along myself since he was on such bad terms with the rest of them. Even if he didn't know it. I could have refused to go and offered to do something else with him, even just see the fireworks on the seafront, but that might send the wrong message. Fireworks, drinking, just the two of us. And I wanted to go and keep an eye on Laurie and Helena anyway. Laurie wouldn't tell me if she needed help – she very rarely did. That big-sister kind of pride. But I felt I should be there.

Out of nowhere she told us she didn't plan on going.

Helena tried to sound casual. 'What do you mean?'

'It's always the same. It's all just Duncan showing off his stuff.'

That was true, if you looked at it that way, partly true at least. But I was surprised to hear her say it to Helena.

She spoke from behind her pint glass. 'I don't think we've got the right to judge him.'

'I'm not judging him. I'm just saying, all he does is show off his stuff.'

'You know what he's like. He likes to entertain.'

'He's an *hôte aimable*,' I tried to wedge in.

'He wants to impress people. He just likes...' Laurie gripped her glass. '...getting a hold of people.'

'Nonsense.' Helena leant back. She wasn't hiding her anger anymore. 'Let's drop it.'

'He just wants to get women into bed.'

There was a silence between us, thickened by the sound of Johnny Mathis from the jukebox. I had no idea how to fill it. It was true to say that Duncan was promiscuous – everybody knew that now – but all I could think about was him and Helena outside the off-licence, his eagerness to have his hands on her and the way she touched his cheek. I still didn't know what bonded them, though I'd hoped Helena would volunteer it. There'd been some incident in Islington – something big, that's what I'd picked up – but whatever it was gave them an ease that Laurie and Helena had never had, not in the same way. It was physical and intimate. If Laurie wasn't referring to that, I don't know what she was referring to.

Helena placed her glass neatly on the beer mat. 'You are so uptight.'

'Me?' said Laurie. 'The guy fucks anything that moves. Besides—'

She didn't see the hand floating above her until it'd already fallen hard onto her shoulder. She jumped and turned and there was Dad who in the heat of the moment I'd forgotten all about. His Crystal Palace tattoo spread its wings across his bare arm, just a few inches from the branch of scar tissue above Laurie's eye. She swore and brushed him off but he paid no notice. He set down his pint beside Laurie's with a satisfied groan, wobbling on his feet. Same old smell of hash. I stood to hug him and he held me tight and welcomed me home. I felt his love when he hugged me, I always did. I was never as sceptical as Laurie. He sat down slowly beside Helena and swooned.

'Come here often?'

Laurie gave an *Oi!* which Dad ignored. Helena inclined her head and let her eyebrows lift like a schoolteacher might with a very young pupil testing their luck.

'Tom Grocott, really. I'll bet you say that to all the girls.' She laughed. 'Honestly George, he's such a cheek.'

It was strange to hear his name – *Tom Grocott*, his real name – in her cosmopolitan voice. He howled and slapped the table and the moment dissolved. We all took a drink but he seemed in no hurry to leave us. I knew he'd get straight on to me. 'So, Georgie. How are you finding it down there?'

He always called me Georgie, I think just because I was skinny and pale and didn't have a bulldog tattooed on my chest. I told him I was having a whale of a time, which is exactly what he wanted to hear. Though he'd have preferred more gory details.

He gave me a look of interrogation. 'Got a bird, have you?'

'Not really, no.'

He nudged Helena. 'What, no bird on the go?'

'Not at the moment, Dad.'

He exhaled through his lips like a horse and his head tilted up towards the Christmas bunting, thinking. His big hands lay palm down on the table as if the idea just coming to fruition was about to bring him to his feet. We waited patiently, watched his look pass between Laurie then Helena, Helena then Laurie, until suddenly he woke up, shrugged and spoke. 'Fair dos, Georgie. It's all benders down that way anyway.'

Smacking his lips as if he'd just downed a drink.

It may have been a joke, it may have been a political statement – I wasn't sure. I hadn't heard the word *benders* for several years. Nobody in Brighton would have said it, even as a joke, and since I'd left the village the sillier nuances of schoolyard banter were a distant memory. But I wasn't upset by it. It was just about the most Dad thing Dad ever said.

Laurie folded her arms. 'I don't find that funny.'

'Yeah, good for them, I say. Fuck whoever you like.' He winked at Helena when he said that. '*Free love, man.*'

'Christ's sake. You've missed the point as always.' Laurie tried her best to sound tempered through the anxiety wobbling her voice. I think if we had not just been speaking about Duncan and his promiscuity she might have let it go.

'I think what Laurie means,' I said, 'is that there's more to sexuality than just sex, Dad.'

Laurie held the table. 'Exactly! It's not just who you fuck.'

But Dad showed no signs of acknowledging her anger. It was the 2000s all over again. 'That's what I'm saying, Georgie. I don't care if you're straight or queer or whatever.' He said it smoothly, disinterestedly. To him we could have been talking about football or the value of the pound. 'You know what I mean, don't you.'

'Don't speak to him like that,' said Laurie. 'And anyway, we're not "queers". It's not the 1970s.'

Again, Dad stopped to think. He put his hands back on the table, his head drifting up, his eyes squinting. Laurie wanted to continue but I think she could feel Helena's gaze on her, begging her to drop it. Helena looked tired, utterly tired. Dad's idea eventually landed.

'Why not? LGBT Q. I can say "lesbian".' Leaning towards Helena. 'Can't I say "lesbian"...?'

Laurie baulked. 'For Christ's sake, Dad, listen. Sexuality is like a spectrum...' But she didn't seem to know where she was going. It wasn't enough.

'Exactly.' And then Dad looked satisfied. 'It's a spectrum, not a rectum.'

He laughed, no one else did. Laurie shook her head and stood. Dad stood as well. They squared off to each other, Laurie's eyes firm and sober, Dad's vacant and content, with the locals watching us and waiting for a proper row. Just like it had always been.

'Laurie,' Helena said, resigned. She looked down into her lap. It was the only time I ever saw her embarrassed.

'Laurie, come on, eh,' I said.

Dad jabbed his hand out in front of her for a shake. Laurie flinched, I flinched, Dad sniffed. He moved away without waiting for his daughter to take his hand.

'Only messing with you, love,' he said over his shoulder. And then he was heading over to the bar – 'Back to work' – and forgetting all about us.

When Laurie sat down I tried to catch Helena's eye but she was busy with her phone, rushing out a message. Laurie didn't seem to notice but I couldn't help but see Duncan's name on Helena's phone.

Music played through the silence.

Mary's boy child.

Jesus Christ.

We drank on steadily under the din of Christmas music and I felt sicker and heavier as the silences got more and more protracted, until eventually the pub groaned for midnight. We passed Dad on our side of the bar with a drink in his hand – it didn't look like he'd done a lick of work all night. He grabbed me and hugged me and the wrapping paper rustled in my backpack.

'You heading off, lad? Your bed's made up, I'll try not to wake you up.'

One of the locals tapped him on the shoulder and offered to give us all a lift home. I guessed someone else was shutting up for the night, as someone else usually did. Though his staff seemed to love him all the same.

'What are you talking about?' His voice was slurred.

The man brushed the flecks of Dad's pint from his overcoat. 'You're pissed, Tom. Go on with your kids.'

He stood up straight with his arm around me, chest inflated, half a head taller. 'Well, obviously I'm pissed,' he announced. 'It's Christmas Eve.'

His friend tapped his watch. 'Christmas Day.'

'It's bloody Christmas Day!'

But he followed us out anyway, chased by the jeers from the locals and the laughter of the boys at the pool table. Outside he fell onto the bonnet of his car – the same souped-up Mini with the chequered roof and the sticker that read SKA'D FOR LIFE, same car he had run us around in as kids – and started trying to de-ice his windshield with a debit card.

'I thought someone was driving you home?' I asked.

I thought Laurie might intervene but she didn't seem bothered.

Dad looked up with his eyes half closed. 'Drive home, Georgie? You mad? I'm pissed.' He straightened out when he saw Helena, approached her unsteadily. 'You want a lift, sweetheart?'

Laurie took her hand. She pulled it away sharply.

'I think we're walking.' Her pleasant facade still intact. 'Why don't you walk with us?'

He leant back on the car. 'What do you think of my pub?'

'I think it's a charming little place.'

'It's shite, love. But it's *ours*.'

Then, out of the blue, he grabbed her free hand. Laurie started forward but I held on to her. We all watched as Dad lifted up Helena's hand quite gently, slowly turned it facedown and gave her fingers a gentle kiss. He let go, bowed and turned back to the car. As he opened the door, one of the regulars from the pub came out and took his keys. I was glad of that.

'You want a lift?' the man offered.

'We're *walking*,' said Laurie.

Dad wound down his window as the car pulled away and shouted *Bloody Remainers* as if to finish us off. I looked at Helena and she laughed, but Laurie was already marching off into the dark. I went to follow her but Helena stopped me. So we set off towards home together, Helena and I, lit by the light from my phone's torch, while Laurie stayed ahead of us, disappearing around the corners, melding with the dark.

I wanted to ask how she was feeling but before I could she said quietly: 'So is Antonio joining us on Saturday?'

'On Saturday?'

'New Year's Eve.'

'Oh.' Dad and the argument and the frost between her and Laurie had put Antonio out of my mind. 'Yes, apparently so.'

She squeezed my elbow. 'And how is everything? Since he tried to kiss you, I mean?'

I'd told her about that a few weeks back, making it clear I didn't think Laurie should know. Still, I didn't get why we were speaking about me and my thing now and not about her and Laurie, but perhaps that's what she needed.

'It's okay,' I said. 'He doesn't seem awkward about it at all. I mean, his behaviour hasn't changed.'

'Do you get the sense he's waiting for you?'

This was one of the things I was trying to put out of my mind. 'I don't know. I hope not. He acts so straight when we're around other people, I thought maybe he just got overexcited before.' *Overexcited.* The word reminded me of Duncan. 'I don't know what he wants.'

'Have you told him what you want?'

'I've told him he means a lot to me. It sounds silly but I can't really imagine Brighton without him. You know. He's my best friend down there. My best male friend anyway.'

Ahead of us, Laurie cut through the darkness with her torch lit, marching against it like she wanted to drive it into retreat.

'Do you think he wants a relationship? It seems like he might.'

I watched Laurie's torch illuminate the little humpback bridge by the church. 'I don't know. Every time I try to bring it up he pretends he doesn't understand what I'm talking about. I mean literally, he pretends he can't understand my English. He might want a physical thing but honestly I think he's just confused. I know it's odd to say because he's older, but sometimes I think he just looks up to me.'

'No, I don't think so.' Her voice was tender now. '*She* looks up to you.' Laurie's light was roving the gravestones in the churchyard. 'I hate the way she plays up around you. She really hero-worships you.'

'I don't get that. She's my older sister.'

'Yes, but you've got something she doesn't have. You've got compassion for people. Not that Laurie doesn't have compassion, but you have empathy. You can listen.'

I thought back to stuffing my denim jacket into the trees and the words crossed my mind as clear as anything: *If I should tell anyone about the riot I should tell Helena.* A car sped past and I watched her face in the orange glow of the tail lights, kind and purposeful.

'You're her brother,' she said. 'She just needs you.'

I looked ahead. 'I know she does. I just don't know what I can do for her. I feel like I've let her down.'

By the light of her torch I could see Laurie had stopped by the conifers at the end of our drive. Waiting for us to catch up.

Helena held my arm tightly. 'How have you let her down?'

I still didn't get why we were speaking about me, about my problems, but another part of me, a part that screamed sometimes, wanted to tell her how I felt. I wanted to tell her how Antonio made me feel, when he forced me to dance on Madeira Drive and pushed me onto the marina boat and pulled me through the crowds at Pride, and about how his vulnerability left me split. I wanted to tell her that I wouldn't be able to look after Laurie if she left her, which I knew at some point she would, not while I didn't have the strength to get through to my sister and while Antonio took up so much of my energy. I wanted to tell her about the riot and my guilt and failure, and then for her to drag me down the country lane and meet Laurie by the conifers to tell her as well.

But now wasn't the time. Too many plates were spinning. So I kept quiet.

'I can't say,' I said.

She breathed deeply. 'Well, maybe you should tell *her*.'

The cold gripped my lungs, I started to wheeze.

'Oh, George,' she said, taking my hand. I loved her then. 'Don't beat yourself up. Just be there for her. That's all you've got to do.'

Before I could say anything more we were already there, and Helena was letting me go and walking over to Laurie who was stepping from foot to foot on the side of the road.

'It's cold as shit,' she said. But neither of us answered.

It was cold, deathly cold, and all I wondered was what Helena must have been thinking, a Londoner wandering through the Sussex countryside, with a woman she was drifting away from. I wondered if she was considering why they'd ever gotten together, as I was, why they had at any point felt they needed each other. Yes, Laurie was strong but so was Helena – stronger even, and certainly more stable and more mature. And yes, Helena was smart, but what did Laurie want with smart, when I knew all she really wanted was *action*?

We stood there in the darkness and I stayed clammed up in my old self without saying anything, and no one else was saying anything either, so the silence of the countryside cut through us with the cold. No stars at all, just clouds.

Before we reached the house a message came through on my phone, 25 December 2016, one week till the new year, half past midnight.

Feliz navidad, camarada x

Merry Christmas, comrade.

Leading Antonio into the school on New Year's Eve I felt that old feeling, the rush and sickness of entering a party, made worse that night by the sense of impending disaster that had hung over me all week. The school itself felt much the same as it had the first time I visited – that first big party back in May – except that now the EU bunting was gone and tinny jazz music rattled down the corridor. A few people arrived at the same time as Antonio and I, giggling and gasping as they walked in, everyone fully costumed for the theme. Bright flowers in vases covered the reception area – a nod to Gatsby maybe. Antonio jumped at the feel of the cloth petals, lifted a vase to examine the water, picked out a plastic stem, nodded approvingly. He looked over the candlesticks, the white feathers in the pencil holder, a printed sheet that read LET'S MISBEHAVE in gold deco lettering, muttering *Wow, wow, wow* to no one in particular. A young man walked between us, shoulders back, with a cane rising and falling in front of him.

Antonio grabbed my elbow. 'Is *muy muy impressionate.*'

He'd told me he was alone on Christmas Day but boasted of how he'd discovered Baileys and didn't remember most of it anyway. He was more interested in the New Year's party, which he told me only that night he was going to dress up for. His pinstripe blazer and slicked-back hair should have made him look like a card sharp but the suit was oversized and he'd made a hash of his pencil moustache. It was the first time I ever saw him in anything except for his own smart clothes or the work shirt with the castle insignia. He might have looked something like his great-grandfather had the whole thing not ended up so crude and affected.

'Yes,' I said, 'very impressive.'

Marta welcomed people at the reception desk. When she saw us coming in, her smile froze so forcefully it made her eyelids twitch. She left the desk and I knew she was going to find Duncan to tell him who'd just walked in. Antonio didn't notice. He was still playing with the flowers.

'Best behaviour, Antonio.'

His smile — lively and oblivious — was always difficult to resist. I warmed to it but I still wanted to be clear, it was only fair to him. 'I mean, no trouble tonight, okay? No trouble.'

His chest inflated. 'Jorge. I understand.' Though even through those words, spoken so firmly and honestly, I sensed that he didn't.

The tinny jazz jangled around the assembly hall, music from between the wars. Antonio was amazed by the number of tuxedos — most of them worn by women with gelled hair and ink moustaches. Most of the men wore plain shirts, suspenders, drooping bow ties. One had a bottle-green bowler, another a fedora and violin case. The flappers wore long dresses made to look like ballgowns, with plastic pearls and elbow-length gloves. Antonio marvelled at the costumes, genuinely, just as he'd marvelled at my borrowed jacket when I ushered him into the taxi that evening. He'd even offered to fetch a flower for my lapel, which I refused because the meter was running. He touched my cheek when I said no, in the dark outside his flat, before he realised the driver was watching us. After that he chatted to him in his most masculine voice all the way to Duncan's place.

At the drinks table he laid out our amaretto, sugar and a box of eggs. We chopped a lemon into a bitter mess and drank two tepid amaretto sours from matching Charles and Diana mugs. A few other people lingered around the drinks table with us, people who'd lost their friends or were too shy to dance. Laurie and Helena stood by themselves in the opposite corner, facing one another in the dark.

I led Antonio through the crowd but as we approached he slipped into a large space formed for a couple who knew how to Lindy hop. He stopped to clap along and almost knocked them over. I pulled him away. Helena didn't see us, so it seemed – she'd already walked off by the time we reached them. Before she did I heard her say something like *Not tonight*, which Laurie didn't answer.

Antonio grabbed her hand and shook it. 'Yes! Laurie! *Impressionate...*'

Laurie nodded absently. She was about the only person not in full costume, though it seemed that Helena had at least managed to hustle her into a button-up shirt. After several seconds standing still as a headstone, she suddenly shook herself awake and her face jolted to life. It startled me.

'Come on,' she said. 'Let's go to the room.' She drew a drink from her carrier bag – a large can with a loud label. Caffeinated vodka.

'You're drinking tonight, then?' I said.

'Looks like it.'

'Everything alright?'

She took a long draw which seemed to impress Antonio. 'Dandy,' she said, and marched off without us.

We walked in her wake, greeting no one, and passed into

the back corridor. I could read by the look on her face exactly how she was feeling – sore and trying to bottle it up. The way she walked told me she was already far from sober. I hoped Antonio would at least not get too far gone – a faint hope in spite of the facts.

The noise of the party was much dimmer by Duncan's door. The slate that read HEADTEACHER was covered by a sheet of worn crate paper with *Happy New Year* written on it in several languages. Antonio slapped it. It tore. '*¡Feliz año nuevo!* You see?'

Laurie walked in without knocking. I was surprised to hear no music inside, no sound at all. We were relatively early – I thought we could get out early, too – and it looked like Duncan hadn't yet brought anyone through to his room. Antonio stopped me in the doorway. He looked at me with the same appreciation he'd shown walking into Marta's flat. The pride of acceptance, the honour of an invitation from a foreign dignitary. Except now we weren't invited.

He tipped back his head and strode in. Inside I could hear Laurie already moving stuff about. A bad start. I took a breath like swimmers do before they dive.

Duncan's lamps were lit for the party – just the deco ones, the ones with stained glass shades. A few clean glasses sat on a tray with a bottle of wine and a corkscrew. All around us the records, the posters and the tatty paperbacks sat statically like objects in a museum after closing time. The ashtrays were empty and the record player was bare. Coats covered the bed. But no one was there, not even Duncan.

Laurie put her can down on an antique dresser and picked

up a book. There were voices in the corridor. I tried to sound casual. 'He's not here. Let's go.'

'No, no,' said Laurie. 'I'm fine here.'

Antonio manhandled a box of vintage postcards.

'Come on, Laurie,' I said, 'let's find—' but I couldn't think of anyone we might want to see. Even Helena was off that list now, at least for tonight.

Before I could convince either of them to follow me out of the room, the door opened and two flappers came in, surprised to see us standing around in the half-light. It was Marta and one of her housemates, the woman who'd pulled her away from the roof at Pride – Paula, her name was. The two of them looked us up and down. In the brief silence before anyone could say hello, Antonio pulled a record from the shelves.

'¡Hostia puta! ¡Flamenco!'

I gestured to take Paula's coat for her but she refused.

'It's quiet in here,' she said. 'Where's Duncan?'

'He'll be here in a minute,' I said. 'We're just dropping off our coats.'

Marta looked unconvinced. 'Was he invited?' she whispered to me, though Antonio must have heard her because he turned around and greeted her warmly in Spanish. He called her *La catalana* as I'd heard him do before. She took his handshake gingerly and then bustled Paula over to the desk, all a-fluster. A few more flappers came in after them and sat down on the chaise longue. Authentic-looking costumes, actual vintage. Friends of Duncan's, *Left Nut* followers, sitting like they belonged.

I watched them from the side, smiling, nodding.

They ignored us too.

Over the space of an hour or so, more flappers and fops filtered into the room, more bottles, more cans, more smoke. People spoke about George Michael, who'd died on Christmas Day, and about how 2016 had been a car crash, total shit, worst year ever. None of them said a thing to me, Laurie or Antonio, which I was glad of, and I managed to keep the two of them sat down beside the bed, out of the way. Laurie's second can joined the first, and then the third, fourth, fifth. She actually got up from the floor each time to stack them on the dresser, despite having to move a little plaster Lenin statue to do so. At five high, the stack was beginning to lean. Marta and the others pretended not to notice her doing it.

'*Impressionate*,' said Antonio. 'There is something very English when…'

He was still enraptured by Duncan's room. I nodded along, let it filter through me.

I wanted to go over and speak to Marta but I was worried that if I left Laurie and Antonio something might happen. Every time the door opened, Laurie looked up through the forest of legs forming around us, stood up sometimes, and then ignored whoever came in. I watched her intently, she knew I was watching her. Antonio noticed too, and he must have clocked that it was unusual for Laurie to drink so much because he helped me settle her down when she got antsy. I was grateful for that, though if it came to it neither of us would be able to stop her. Eventually Duncan walked in with his lips around a fat Chianti bottle, fully tuxedoed with a red cummerbund and a little plastic flower stuck in his lapel. He actually looked a bit like Antonio, with his pencil moustache and hair slicked back. Dark and charismatic and a danger. A string of flappers trailed behind him, all holding hands in single file. At the back of the line was Helena. She looked the part too, in her gloves and fascinator. For the first time ever I caught the unwelcome sensation of not being pleased to see her.

Laurie staggered to her feet but a few more partygoers followed and blocked her path. Helena found her way to the desk before Laurie had managed to straighten out her clothes. She let Antonio and I hold on to her, perhaps even appreciated it. Beneath her drunkenness, she was still my big sister, and she still may have grasped that there was now a potential for things to become messy.

Duncan saw us on his way over to the desk and by the way his face didn't change I knew he was surprised. He ignored us completely, bent down and smothered Marta with kisses that she squirmed away from. Helena hung off the edge of the desk with one of Duncan's tatty orange paperbacks and within a minute he had taken it off her and was reciting from it into her ear. *The Ragged-Trousered Philanthropists*, I could see it from here. He glanced at us as he read, drunk-looking and faintly sad. I held on tighter to Laurie, and Antonio offered her a drink from his Lady Diana mug but she refused. She just stood there, breathing heavily.

I put an arm around her. Her sadness washed into me. 'Why don't you sit down here?'

She brushed me off without looking at me, but then took the chair. I thought if I could hold her there at least until she was sloppy drunk and couldn't talk at all, we might still be able to stave off the disaster.

Antonio whispered in my ear. 'She has a love problem, I can see...'

He was about to go on when a young man — seventeen perhaps, one tracksuit leg tucked into his sock — barged past him and approached the desk. The only person but Laurie without a costume.

Antonio nudged me. 'Who is?'

'I don't know,' I said. I didn't want to tell him the kid sold mandy — Antonio never liked that kind of thing. Luckily his attention was elsewhere by the time the boy left and Duncan tipped out a little white mound onto his Robert Tressell. As he chopped up lines with his debit card, the room seemed to close slowly around the desk, the chain of flappers reassembling around it, with Helena and Marta and her friend Paula on the inside, and the rest of us on the outside. Laurie groaned like someone half asleep.

'Laurie, why don't I get you some water—'

She gripped my shirt and looked me in the eye, then let me go. I looked down at her slumped in Duncan's chair. She was ruddy and lifeless and said nothing. And I thought, hoped, prayed that she'd stay that way.

Luckily she did stay that way — limp and lifeless in the chair — while I made small talk with strangers and tried to keep an eye on Antonio and never even went near Duncan and the others, until about half an hour to midnight. I remember looking at my watch and then around at the room, wondering how early I could convince Laurie to leave. Marta and her friends were speaking seriously by the bookshelves. At the desk, Duncan was looking into Helena's eyes, stroking her, trying to hold her attention. I knew if we waited until the countdown and saw in the new year in this room with everybody laughing and hugging and kissing, we would see something irreversible. I dragged Laurie to her feet and took her and Antonio by the waists.

'Come on. It's New Year's Eve. We should dance.'

Antonio, drunker now like the rest of us, shuffled out from my grip with a flamenco twist of his hips. Laurie could barely stand. Her eyes were vacant windows.

'Come on, Laurie. It's almost midnight.'

A spittly *pfffft* left her lips. A sound like Dad might make.

'Let's get a drink from the table,' I said.

She held up the bottle she'd been drinking from for the last hour, something gold with the label ripped off. The liquid sloshed at half-mast. 'I don't know why we fucking come to these…'

'Laurie, please.'

'No. It's a fucking nightmare. I'm going to *get her*.' She meant fetch Helena to leave but her tone came out spiteful and wrong.

I could see Duncan's hand running down Helena's arm and her doing nothing to stop it. Marta was trying not to look and a few others stared at us openly as if waiting for something to happen. So that it really was like a nightmare.

'Laurie. Maybe we should just go.'

Antonio must have picked up on the shudder in my voice because suddenly he was moving me aside and taking Laurie by the arm.

'Don't, Antonio.'

'Laurie…' he said. 'Laurie, what is?'

He followed Laurie's eyes to the desk and I followed them too. Duncan had his arm around Helena's shoulder, and both of them were laughing, just as friends might laugh, more-than-friends. Laurie's face slumped into exhaustion. Like there was no fight left in her at all.

'Come on,' I said as the music dropped. 'Let's go home.'

She agreed without nodding and we turned towards the door. Antonio stood in our way, glancing over our shoulders at the people by the desk. Then he puffed up his chest and strode past us.

'Antonio…' I said, but by the time I reached him he'd already pulled Duncan to his feet.

Duncan wore a white polo around one nostril – flakes of it had come off onto his jacket, onto Helena. Antonio's voice, with that perfect clarity he achieved only very rarely, bellowed through the room. '*¡No!*'

Immediately, half a dozen conversations came to an end.

'You,' with that hard J, pointing Duncan in the face. 'Not to fuck.'

I reached him. 'Antonio.'

'You listen. You not to fuck.'

Helena tried to speak. I froze up. I should have been doing something.

Duncan spoke evenly. 'This is none of your business, Antonio. None of your—'

He pushed Antonio hard against the chest with both hands – a slow, deliberate gesture that Antonio did nothing to resist. *Fuck's sake*, someone shouted and then all at once the room filled with violent noise. Swearing, falling glass. Antonio looked back to me for guidance. I had no answer. Duncan pushed him again.

'*How dare you fucking… How dare you*—' Duncan was all

red, suddenly shouting, ranting. Long, abusive words, slurred into one snotty string. I couldn't understand all of it but the words that came most clearly were *You little Spanish shit*.

He didn't move at all when Marta barged past him and ran out of the room with Paula following. Antonio faced him still – stunned, I think, or just confused. He looked to me again. I had no answer. Someone turned on the main light and my nerves swam up in bright blotches over my eyes. I just stood there, perfectly still, feeling the waves of nausea wash over me. The feeling like my lungs were filling with water, like my hands were about to rise in surrender. Any clarity and courage I thought I'd picked up from Antonio vanished, and all the ugly fears I'd hidden for so long were suddenly illuminated as if in the headlights of an oncoming car. All I did was stand there.

Duncan's eyes were half closed and clouded over and his jaw ground his teeth automatically. He didn't notice Helena pulling at his jacket, slipping back, knocking a flapper off her feet. He was fixated on Antonio in a blunt, contorted way that made me forget he'd ever been witty and verbose. I carried on watching, we all did, until a face I'd forgotten all about appeared in the opening.

She was dark around the eyes and heaving. Duncan turned absently.

When Laurie hit him it was sloppy and weak. The punch found his chest – a wet fist splashing onto his black lapel. It knocked out the little plastic flower from Duncan's buttonhole, which Laurie followed with her eye as it flew through the air. She followed it all the way to the floor, lost her balance before it landed. Before Duncan could react, she slipped and fell stiffly and awkwardly like a scarecrow.

'Oh, Jesus,' I said.

I pulled her to her feet alone – no one came near us. I looked across to see Antonio, drifting out of the inner circle. He simply stared ahead as if he still had no idea what was going on. The room held its breath.

'Let's go!' The only time I ever heard Helena lose her temper. She stepped into the circle, snatched Laurie away from me and marched out of the door without looking back. Duncan was immediately surrounded by people consoling him, running their fingers through his hair, straightening out his tux. I moved towards them but the group hardened around him and I heard someone behind me say *Just go*. They were speaking to Antonio and I, again telling us to leave. I should have said something, while people were still listening and my blood was up. Instead, I took Antonio by the elbow and pulled him in silence out of the door and into the assembly hall. We stumbled through the countdown to midnight, knocking into people, spilling drinks. We got stuck by the climbing ropes where the guy with the leather jacket had made a fool of himself, all those months ago. I had to force our way through. As the countdown reached *Three! Two! One!* I flinched and the whole room burst into violent celebration. Confetti filled the air. A party horn screamed. People grabbed each other and kissed with their eyes open. Someone grabbed me but I wriggled past.

'Fuck's sake, get out the way.'

Antonio trailed behind me, confused but with no sign of shame. When he stopped at the reception to again rub his fingers over the cloth petals of the flowers I physically pushed him out of the door. The alcohol spun in my head, tipping me off balance.

Even before either of us spoke I knew that something was over.

The car park was cold and empty. Under the white lamplight of the front gate, I could see Laurie standing with her head down, down far enough to fall asleep, and Helena checking something on her phone, talking over her. No sign of Marta or her friend.

The noise of the party rang through the night. Suddenly I was desperately tired.

I pointed Antonio in the face. 'Jesus, what happened?'

But he didn't understand. He just looked at me like a cow chewing cud. I said it again, drawing out the words, but he was still blank.

'Honestly,' I said. 'You know we're friends but sometimes you're a real liability.'

Still he looked at me, totally blank, saying nothing. The smell of his aftershave got into my lungs and made me cough.

'It's like sometimes you don't understand how the world works.'

He stepped forward and tried to touch my face but I shrugged him off.

'Jorge. I understand.' His voice was meek and pleading like he was saying *Love me*, and then his sister's question was ringing in my mind with the tinnitus and that made me more upset than ever. My chest was wheezing, my breath short in the cold. He lurched forward then and I felt his lips on mine and his hot breath rushing up my nose. Booze, lemon, egg. I pushed him back, hard enough to make him stumble.

'My name is *George*.'

I could see Helena guiding Laurie onto a bus and then walking off in the opposite direction when the doors shut. I looked again at Antonio. The certainty had melted from his face so that all that was left were the last searching glimmers of hopefulness.

'Christ, Antonio. We're *friends*. I'm never going to sleep with you. I'm sorry if I made you think otherwise. Actually, I'm not sorry. For God's sake, I've never led you on. You're forty years old for one thing. How haven't you understood that?'

I struggled for breath.

He said just: 'Jorge?' and held my eye with that total lack of comprehension that at that moment I couldn't look at any longer.

As Laurie's bus pulled away, I pulled my borrowed jacket around me, swore and walked off alone with the scratch of his stubble still raw against my cheek.

3

HOW THE WORLD WORKS

2017

Brighton can be bleak in winter, when all the colour drains from the streets and the city resembles the other seaside towns that have died before it. The habitual hibernation, the end of the party. That year I caught a sense that it was especially cold, especially void of life. It wasn't just the grey clouds that blew over our heads all through January – it was a deeper feeling that hung in the streets like a cold mist from off the sea, invisible up close but quietly freezing us to the bone.

I felt it soaking into my skin, chilling me from the inside out. That's how the first few weeks after New Year's went, with me trudging to work through the wind and rain, marching with my head down, trying not to bump into anyone. Most of the messages I got were from Antonio – poorly spelt and coming at odd hours of the night, with lines of smiley faces and Spanish words I never translated. I kept my replies vague and non-committal and only saw him when I had the energy, maybe once a fortnight or less. I wasn't ready to deal with how I felt yet. But the messages never stopped. The only other regular messages I got came from Laurie, who I knew was suffering but still, in the weeks since the drama, hadn't said a single word about it.

So it was a surprise when, walking down to the Old Steine on her instructions, a year since I'd first arrived in Brighton, a message came through from Dad, who never usually messaged, always rang, normally at the worst time.

It was a simple message and I could hear it clearly in his broad, Sussex country voice.

Look out for ur sister pls Georgie

Dont let her go off the rails

It was freezing cold at the Old Steine, with the wind washing up the opposing slopes that rise towards Kemp Town and North Street. The protestors were easy to spot – they'd put up a yurt between Victoria Fountain and the pavement and had planted two large tricolour flags either side. Red, white and green, with a yellow sun fluttering in the centre. The Kurdish flag, which since New Year's I'd become all too familiar with. There were about a dozen people out on Old Steine Gardens – Laurie's friends from the Cowley Club, students with red-and-black bandanas over their faces, an old couple in camo gear and six or seven Middle Eastern-looking men that I guessed were Kurdish. At the front, Laurie handed out flyers. She didn't see me as I approached so I got to stop and look at her. It looked like she hadn't slept. She pushed the flyers at everyone who passed – absolutely everyone – and then said something just briefly and moved on to someone else. Flyer after flyer after flyer. She pushed one into my hands before she realised who I was. All she said was *Remember Rojava* and then moved on. I waited there until she noticed.

'Oh, George.'

I could tell by the faint light in her eyes she hadn't thought I'd show up.

'We're passing these out,' she said. 'Give me a hand.'

On the flyer was a message about the Kurds in Rojava. I asked her how long she'd been out that morning but she didn't hear, she was handing out more leaflets. I heard her say *Remember Rojava* to an old woman with a walking stick. She shuffled off like Laurie was going to mug her.

As I went to hand out my first leaflet, my phone pinged. A message from Antonio. This one came appended to a stock photo of beer bottles.

Jorge something very good for you

Must need you weekend

'Bloody hell,' I said, and put it on silent.

I hadn't been surprised when I found out Helena had left Laurie, though it still took a few weeks to process. It wasn't as though they'd never cared for each other, or that either of them had led the other on. Whatever they'd felt they felt sincerely, but whatever that was didn't match and I knew that now. They were different people on different trajectories. I think it was only Laurie who never realised that.

It bothered me most that she didn't tell me herself, and that by the time she opened up about it, weeks after it happened, she was already saying it was *the past*, and she didn't want to talk about it, and would I just let it go. I spent the whole of those first months trying to get her to open up to no success. I'd seen nothing of Helena since New Year's, only messaged her to say how sorry I was, which she thanked me for. I wanted to see her but I couldn't picture myself there, not with Duncan around, if he was around. I'd bumped into Marta the day before she moved back to Barcelona – she told me she was packing it in because of the referendum *and all that shit*. Though I didn't believe her. I was sad to see her go and even more angry with Duncan than I was before, but there wasn't much to do but stay out of his way. Besides, I had my hands full with Laurie, going along to her marches and meetings and supporting her political interests, of which this Kurdish thing seemed at the moment the primary one. I still didn't know much about it, except for what she read aloud to me from the internet. But I turned up anyway, hoping we'd get a chance to talk, and agreed to hand out her leaflets.

I tried at first to say *Remember Rojava*, but it didn't sound like it did when Laurie said it. I watched her as we worked – purposefully, erratically, bothering people. I didn't like to see it. I tried to give one to a butch-looking local in an Albion shirt but he actually stopped to tear it in half in front of me. I snuck a few of the leaflets into my backpack so I'd run out quicker, and Laurie seemed pleased I'd done so well and told me to go through to the yurt. On my way there, my phone vibrated.

Jorge come today this afternoon

I read the notification without unlocking my phone so Antonio wouldn't see I'd read it. I noticed myself doing things like that more regularly – I had to shut out that feeling too. Then I was thinking about the message from Dad, whether I'd get a call about it, and how Laurie might react when I told her, and I didn't even realise I was standing stock-still in the middle of the pavement, shivering.

Laurie's voice startled me. 'You alright?'

'Oh, yes.' Hiding my phone away. 'See you in a minute.'

A folding table blocked the entrance to the yurt. Two men sat behind it – middle-aged men with black moustaches, hairy forearms, jewellery. These weren't boys you might meet down the pub when a march is over, these were real men from the real world. The awkward part of me wanted Laurie to take me in there with her. I looked back but she'd crossed the road to harangue a couple of Jehovah's Witnesses at their stand. I sank a little then. Again I knew this would not be the day we'd speak about Helena. Though I would have to tell her about the message from Dad.

The men at the table offered me some of their literature. There were photographs of mangled bodies among the books and pamphlets – bones sticking out from rubble, battered faces. It got under my skin. In the darkness of the yurt, a few people sat cross-legged on the floor making signs. All around them were pictures of people I could just about make out – protestors, martyrs, a man with his face turned in profile who looked like a politician. Staring out like idols.

'Laurie said I could come in.'

The Kurdish men looked at each other – they didn't know Laurie by name. The people on the floor stopped talking and I thought suddenly *God what if they think I'm a policeman.* I didn't look like a protestor, anyway. One of the Kurdish men asked if I'd mind opening my bag. I looked at the pictures of young martyrs around the yurt and the sadness of it all got mixed up with my bumbling British embarrassment and I didn't know what to say. A hand landed on my shoulder, made me jump.

Laurie said: 'He's with me.' She greeted the men at the table with their names but it didn't look to me like they knew who she was. 'You can put your stuff down there.'

They watched me as I squeezed past, speaking in their own language. I caught sight of a picture peeking out from under their pamphlets. A young man in denim lying on a pile of concrete, covered in blood. It went straight to my stomach.

We sat down by a couple of the students wearing the red-and-black bandanas, anarchists maybe. They spoke about the Turkish government with such hatred I had no idea what to say. Laurie knew I'd been in Turkey during my time away – I thought she might bring it up as she sometimes brought up my visit to the West Bank. I was grateful she didn't.

'I need to talk to you,' I whispered.

'Yes, of course.' Though she made no offer to take me outside.

The protestors spoke about President Erdoğan, who had at some point joined up with a far-right party to *fuck the Turkish parliament*. The rest agreed he was a cunt and then that Theresa May, who'd signed an arms deal there in January, was also a cunt, as was Boris Johnson, Nigel Farage and Jacob Rees-Mogg – all cunts. I spent most of the conversation snatching glances at a boy in the circle who I thought I recognised – a dark-skinned young man in a leather jacket, though I couldn't place him. When the conversation turned to the British public, Laurie lit up.

'The British public must be the most complacent people on the planet,' she said. 'I don't think anywhere people are this lazy. All they're interested in is *stuff*.'

She spoke generally but I knew she meant Duncan. She'd

rarely said anything directly about Duncan or about how the others had never really taken their political life seriously. Even Helena, who was just as active as Laurie was, had never really been as 'committed' as her, in her own mind. Now she was rid of them, and I knew there'd be no more parties. Not now she was on a mission.

Someone said something about the first-past-the-post system and Laurie said: 'The whole system is broken.' The students were looking at her dotingly now, quite openly. It made me feel ill.

'I think we just feel deflated at the moment,' I said. 'After losing so many battles.'

One of the students rolled her eyes. 'If people had been more on it in the first place, we wouldn't be in this position. It's the English who vote in the Tories.'

Now Laurie was looking at her as if inspired. I remember thinking it would be much more bearable if anyone I knew was there with us, even Duncan. Or, better still, Helena. I said: 'Not all English people, though,' like she might have done, and hoped that would soften things.

'No,' said Laurie. 'Not all.'

It was only when the boy in the leather jacket started to speak did I realise who he was. It was the guy who climbed the rope at Duncan's party the previous year, the drunk one from the hostel who shouted at us and who Antonio escorted out. He wore the same jacket with the pins and badges, though sitting here now, perfectly sober and fresh-faced, he looked like a completely different person. His voice had a heavy Spanish inflection. I guessed by the little ETA pin on his lapel that he was more likely Basque.

'I met a volunteer last month,' he said. 'He gave me an encrypted email address to get in touch with the YPG.'

I seemed to be the only one who didn't know what the YPG was. I tried to ask Laurie without the others hearing but the Basque guy answered for her. He seemed to have no idea who I was, or that just under a year ago I'd planted a dainty wet kiss on his nose.

'The People's Protection Units. In Rojava. Some Brits have already gone over as volunteers.'

'To fight?' The concern in my voice must have been obvious.

'To preserve the freedoms of the Kurdish people,' and he went on to explain the hows and whys and *by-any-means-necessarys*, though I didn't pay attention.

Laurie ran a finger across her scar as she listened. My eye wandered to the pictures of the soldiers above our heads, who I noticed now didn't all look Middle Eastern. Some of these might have been volunteers, men and women our age or younger, who had decided to leave their home countries to fight for people they didn't even know, just as Arthur John Martín had done. Men and women with an ideal of the world they were willing to take up arms for, heroic in a way that Laurie and I had idolised as teenagers. Though the sadness of it was all that came to me through their static portraits.

My phone buzzed again. Another message from Antonio. I wanted to ignore it but it was frustrating me now.

Need you today

Laurie seemed relieved when I put my phone away – I could see she thought I was going to walk out. I wanted to, but if I did she wouldn't understand. One of the students played us a video on her phone – protests in Haringey, chants in a foreign language – but she was interrupted by the sound of a loudspeaker outside. From the table, one of the Kurdish men told us it was starting and Laurie stood and helped me to my feet. I stared at her but she couldn't hold it.

'I need to talk to you,' I said, but she just rushed ahead of me, already shouting.

I followed her into the red flare smoke outside.

The word was *Rojava* – one of the students was shouting it out over and over again through the loudspeaker. More people had bandanas over their faces now, which made me uneasy. They had worn bandanas at the riot in London, lots of them had, so that you could only see the slits of their eyes staring down the police. The sight of them brought back the sound of the first baton cracking against a young man's skull. Red blood, black cloth.

The speech was indistinct. Something about Afrin, Erdoğan, Trump, the Russians. In between the proper nouns all I could catch were muffled snippets thick with spite. When the student was finished the chanting began and I found myself next to the boy with the pins and badges who was almost screaming the words. I chanted along, whatever they were saying. After that an older man took the megaphone, one of the Kurds. He spoke passionately about Syria and Bashar al-Assad and someone called Apo, all with such violent sincerity that it felt like being at a rally over there, where it is all so much more real.

Laurie listened intently, nodding away. I thought *Maybe I shouldn't have come after all, maybe I should've skipped it* but I was here, with Laurie beside me, and where else was I supposed to be?

'I got a message on the way down,' I called over the din, but she wasn't listening. 'Laurie.'

She held up a finger for me to wait. That bothered me. She gestured for the megaphone and I stood there waiting but she didn't look at me. She just lifted the thing to her lips and started shouting.

Her first word was *Fuck*, and after that all I heard was a torrent of rage against absolutely everything. *Fucking May, fucking Trump, fucking* everyone. She shouted about arms deals, about capitalism, exploitation, tax. She said: '*It's time to rise up and fuck the people who are fucking us.*' I saw the anger that came out when she was at her worst – the anger of a girl who has never got over the sight of her mum in bed with another man. Every time her fury peaked, the crowd cheered. I hated it.

I felt my phone vibrate in my pocket – once, twice.

'For Christ's sake,' I said under my breath.

Jorge

Today

The crowd was all fists and bared teeth. The anarchist-looking ones were the most riled up, along with the students and the old couple in camo. Only the Kurds chanted methodically, purposefully, with a clean, directed anger I hadn't seen at any protest before. Yes, everyone was serious, everyone meant it, but these people were fully invested.

I looked around to see if any police had shown up – I saw none, I was grateful for that. All I could think about was batons and shields and horses, the nerves rising up in my throat. The boy with the leather jacket held a sign for me to hold but I refused. It was an image of a woman in a burqa lying on a stretcher. Another buzz in my pocket. *Christ's sake*.

Please, it read simply.

I wrote without thinking:

Jesus

Busy mate

Later

The crowd roared as Laurie finished her speech. They actually liked it, all this fire and brimstone. I turned away, hoping the sight of the normal people going about their normal business on the pavement would calm me down, but it didn't. Laurie came straight over to me.

'Are you staying or what?'

'Yes, I'm staying.'

She turned away frustrated, as if she'd struggled to convince me. *Next time I'll say I'm ill*, I thought.

'Laurie.'

'What is it?'

But then all the words I'd prepared on my way down

evaporated and I had no idea what to say. 'I got a message this morning.'

'Yes, you said.' Clearly I was bothering her. 'What was it?'

'It was from Dad.'

She was still looking over in the direction of the megaphone but now it looked more like she was pretending. She shouted something along with the crowd, half focused, and then her lips formed the words *Let me see it*, though I couldn't hear her voice.

'He was just asking me to look out for you. Have you spoken to him lately?'

She sniffed and met my eye. I could see her pushing the feelings down into her chest. The sound of violent uproar rose around the fountain. I was sure the police must be on their way. She snatched my phone off me but it was locked.

'George, just let me have a look.'

I didn't want to but the swell of the crowd was in my blood then. The rush of raw emotion I had felt at the riot was rising in me. *God when will I ever get rid of this*. I unlocked the phone and gave it back to her.

It opened on Antonio's messages – Jorge, Today, Please – which she ignored. She found the message from Dad under the little picture of his gurning face in the top corner. And under that, my reply.

Of course Dad

I'll keep an eye on her

Ring you later

Laurie held the phone just a little longer, and then thrust it back at me. She laughed spitefully, dismissed me with a wave of her hand. 'What are you, a policeman?'

As she rejoined the crowd, I saw a few community support officers watching us from the other side of the road, chatting with the Jehovah's Witnesses, who looked like they were getting ready to leave. I decided with my heart rather than my head that yes, they had the right idea.

I left Laurie with the Kurdish men and the students and anarchists, waving their red-white-and-green flags under the freezing sun. I didn't bother to say goodbye.

I messaged Antonio a few days after the protest but for the first time since I'd given him my number, he never replied. I thought perhaps he'd picked it up drunk and forgotten about it. He'd definitely read it, I knew that – I'd watched the little confirmation ticks turn blue before the words under his name changed to *last seen today at...*

I messaged again to suggest we meet, and again to ask if he was alright. After that I found myself checking to see whether he'd answered, when the last time he'd been online was, just waiting. It made me angry. I tried to ignore the feeling, but then I was bothered by the fact that he was making me carry this burden in the first place, the burden of my own feelings, which I still didn't fully understand. I'd gone out of my way to be a good friend – it was him who behaved poorly or at least not sensibly. And yes, if he hadn't made things escalate at the party I'm sure Laurie and Helena would have broken up anyway, but he was still a part of that. Sometimes it felt like he was in the dead centre of it. I remembered what the young men at Hostelpoint used to say about him – that he was *craaazy*, which I'd thought just meant wild. And I remembered how his sister had treated me, as if I was the burden on him, as if I was the one confusing his feelings. That bullshit. At least that's how I felt when I was upset, or maybe just when the guilt in me was growing and I needed something to bat it down with.

It wasn't until a couple of weeks after the Kurdish thing that he got back to me, and when he did his message was curt and flat.

Free Saturday

I invite you my home

I was working at the bar Saturday so I suggested Sunday but he didn't reply. I suggested the following Saturday but again nothing. He might have avoided me completely, if Brighton wasn't the village that it is. But eventually we had to bump into each other.

The persistent winter chill had finally given way to a wet, late spring. Rainclouds hung above the Clock Tower, where street sleepers huddled on the steps with their dogs and sleeping bags. As I waited to cross the road, I saw Antonio on the opposite side. His shoulders were slumped and his mouth hung open. He was staring into space with a vacancy I'd never seen in him even at his drunkest. I thought maybe he was drunk, but it was mid-morning and he wasn't dressed like he was on a bender. He wore his work uniform, so I thought maybe he'd been on a night shift and was just exhausted. Though really it didn't look like that either. It looked like a part of him had been hollowed out. I could have walked off without him noticing – he was that absent – but I could see by then how wrong things were. He walked through the people like a ghost.

'Antonio,' I said, and he blinked at the sound of his name.

When his eyes fell on me, he slumped even further. It made my heart sink, I felt my skin tingle with nerves. I couldn't remember having that effect on anyone, ever.

'Oh. Jorge.' He met me with a hug that was so limp and apathetic it was like hugging a different person. It was an automatic hug, a nod to the usual pattern of our friendship. I baulked at the feel of it. In the absence of his aftershave I caught the sharp smell of unwashed clothes and booze coming through the skin.

'Good to see you,' I said, and it was, though I'm sure he could see I was concerned and confused.

'It is shit morning.' He laughed and I saw a glimmer of life and energy. But it faded with his smile.

'Yes, it's been shit all week.'

I thought *Jesus we can't talk about the weather, not us*, but he didn't seem to want to say anything. We stood there in silence while the shoppers jostled past us. Someone knocked into me from behind and told me to watch it. Neither of us moved.

'Shall we go to yours?' I said.

Normally he would have jumped at the suggestion. He was always trying to get me into his flat, always suggesting I stay over though I never did. I'd been avoiding the place since New Year's and he knew it. He paused for a long time and only eventually shrugged. That shrug sent a shiver through me.

'Why not.'

It was the least enthusiastic yes he'd ever given. He said it like a Brit.

We walked through town slowly – it was so crowded and Antonio was so quiet I could barely think straight. He just let the people bustle around him so that I had to steer him physically around a couple arguing outside Poundland, his body cold and unresponsive to my touch. When we got to his flat I noticed some new graffiti near the door of his building, a six-inch scrawl in red ink. *£500 PCM Bills Inc*, and an arrow pointing to a hole in the brickwork. The kind of graffiti you get in Brighton, the sarky kind that sticks in your head. I tried to ask him if he'd seen it – it was the kind of thing he'd find funny – but he walked in without looking.

The light wasn't working in the staircase so I had to feel my way up with the banister. I was thinking then how all this must be because of me, though I had thought he was taking it better than this. I hadn't thought he was the type to hold a grudge, but then I was thinking about his birthday and Alejandra and the way she looked at me on the boat. So that I had no idea where all this was going. At the top of the stairs, Antonio pushed hard against the door and then stepped over the pile of folded clothes that had fallen across the doorway. The smell wafted into the corridor – cooked food and tobacco smoke. I followed him in and stood awkwardly on the small square of visible carpet.

I hadn't been in his flat since before Christmas. In that time, his collection of reclaimed *objet d'art* – the stuff his sister had looked at so disparagingly – had become a hoard of pointless street junk. I counted four sets of golf clubs in rotting cases, and other putters and drivers suspended with nails from the wall. Two cracked flat-screen televisions lay on his original low table, supporting cups, glasses, a Buddhist prayer bowl encrusted with yellow sauce. There were posters not just for films and concerts but for household products, library events, takeaways. On the back of the door was a painted picture on frayed cardboard – white horses, green grass, blue sky – with the words 1,000 PIECES in the corner. At the far end, stuck onto the headboard in front of a picture of an astronaut, was Alejandra's goalkeeping glove, now faintly soiled.

He asked me to sit.

'Where?'

The sofa was covered in second-hand books – all on the Spanish Civil War. He moved one from the arm, tossed it aside. I perched. The air was thick with the smell of dust and smoke. I pushed my finger through the curtain. Clear tape sealed the window frame.

'Shall we go to the beach?' I ventured. We hadn't been yet that year.

He said nothing. There was food on the counter – pointed peppers and blood sausage his sister sent from Spain. I thought he might offer to cook as he usually did, but I was grateful he didn't. The peppers were wrinkled and the sausage looked warm.

He shuffled about, moved dishes into the sink. I had no idea what to say.

'Have you spoken to Alejandra lately?'

He answered without turning. 'No. My sister is busy in Madrid.'

The clatter of crockery. I'd never seen him like this.

'Antonio.'

I noticed his swimming shorts draped over the radiator, sopping wet. He must have been swimming already that day, though it was freezing.

'*Antonio.*'

He turned. I tried to look receptive.

'Let's have a drink.'

It was never me who suggested we drank but I had no idea what else to say. His lips turned down, I thought he was going to cry. He took two bottles of beer from a second fridge with no light – cheap stubbies at room temperature. He took a long draw from his, I did the same. I was feeling hemmed in and nervous and for the first time, in one idle corner of my mind, I considered how infinitely easier it is to drink alone.

I asked him what'd been going on.

'*¿Qué está pasando? Dios.* You know in Spain, they want…' He made the action of heaving something into his lap – it spilt a dribble of his beer. '…the *cadáver de Franco.*'

'Oh, yes.' Carlos my manager had mentioned it one night – a rumour they wanted to exhume General Franco's body from the big stone monument he was buried in. 'I mean, what's been going on with you?'

'*¿Que? Nada.*' He muttered a simple song under his breath: '"*Franco, Franco, que tiene el culo blanco…*"' I think it was to the tune of their national anthem.

'No parties?'

'I don't want.'

'Do you have to work this weekend?'

He stroked his stubble. 'Two week ago – three week ago – I was in my home and my work call me. They say me, *You come early tomorrow, sis o'clock*, so I went sis o'clock. My manager was waiting me there…'

I knew he struggled at work sometimes but he never usually complained. Now his voice was full of emotion and his accent thickened so much he was hard to understand. He stumbled over his words, skipped a few of the more difficult ones. He stood up and started rummaging through loose papers.

'He say me, *Antonio, you was late today, you was late last week, bla, bla, bla.* I wasn't late never. One time, is all. *Antonio, you smell, you uniform is a smell.* Is bullshit, I know.'

I don't know how you tell people they smell, never mind people like Antonio. And he didn't smell *that* bad anyway. Just that he was due a shower and a week off the booze.

'What a bastard,' I said.

'Bastard *cabrón*. But… I am not a stupid. I say him, *You hate all Spanish people*.'

'You told him that?'

'Yes, I told him. You remember Iker, *el Sevillano?* He was told one day, *You go*, and no reason. And Marco, *el futbolista del hostal?*' He threw a click over his shoulder. His voice was getting hoarse. '*Go!* No reason, nothing. So I say, *You are a racist. Racist, racist, racist*. He told to me, *No, I treat everyone the same*. I say, *You are the worst English man!* The worst — *¿como lo llamas?* – *type* of English man.'

I tried to ask if that meant he'd lost his job but he wouldn't answer, kept on with his story, which I believed even if it didn't wholly make sense. After he'd finished, his head hung low. I took his empty bottle from him and put it with mine on the counter.

'Antonio.'

His chin lifted.

'Come on. Let's go to the beach. It'll help clear your mind.'

He wasn't buying it.

'Anyway.' I tried to sound light. 'We're out of beer.'

Antonio looked at the bottles and nodded. Then he turned to his bed, rifled around among the sheets and the dog-eared Civil War books and pulled out a bottle of cheap red wine. He unscrewed the cap and poured a long stream of it down his gullet so that a rivulet of pink ran off from his lips onto his shirt. I wanted to take the bottle off him, less because it saddened me than because it disgusted me. It was those judgemental feelings that mixed with the sadness and confusion in me, so that I had no idea how to feel.

'Jesus, Antonio. What's happened?'

His lips smacked when he stopped drinking. '*Vamos*.'

He put his coat on and led the way out. I followed behind him, watching his unsteady old man's walk, thinking of Alejandra and the way she made me hide the bottle of Bacardi on his birthday. Wondering what on earth could have happened since New Year's.

We walked to the beach but he didn't want to sit in our usual spot. Instead we walked west over the shingle that had been thrown up onto the pavement. He led us to one of the shelters on Hove Lawns. It smelt pissy but he sat down anyway. I pushed aside an empty Pringles tube so I could sit beside him.

The sea was rough that day even though the wind wasn't up, so rough that I couldn't believe he'd already been out in it. I felt the prickles of cold under my skin. We drank quietly and I hoped to coax whatever was wrong out of him, but he held on to it stubbornly. After half an hour I needed to say something but I was tipsy already, surprisingly so, and I wanted to get drunk. The words wouldn't come – nothing useful for either of us – and it frustrated me. Eventually I thought of something that would cheer him up.

'You said you were looking at the family tree?'

'No,' his hands deep in his pockets.

'Come on, now. You were all excited last time we spoke about it.' Though that had been many weeks ago now.

'No.'

There was a new look in his eyes, something violent. Just like Laurie when she'd squared off to the CSOs on New Road. It was like Antonio was suddenly aware of the power of his age, his strength, the years he'd already lived. There was no love for me in his eyes. Still, he wasn't willing to turn away.

'My *grey gran-father* was a *cabrón*.'

The hard R startled me. He kicked a Stella can out from under the bench. It almost hit a pram – the mother steered it away from us.

'Antonio, what do you mean?'

His face was blank drunk. 'My *grey gran-father… ¿Como pude haber sido tan estúpido al pensar que este inglés que nunca conocí era un héroe, cuando en realidad no era más que un cobarde, un jodido cobarde…?*'

'Antonio, I don't understand.'

He took the photograph of his *bisabuelo* out of his pocket, held it in his hand without looking at it. 'I was looking the people my relatives. All Sussex people. Brighton, Hastings, all people. I was looking one man. The son Arthur John Martín. His name Re-ginn-al.'

'Reginald?'

'Reginal, *si*. He was son Arthur John Martín.'

'That's great. So he would have been your great uncle…?' I had no idea.

'He was son Arthur John Martín, is all!'

Usually when he got angry there was a liveliness to it, something performative, like when the kids at the hostel used to tease him about his age, his manners. Now his anger was real and bitter-poisonous. I sensed that whatever had upset him had already settled into his blood, and if that was the case it might be impossible to draw out.

'Jesus, Antonio, what's the matter?'

He slumped back onto the bench. 'I know, I found. Reginal is alive – seventy-seven years old.'

'Oh my God.'

'In the town Lewes.'

'He's in Lewes?'

'Yes.' He kicked another piece of rubbish.

'Antonio, that's wonderful. Do you want to see him?'

'I have seen.'

The rain started then, falling lightly on the stones. I put my hand on his shoulder, the nerves running through me, but his face didn't change. 'Antonio. When did you see him?'

His voice grew quiet. 'I have seen, few week ago.'

'For God's sake, why didn't you tell me? I would have gone with you.'

'I went alone.'

So this was what he'd needed me for, the weekend I was busy helping Laurie with her Kurdish thing. It had been important, and I'd missed it.

'Well, what happened?' I said.

He held out his hand to feel the rain. I watched the droplets spattering his dry palm.

'Nothing.'

Now I had no clue. 'What did you talk about?'

'Nothing.'

He wouldn't look at me.

'Antonio—'

'Forget.'

'Please—'

'*Forget.*'

'I don't understand.'

He gazed out at the sea without tears. Then he looked across at me, looked right through me so that it was hard to hold his eye, and poked me gently in the chest.

'You understand nothing.'

'What? What do you mean?'

'You.' His voice cold and lifeless. Like he was speaking to nobody. 'You understand nothing.'

He clambered up and walked away with his head held high against the rain, with the faint sound of ¡*Ay Carmela!* ¡*Ay Carmela!* trailing behind him. When I looked down at the bench I saw the photograph of his *bisabuelo*, abandoned there with the young man's profile still lifted proudly against the West Pier, dotted faintly with rain.

When May finally came I was so desperate for the sun I pulled a sickie and took myself down to the Level. I sat there watching a hippie boy balancing on a slackline tied between two of the Dutch elms that line the park, the grass dry underneath me. This is where I'd first properly met Antonio, among the waiting crowds while Duncan and the other naked cyclists prepared for their route around the city. I kept half an eye on the central path since I knew Antonio crossed the park sometimes on his way to the supermarket. A part of me believed I'd see him sauntering past as normal and we would hug it out and make everything understood. But he never did.

After what he told me at the seafront, his messages dried up. I wanted to get the truth out of him about *Reginal* or Reginald or whatever he'd been saying, this man he went to see. Whatever was going on, he didn't want me to be any part of it. I told myself that was for the best. I'd wanted that feeling – the feeling of solitude– but now I had it I wasn't sure what to do with it. It was the perfect day to toast the fact that summer was on its way but I sat there alone and sober.

As I slipped off my shoes, a message came through from Laurie.

Can we meet?

I sat up straight. I hadn't seen much of her either, not since she told me point-blank that pubs weren't her thing anymore and that she wanted to *focus*. After that, getting her by herself was almost impossible. She was always with people from the activist groups, people I didn't want to know. They didn't trust me – none of them did. I could tell by the way they watched me when I spoke. They knew I wasn't part of their thing.

Of course

When?

She messaged back to say Now, which surprised me even more, and I told her where I was and within a few minutes she was on her way.

Of the two of us, it was Laurie that never mentioned Mum. She'd hardly said two words about her our whole lives, and so I knew she was one for bottling things up and I learnt never to push her too hard – I knew what happened when you did. So it was a relief to me when I saw her tramping across the Level in her heavy Doc Martens with her shoulders swaying to and fro. I was relieved to see she was smiling, too – I'd assumed by her urgency something was wrong. She hugged me tight as she hadn't for some time, and then sat with me. It felt like we hadn't been truly alone together for ages, at least not since before New Year's. It didn't take long for her to get round to what she wanted to say.

'I'm sorry about how I was with you at the march. I was just upset about Dad.'

'That's fine,' I said, and it was. I only wanted to hear her say it.

'I've been selfish. I'm sorry if I've made it awkward for you.'

I told her it was okay but she seemed to understand already.

'I don't know why she was ever with me at all,' she said.

She, Helena. I'd waited all winter and all spring for her to open up and by now I thought it would never happen. The tears had already passed and like always she'd shown me none of them. But at least now it was coming out.

She mused. 'It didn't quite make sense, did it?'

'How do you mean?'

'She clearly wanted someone around.' She spoke calmly, even breezily, and I searched her eyes for signs of uncertainty but found none. Maybe she really was over it. 'I'm sure she wanted someone who'd listen to her and everything. She did say over and over that I was a good listener. But then when I think back I can't remember her ever really saying anything.'

'You mean emotional things?'

I was thinking of whatever had happened to Helena in Islington, her past life. Neither of them had ever explained what it was, if Laurie even knew.

'Yes. We only really talked about films and music, and political stuff. Then she would say, *You're such a good listener*. What does that even mean.' It wasn't a question.

'Maybe she still felt like she was getting to know you.'

She picked up a fag butt, flicked it away. 'I didn't really realise until we were back home. What I mean is, if she wanted someone more like one of those people...' She meant Duncan, I think. '...why didn't she go for one of them? They're more her people, aren't they?'

I supposed they were. Antonio had seen the whole group as one homogenous whole – the cultured English perhaps, socialists and poetry readers. Less like a string of connected islands than one solid land mass with high cliffs all around it. I wished I could tell Laurie how I was feeling about Antonio, about how it was all changing. Though it wasn't the time.

She repeated: 'Don't you think they are – more her people?'

A couple of hippies ran past us with their dog, kicking up dust.

I decided to be bold. 'Laurie, have you not considered you might have pushed her away?'

She tried to hide her surprise. She failed. 'What do you mean?'

'You obviously made the effort. That's fine. She made the effort too, I think—'

'What do you mean "made the effort"?'

'To accommodate you. To accommodate each other.'

She laid down flat with her eyes shut. 'I have no idea what that means.'

The sun beat down on my head. I was feeling sticky for the first time since last summer and the day was still getting warmer.

'The thing is…' She seemed less sure now. '…she just has a different view on the world than we have.'

'How?'

I followed a Frisbee with my eyes before she answered. A lime-green disc arcing across the sky with a black dog chasing underneath. Its white teeth snatching the air.

'Do you remember the day of the referendum result?' she said.

The memory of Duncan and Helena outside the off-licence came rushing back. Maybe Marta had told her before she left the country, though I couldn't picture that. Maybe she'd seen them herself and bottled it up this whole time. Which meant she knew I'd been there. I noticed suddenly how the Level was filling up with people – hippies, skateboarders, the homeless.

'Hard to forget,' I said, picking at a hole in my sock.

'I was upset that night and I thought I knew what I was upset about but maybe I didn't.'

'You were upset by the result.' A couple of kids screamed as a football floated over our heads. 'We all were.'

'No...' She was concentrating now. 'I think I knew how it was going to go.'

It was true that of all of us, Laurie had been the least convinced it would turn out the way we wanted. I could have given her her dues and put it down to shrewdness, but I don't think it came from there. If Laurie knew we were going to fail, it was only because she had no faith in the British people. And even less now. To her we lived in a nation of Tom Grocotts, one great Shoulder of Mutton.

'Then what were you upset about?' I asked.

The door was wide open for her to tell me how Helena had hurt her – even if it wasn't Helena's fault, just because they weren't right for each other, because Laurie needed someone who was as dependent on her as she was on them. She closed that door with a gentle push.

'That voting just doesn't cut it.'

I sensed then she had said her last word on Helena but I had no desire to get into a discussion about parliamentary democracy. I'd been surprised not to have received a message from her about the snap election due in June – the Tories' obvious, unashamed attempt to hold on to power. Even now, seeing her a week after it was called, she didn't mention it once. It felt like her focus had fallen on something else, something I wasn't a part of.

'I want change,' she said, 'revolutionary change. There are people all over the world actually trying to make a difference—'

'Helena makes a difference.'

She didn't flicker. 'People who actually put their lives on the line for what they believe in.'

'You need to pick your battles,' I said.

'Exactly. It's time to choose.'

That wasn't what I meant but she stood up to show she'd had enough. The boy on the slackline was still balanced between the elms, rocking slowly on the line, up and down, up and down, looking like he'd fall any second. More than anything, at that moment, I wished we could have a drink together – Laurie and I, Antonio too. All three of us. I stood to meet her and her shoulders broadened. I touched her arm, wet with sweat. The sunshine was boiling my brain.

'Come on,' she said.

Her body was all tense now, the armour was back on. I knew that the pain was still in there, whatever she said. She started to walk off and I hobbled to squeeze on a shoe. 'Wait!'

I called but she marched on and I considered not following at all but I knew I had to.

For some reason, perhaps just because of the way she marched ahead over the dry grass and across the main road, it seemed like she knew exactly where we were headed.

The Cowley Club is a little place that runs a cafe and bar, punk gigs, action meetings, spoken word nights. There's a window by the entrance with books on Palestine and permaculture, and more books inside that you can buy or borrow – far too intense for me, I could barely look at the covers. The few times I ever went in the people were friendly, welcoming even, though for some reason I always felt as though I stood out in there, like a policeman in uniform. Paranoia, perhaps.

That afternoon it felt dark inside, just because the sun was out and we weren't in it. I thought it was empty at first, until I noticed that Laurie had stopped to stare at something by the entrance. I don't know if she knew already that they were inside – how could she? – but when I heard a bubble of elegant laughter burst underneath the window and looked towards the disaster waiting for us, she didn't look in the least surprised.

Helena sat there, laughing gracefully in crisp summer clothes, holding on to a paper straw in a perspiring tumbler. Across the table, Duncan laughed too, sitting there with his torso obscured by shopping bags, collar open. It was months since I'd run into him – before *Left Nut* had got a feature in *Viva* magazine and his Twitter followers had spiked beyond fifty thousand – everyone was talking about it. The thought once again skipped through my head, plain and simple and horribly immutable. *Brighton is just a village*.

'Come on,' I whispered. 'Let's go.'

They still hadn't seen us and we could have left quite easily. Laurie shrugged. 'I've seen her since. It's no big deal.'

'Laurie, if you want to—'

'You go on home, if you want.'

But there was no chance of that.

She turned to the woman at the counter with an amiable smile, ordered lime soda and a white wine for me without me asking. I glanced around at the empty tables, the bookshelves. Helena and Duncan still hadn't seen us. They were leaning in towards each other though I heard Duncan say something like *Just let me call him and see if there's anything coming in.* Maybe I should have just walked out by myself.

Laurie took us to a table by the bookshelves. I sat opposite her with my wine. She passed her hand over the flame of the candle. 'I used to love it in here.'

She said it loudly, pointlessly loud, just as the music faded out. The woman working there lifted her head. I hid behind my wine glass. 'I thought you liked it.'

'I don't know,' she said. 'There's something kind of showy about it. Sometimes it feels like it's just full of posers.'

No one spoke. I drew the strength to look up and when I did, Laurie was staring towards the window and they were staring back. When the music restarted, she got up immediately. I stayed.

'Hello, you two,' I heard her say. 'Good to see you both…'

Her voice remained loud and much too quick, stuck on the wrong speed and volume. They exchanged pleasantries and Helena waved at me timidly. When I waved back I felt like we understood each other. The eyes of two people desperate to vanish.

'Dark in here,' Laurie said to me as she returned to our table.

But she didn't sit down. She picked up her glass without looking at me, walked back to the window and took the chair beside Duncan. Helena sat dead still with her eyes wide open. I hurried over with my wine and sat beside her. We hugged but neither of us committed to it. I watched candle wax edging down the side of a pastis bottle and onto the table. The flame flickered between us.

'I hear you've gone full time for the party,' said Laurie.

'Yes,' Helena answered, her voice quiet.

I'd seen online she'd been taken on as a personal secretary to some political candidate I'd never heard of, someone for a constituency outside of Brighton. She didn't seem to want to talk about it.

'What are you shopping for?' Laurie's voice still over-loud.

Duncan's voice was quiet. 'Nothing special.'

Laurie spoke to him without looking. 'You look tanned. And you've got a moustache.'

'I've been away for a couple of weeks.'

'Where?'

'Barcelona.'

Laurie surprised me when she said: 'Oh, nice,' though I could see she was biding her time. I wanted to run.

I turned to Helena, spoke without thinking – 'Did you go as well?' – and then realised what an awful question I'd asked. She said no, thank God.

Laurie stroked her chin. 'What did you do in Barcelona?'

It was only when Duncan paused to answer did I wonder whether he'd seen Marta, whether he'd gone specifically to see Marta. Maybe to win her back. Maybe just for a fuck.

'Nothing really,' said Duncan. 'Saw the Sagrada Família.'

'Fun,' said Laurie.

'It was very beautiful.'

Helena's drink disappeared in one. I finished mine too. An ideal space was left for us to make our goodbyes and leave. It passed.

Laurie leant back in her chair. 'Do you think it's right, necessarily, to join in with that lot outside?'

She nodded to the window, where a few shoppers with Poundland bags were walking past. *This is awful*, I thought. *This is the worst.* I wanted to lower my eye onto the candle.

'What do you mean?'

'Shopping for crap.'

Helena gathered up her things. 'Speaking of which we still need to get to Tiger.'

I started to shuffle out of her way but Laurie held my hand. 'I mean, if we spend all our money on crap, aren't we just as bad as the Americans?'

Something inside Duncan slipped just then, revealing a flash of sincere sadness that lit his face an unfamiliar tone. I wanted to know if he'd seen Marta, why he'd gone, what was happening. Even though it was none of my business. Maybe he'd flown over and got on his knees on Las Ramblas and begged her and she'd sneered, flicked her hair, refused to come back, good for her. Whatever it was he wasn't sticking around to explain. He collected up his things. Laurie was in his way.

'You haven't finished your drink. I was saying – it's easy to be moral when you've got a bag full of Marks and Spencer.'

Maybe Duncan just wanted to tell her to piss off, but if he did he lost his nerve. He laid his gloves on the table. 'It's a present.' He fumbled with a pouch of tobacco.

Laurie laughed. 'And how do you square with that?'

'With what?'

'You've got a pouch of Golden Virginia. And a few bags from the high street. Maybe we should go out and buy some cocaine. Go to a strip club.'

Laurie's voice was going all Sussex now and Helena was getting up. I moved aside for her and Duncan tried to follow. Laurie sat still for just a second while she finished her lime and soda, and then moved out of the way.

'I'm sorry,' she said. 'Just trying to make conversation,' and everyone swapped goodbyes before the couple rushed out. I saw the look on Helena's face as she went – real pain and embarrassment. A breeze whipped in from the open doorway and shook the flames off the candles.

I stood in the empty place with my mouth bitter and dry. 'Feel better?'

Laurie let all the breath leave her body. She tried to look unfazed but her hands were shaking. Outside I could see Helena and Duncan arguing with each other, just briefly, and then walking off in separate directions. Laurie sat back down. I didn't.

'That was bloody embarrassing.'

She ran her finger over the lip of her glass. 'Calm down, George.'

I was angry like I hadn't been for a long time. The woman at the counter stared at us but for once I didn't care. 'No, Laurie! That was awful.'

'Fuck them,' she said.

Fuck them? I felt so angry I could burst. 'No, fuck *you*.'

That shocked her.

'Look,' I said. 'Like Dad said, you're obviously in a bad way. It seems like you might not be coping at all.'

She froze then. Only after several seconds of staring into my eyes did she sniff, and I watched the armour fall back into place. 'I'm fine,' she said. 'It's you that's freaking out.'

There was desperation in my voice now, she could hear it. 'I'm worried about you, for Christ's sake.'

'Worry about yourself.'

She stood to leave. I grabbed her by the wrist, something I'd never done before, not like that. The woman at the counter was watching us. I remembered Laurie at the riot, squaring off to the line. I wanted to tell her the truth – actually I wanted to shout it in her face, just to punish her. She stopped and shook me off with ease. Then she stepped forward, right up into my face so that the whole of her was over me. Our noses touched.

'Go on, then,' she said, like a lad might.

My heart thumped in my chest. It was like I could hear it smashing against my ribs. She stood there several seconds, then huffed an older-sister huff, and walked out.

It's you that's freaking out.

After what happened at the Cowley Club I decided to give Laurie some space, and since Antonio was no longer even reading my messages I saw nothing of him either. I knew if I went outside I'd bump into someone – either them or Helena or Duncan or someone else – so I just watched the city getting hotter and hotter from my window and tried not to spend too much time on the internet. It was all bad news or fake news or a combination of both. Those were the months when the Manchester Arena was bombed and we watched Grenfell Tower burn with seventy-two people trapped inside, the decade getting darker and darker with no respite. After that I imposed myself with a blanket ban on the news.

Instead I took out library books, dozens of them, thinking I could read like I'd read my way through the more difficult years of school. Only now the old crinkled novels looked long and self-important and the new ones felt insincere and predictable. The same went for films, albums. To kill time one night I made a collage out of pieces of an old *Cosmopolitan* – a face with borrowed hair, borrowed eyes, a borrowed smile. I flambéed it as Antonio used to do with his chorizo. Fierce, brief flames. The smell of burnt glue stuck permanently to the curtains.

Looking back, I was 'wallowing', which I guess is meant to evoke the indulgence of it. Really it was plain old-fashioned self-pity. I behaved in the shy, withdrawn way I had at school, though without Laurie to pull me back into the action. And without Antonio, who had stumbled in and then out of my life and who I knew I needed now – though I thought I hadn't. So many of my feelings at that time were hard to process, but that realisation had come quickly, as soon as the hole he had left behind was made clear. Though I still didn't know what to do about it. I beat myself up for the clichés rolling around in my head – *you don't know what you've got till it's gone*, in Joni Mitchell's voice. It made me feel fickle. I especially tried not to think about him on those long nights when I avoided my own eye in the mirror. Once I dug out the picture of Arthur John Martín, which I'd kept, just to look at and see how I felt, but I couldn't stand it. I hid it away under the sink and slumped down against the cabinet to think.

Phone off, laptop closed. Nothing to see here.

It was around that time that the rashes appeared on my skin. The first one spread across my throat – a dry red Australia growing into a long, bloated Russia, bordered with an outline of darker red raised above the skin. Looking in the mirror one morning my whole reflection looked saggier, sadder, like a dog in the first black-and-white frames of a rescue advert. I tried to look stronger but my face was unconvincing – it made me think of the Prime Minister, who I guessed might win her snap election but who I couldn't help feeling sorry for. She was all haggard now too, though she didn't have the rashes. They itched so much that eventually, one morning in June, I decided I couldn't put up with it anymore.

I took side streets all the way to the pharmacy, hood up, not recognising anyone. It was a busy Saturday and I had the day off, which more and more seemed like a heavier burden than work. The sun frazzled my hangover. The heat made my rashes burn. I stopped by the benches and then looked up to see Marta, standing outside the pharmacy with a guitar case on her back and a few orange bags at her feet. Like she'd never been gone.

I thought about turning away but I couldn't. 'Jesus, Marta, what are you doing here?'

'George!'

I was amazed when she hugged me, since she never normally touched me, never touched anyone, so I thought.

'How long have you been back?' I said.

'A few weeks. Duncan came to Barcelona to get me.'

So he had been. And she hadn't turned him away on his knees on Las Ramblas. I didn't understand any of it. Still, *none of my business.*

'And are you okay?' I said. 'I mean, are you alright?'

She smiled. 'Yes, George. I'm fine.'

She touched me again, just gently on the arm this time, like she never would have done, and something about it fitted with the new confidence in her voice. It was like whatever timidity she'd had before was gone, replaced by a new glint in her eye. It startled me, I didn't understand. She caught me looking at the bags.

'There's a party,' she said. 'Duncan's moving out of the school.' I could see the kindness in her face, something like pity. She wanted to invite me, for my sake, but knew also that that wasn't the right thing to do. 'Actually, we're getting a place together.'

'You're kidding.'

'No. I'm staying at my old place just till we sort something. We're looking at a house tomorrow morning.'

I felt the anger rising in me. 'But Marta, it's Duncan. I mean, you know what he's like, he's—' I stopped when I saw him through the window of the pharmacy, standing in the queue, tapping away at his phone. That's when I changed my mind about going in.

I looked at my wrist, I had no watch. 'I'd better be getting on.'

'No.' She grabbed my hand. 'Wait, George.'

I was shocked by her hand on mine, her grip. Something had definitely changed.

Before she let me go, Duncan came outside. He saw us and paused. Marta kissed him on the cheek and then leant into my ear to whisper *Message me soon*, before walking down the street with her phone to make a call.

I'd seen him a few times in the weeks following the Cowley Club thing, wandering the streets, sitting with strangers outside the pubs. I'd even taken the time to read the *Viva* article on him, and the other in *The Argus*, though I wished I hadn't. I already had *Left Nut* muted on all platforms. He caught me staring, just as he'd caught me outside the off-licence, when I'd witnessed whatever I'd witnessed.

'Hello, Duncan.'

'Greetings, comrade.'

Prick. I noticed then he looked cleaner, fresher, more relaxed, and that the red flush had disappeared from his face. He wore Labour Party badges, the first time I'd ever seen them.

'I hear you're moving out of the school,' I said.

'Bit of bother with the agency.' He feigned nonchalance but I could tell he was embarrassed to have bumped into me, since I wasn't invited to the party. 'Will miss the old place though.'

I felt my frustration rising but I didn't want to punish him, not really. Still, I struggled to talk small. 'It was awkward, wasn't it. What happened.'

'When?'

I suppose I could have meant any time. 'At the Cowley Club.'

'Oh, that?' His facade struggled. 'Nothing to worry about. Laurie's not a bad egg, I don't think. I hope she's alright.'

Then it was my turn to feel guilty. Because I didn't know.

All I could say was: 'She'll manage.'

I wanted to know if anything had gone on between him and Helena while she was seeing Laurie but I couldn't find the words. Anyway, I couldn't believe Helena would do that, even if Duncan tried it on.

Still, he looked embarrassed. 'I'm not sure I could be her friend, as such – not after everything.' He got out a comb and ran it slowly through his hair – an emergency affectation, I'd never seen it before. It made me angry.

'You behaved badly with her. And with Antonio, very badly.'

He mused for a moment. 'I did, didn't I? I turn into such a rotter, sometimes.'

'Please, Duncan, you don't have to talk like that.'

'No, I want to apologise.'

'No. Like that, in that bloody voice.'

He looked away. 'I don't know what you're talking about. Bloody scalding out here, isn't it? That rash looks sore.'

He picked up the orange bags that had been left at his feet and turned to walk off but I moved into his way. That amazed him, I think, but he didn't get angry. Actually he looked frightened. I think that was the only time I ever frightened someone.

'I'm sorry, George,' he said, the bags clinking with his shrug. 'I'm in love with Helena. What can I do?'

'Ridiculous.'

'Don't worry,' he went on, 'she doesn't love me back.'

'What do you mean? What about Marta?'

Further down the road Marta had taken out her guitar and put her case on the ground for change. She strummed idly, quite happily, out of earshot.

'Yes, well,' said Duncan. 'I know it sounds stupid. But I love her as well.'

Perhaps that should have made me angrier, the absurdity of it all, but whatever he meant, he meant it. Suddenly I felt sheepish about being in his way, as if I'd stopped a stranger who was just trying to get his shopping home before a party. I stepped aside. Before he turned around I saw the old familiar visage on him – the proud look, the performance. I suspected that whether it occasionally faltered or even slipped, it would never fall.

'Anyway, we all have our crosses, *et cetera et cetera*. Helena's getting prepped for the election, I'm sure you've heard. Not a Corbynista like me and Marta, but still. Nobody's perfect.' He turned to go, turned back. 'Almost forgot. I've just seen your mate reposing on the New Road.'

'Who?'

'Antonio, of course.'

And then he walked away briskly after Marta with a clank of his shopping bags, whistling as though nothing had happened.

*

New Road was quiet. Blinding sunlight reflected off the theatre bar windows. I passed the Israelis with their blue-and-white flags and the protestors opposite with their red-black-green-and-white – no one I knew this time. The eye of the sun bore down on me and I felt the sweat prickle up from under my skin. I looked through the glare at the benches that line the street opposite the cocktail bars and the nice restaurants. That's where he was, sat there with the others with a beer in his hand.

He sat in a long line of men sprawled out along the benches. There's always people sitting there when it's dry, summer or winter – men and women of varying ages with all kinds of stories, all kinds of things going on. Working people, homeless people, people who sell drugs. Sometimes you see one of them crying, other times asleep. Mostly they just sit there, absorbed in their own private jokes and dramas, ignoring the street.

Antonio was slouched back halfway down the line. He spoke heatedly with the man next to him, oblivious to everything else, even to the Staffie barking at his feet. There was hair on his face – a thin beard with grey patches along the cheekbone. He rubbed absently at his forehead where the skin was deep brown, even darker than usual. He sat there with one leg trailing into the paths of the other men as they walked along the row to compare something on their phones, or fetch drinks and snacks from each other's carrier bags, or pass each other cigarette papers and filters. They were a quiet bunch that day – all men, no laughter, as if waiting in a queue.

As I approached, their voices rose. I caught an impulse to

turn and walk away. Antonio hadn't seen me and he probably didn't want to. I flinched at each bark of the Staffie, I couldn't hide it. But I made my way slowly towards him anyway. How could I not.

My shadow drew over him. He shielded his eyes to see me, left his hand there for a long time. He stared at me without saying anything – it felt like forever – and then stood.

He didn't hug me, he just stuck out his hand. It was warm and clammy and we shook awkwardly, like strangers. Up close I could see the bloodshot in his eyes and the way they moved shiftily and unfocused from side to side. I wanted to take him away from there but I had no idea where. He offered me to sit.

The man he'd been arguing with greeted me with a heavy Spanish accent and shuffled along the row for me. He gave me a long name that my brain couldn't untangle.

'You no work today?' Antonio asked me, flat and hoarse.

'No. I'm trying to get something for my...' but I didn't finish. 'And you? Have you got a day off?'

He didn't answer. I wanted to ask how he was but I could already see. I thought again I should draw him away but it didn't look like he was planning on going anywhere.

His friend whistled and informed him that someone named Queenie had arrived. Antonio swore in Spanish and walked towards someone in the street – from the garbled insults I could overhear I took this to be Queenie. The man wore bits and pieces of an old linen suit, oversized and damp from the rain. His eyes were buggy like Peter Lorre's and circled with light-blue eyeshadow. He seemed very unpopular with the men on New Road, who rose in an angry Mexican wave as he tried to walk by. Antonio jabbed a finger in his face but I couldn't understand what he was saying.

I sat beside the Spanish guy with the long name, nodding away at nothing. After a minute, he tapped me on the leg and leant in close. His English was perfect but his accent was so thick I had to wade through each word.

'Listen, you're a friend of Antonio's, right?'

I watched Antonio patting down Queenie's pockets. 'Uh-huh.'

'You look like a good person. I have a problem at the moment...'

He launched into a long story about a friend of theirs who'd drowned in a pond trying to win a bet, which I only half listened to while I watched Antonio. There was something in it about poisonous algae – I remember because he pronounced it *aldgy* – and the drowning man having a heart attack in the water and other things, but I couldn't concentrate. At the end of his story, he said firmly: 'So perhaps you can help a brother out.'

Antonio had Queenie by the elbow. Passersby slowed to sneak a look.

I said: 'I think I'd better—'

'He's okay. Listen, we're trying to raise money for the headstone.'

'Hm?' I watched Queenie wriggle free and try to shuffle off. 'Oh.'

I held my hand in my pocket and he could see there was something in there but I didn't really want to pull it out. I believed his story – I really did – but with every second that passed I felt more awkward. In the end, I had no choice.

His face lit up when I produced a tenner, the money I'd put aside for whatever I was going to get from the pharmacy. 'That's so generous,' he said, and then called out something in Spanish to a man down the line, which I hoped was about the headstone. The man named Queenie fled around the corner. Antonio was collected up by his friends to sit back beside me. He took up his can from the bench.

'What was that about?' I said.

'He stole me. Money.'

I didn't want to know. 'Please, Antonio. Have you got the day off? I've been at the supermarket a couple of times, I haven't seen you.'

'Is nothing. You forget.'

'What did I forget? I don't understand.'

He crumpled the can in his hand, made a show of it, took another. 'Forget – about – the work.'

So he probably had lost his job, as I'd been wondering. I looked him over properly as he complained about the situation with Queenie. He didn't look that bad, really – just tired and a bit unkempt. It looked to me like he was in a rut, and I was sure if he'd lost his job he would find another, when he was ready. I just assumed that whatever he'd found out when he visited the old man in Lewes had knocked him for six. *Yes*, I told myself, *he was just in a rut*. Eventually he'd snap out of it and hopefully when he did, he'd forgive me. When he was ready.

He shocked me when he finally leant back on the bench and said: 'This year we go to Spain.'

I'd forgotten all about his invitation. I had no idea it was still on his mind. It made me panic and freeze up but he didn't seem to expect an answer so I just stayed quiet. But the longer neither of us said anything the worse it got, until I was so desperate to leave I thought I'd have to run away. My rashes burned and my lungs rattled in my chest but I hadn't bought the cream and I didn't want to use my inhaler. Then when I thought it was all getting too much, Antonio sprang to his feet.

The men around us went quiet as he marched back into the middle of the street. I thought Queenie might have returned but instead he went and tapped a random woman on the shoulder. My first instinct, despite everything, was that he must be trying to help her with something. When she turned to see him I recognised her – not by her face but by the red cap she wore, bold as anything. MAKE AMERICA GREAT AGAIN. Unbelievable for Brighton on a Saturday.

'*Ey*, you,' said Antonio, '*ey ey ey…*'

It took a moment for me to properly place her – Antonio's landlady, the one who'd been handing out bagels with the Israelis, the one I'd dragged him away from with the cream cheese all over his mouth. By the time I remembered, Antonio was jabbing a finger in her face and she was backing away.

I jumped up but the man beside me said *Wait* so I just stood there. I could make out snatches of what Antonio was saying, though it was hoarse and garbled.

'This money is no pay… I call you three weeks… Nothing, no nothing…'

The woman held her ground but he didn't stop. Now he was shouting in Spanish and she started to walk away but he followed her.

'Oh, Christ.' I jogged after and came alongside him.

He shouted after her. '*¿Cómo esperas que pague cargos por cosas que ni siquiera entiendo?*'

He was still shouting when she dipped around him, and as she did he tipped the cap off her head and let it fall to the wet pavement. She broke into a jog, with the protestors out on the street pausing to watch and the people in the theatre bar pressed up against the window. I eyeballed them but none of them looked away. Antonio picked up the cap and dusted it off.

'Antonio.'

He didn't want to follow her, I was glad. 'Fuck woman. I call three weeks.'

'For Christ's sake, let's go.'

I put a hand on his arm but he threw it off. He stood there panting in front of me, belched twice. It smelt like vomit. His words were slow and deliberate and horribly strained. 'Fuck off.'

I was so shocked I thought I'd misheard.

'What?'

'Fuck – off – George.'

My name fell out of his mouth in a mangled mess, like half-chewed food. It was the first time he didn't call me Jorge since the day we met. It broke my heart – it shocked me how it broke my heart.

He held my eye. 'No call, no visit, no nothing. Only fuck off.'

'Antonio—'

But he just pulled the MAGA hat onto his head and went back to the benches without me while the men cheered for him and his little victory.

I stood there in the hot air and let it blow through my body and thought clearly: *Fuck, it can't be over, not like that.* I watched him, just briefly, before walking off, back to where I'd come from.

When I got back to the pharmacy, I stared for a few minutes at my reflection in the window, saggy and old-dog-like in front of the sign that read CLOSED.

Eight o'clock in the morning, the beach was quiet. I walked down Hove Lawns with the Palace Pier ahead of me and the bright morning light rising behind it. The sea tossed violently. Posters had gone up at bus shelters around the city from the coastguard– an advertisement for sea safety.

Alcohol and seawater
A deadly cocktail

– followed by diagrams about what to do if you fall into the water. You're supposed to let yourself float so you don't go into shock, and then swim calmly to shore like the little faceless man in the diagrams. It was a matter of life and death for the little man. Evidently, he chose life.

Those were the kind of daydreams that came to me now, without Laurie and Antonio to distract me. My own thoughts, my own unbearable company. I passed the black skeleton of the West Pier, the basketball court wet with summer rain, the upturned benches all chained up outside the bars. The carousel was covered and fenced off and beyond that I could see the black empty space under the pier. I paused in front of the fishing boat, the one Antonio had wept in. A dirty hull with empty cans at the bottom, a splintered bench. Just wood, nails and paint. I almost slipped climbing into it. A dog-walker sped up as she passed, maybe she took me for a drunk. I sat in the hull of the boat with my fingers resting on the oarlock. The wind blew around my face and the roar of the sea picked up and I could feel the salty air aggravating my rashes. I imagined myself as a sailor in a lifeboat, drifting through a storm. Then I got out my phone with no intention of using it and scrolled through my contacts. At the top of the list – my only A – was Antonio.

I could have called him at any point but I couldn't picture the conversation. It was rare I called anyone then and if I did I wrote down what I wanted to say in advance – *I'd like to book an appointment with the nurse, please* – and stuck with it. I found any deviation came out awkwardly syncopated, off-rhythm and confusing. And since Antonio had told me to fuck off, and used my name, my real name, which sounded so bitter in his mouth, I had no idea if a phone call would be well received or not. Perhaps he wouldn't even answer. Maybe he would answer and tell me to go fuck myself. Best let him call me.

My phone rang while I was still holding it. The shock of it made me drop it and I didn't see who it was till I picked it up again.

Helena is calling

That was the first time she'd called in a long time, since before our Christmas in the village. I had nothing pre-prepared to say to her. My mind swam with all sorts of irrational things, images of Duncan and Laurie and things happening to them – accidents, injuries, fights, fall-outs. What if Laurie was in trouble, in hospital maybe? I thought about her face at Whitechapel, like a little girl's. The blood on her jacket and mine.

'George, hi.' Helena's voice was quiet and shy.

'Helena, what's happened?'

She told me it was nothing, that she just wanted to see me, and I asked her why and then apologised. I suggested tomorrow, my day off.

'I'm out of town tomorrow,' she said. 'I'm canvassing in Ringmer.'

A village outside of Lewes, pretty little place. I told her I'd be there at one.

'Are you sure?' The first time she'd ever asked if I was sure I wanted to see her or not, the first invitation that was anything less than an expectation.

'Yes, of course.'

'Okay, George. Thank you.'

She hung up and I sat there in the empty boat with my phone in my hand. The place Antonio had cried in front of me – *¡España! ¡España!* I should have known then that letting life take its own course, make its own plans, might not work out for either of us.

Tomorrow, I thought through the tiredness. *Even just to get me out of my own head.*

I hadn't been outside of Brighton and Hove, not even to the edges of the city, in six months.

I spent the whole bus ride that morning staring out of the window, genuinely relieved when we passed the university and the football ground and trundled onto the dual carriageway. I looked down at the cars and lorries heading inland – life carrying on in the rest of the country, people getting on with things. The sound of their engines drowned out the few people on the top deck so that all I could hear was a low coarse rumble and the wind whipping through the open window. We passed a horsebox with an address for Cheltenham on the back, and a beat-up yellow banger strapped to a trailer. I felt like I'd forgotten about all these other things that people did outside of Brighton. It was a relief to know that whatever was happening in my little bubble, everywhere else it was business as usual. It made my own problems look smaller. If only temporarily.

I got off at the village green at about one. Ringmer is pleasant enough – to me it looked a lot like the villages back home, only posher, brighter and less knackered. I messaged Helena and did a lap of the green. The few old people milling around just ignored me. An image came through – a red point on a map. I followed it to the edge of the village. A country lane with cottages, lined with trees. Idyllic in the sunlight.

I didn't recognise her at first. She was at the front door of a thatched cottage speaking to an old man in knitwear. I took her for a charity con woman, a clipboard carpetbagger, except for her black blazer, too smart. When she turned I saw the satchel with the literature sticking out of it, the headed green paper, green name badge, green lanyard. I waited at the end of the driveway. She saw me only eventually, looking up from the clipboard, and her smile was warm and genuine as ever.

It was ten loud crunches at least along the gravel while we looked at each other, looked down, looked at something on our clothes, looked around. I covered up my rashes, suddenly embarrassed of them. I thought she might shake my hand formally or not touch me at all – no one had touched me affectionately since Marta outside the pharmacy. So when she held me so firmly as to crush the air out of me, with her fingernails under the hair on the back of my neck, all the awkwardness I'd expected was squeezed out of me and I knew that nothing between us had changed.

She wore perfume that day, which I never remembered her doing – sandalwood, maybe. I anticipated her first words to the letter. We spoke them at the same time.

'Fancy seeing you here.'

She laughed sincerely, the open laughter that had drawn me to her in the first place. I asked how the canvassing was and she gave me a leaflet. Party political stuff.

'Don't worry,' she said. 'I shan't work my spiel on you.'

I laughed. *You would be good at the doorstep*, I thought. *I would invite you in for tea.*

She took me by the arm and we walked.

There weren't many houses after a while, just hedged fields, trees, a doggy bin. Our conversation flowed with an even rhythm – Helena brought it out of me, out of most people. I wondered if I should apologise again for Laurie's behaviour. But it felt as though she didn't need it. She'd probably ask why I was apologising. Why did I even want to? In the end, it was she who apologised to me, just as we circled back towards the village green.

'I'm sorry I haven't seen you.' She sat down on a bench on the main road through the village. A bus for Brighton passed. I guess she really did want to talk. 'Tell me about work. How is the old place?'

I never really thought about the bar when I wasn't there, and I never talked about it to anyone. I mean, it was fine, it was always fine, even if it was getting more hectic now with the rising temperature. What I tried never to think about was the fact that I'd been working there for well over a year, much longer than any of Carlos' other staff. It was a revolving-door kind of place, a stop-off, even Carlos knew that. Though that didn't unsettle me as much as the thought that other people knew it, were thinking it, were judging me for it. They used to come in sometimes, Helena and the rest, though it had been quite a while now. *Still there*, they must have thought. *And how is the old place?*

'It's fine,' I said, and left it at that.

'I didn't mean to be rude in not inviting you out lately.'

'No, I understand,' I said, and I did. 'I know how you must have felt.'

'Things have been changing so fast.' She looked into her lap. 'Have you seen Duncan at all?'

'I saw him a few weeks ago. He said he was moving out of the school.'

'Yes. Someone smashed a bunch of windows at one of his parties. Him and Marta are getting a place together, a proper place.'

'Yes, I heard. I don't get that.'

I couldn't help but feel angry, that she was going back to *him*, of her own accord. Even if it was *none of my business*, that old mantra. I'd thought Marta looked stronger, more purposeful, but maybe not. It made me think that nothing made sense. Duncan and Marta were moving in together after everything and Helena's career was taking off and somewhere Antonio was sat about with his legs splayed into the street, pissing away his life. And really none of it had anything to do with me. Not now Laurie was no longer a part of things.

I didn't want to push it but there was nothing else to say. 'You two never got together then?'

She shrugged. 'No. No, I don't think we could ever be together.'

'Why not?'

'We're different people.'

I scoffed, I was still angry with him. 'That's the truth.'

'Did you always dislike him?'

'Yes.' Though that was untrue. 'I don't understand why you tolerated him at all.'

'He means a lot to me.' She thought for a second, then made a decision to go on. 'I was off the rails for a while – in London, I mean. I'd been seeing someone for a long time and I didn't deal with it well when they broke it off. You know, I was still me, I still had lots of friends, but my self-esteem really dipped. I started fucking around, doing stupid things. I hurt a lot of people, guys and girls. I ended up in hospital a couple of times. Then I met Duncan and he just sort of picked me up...'

She told me how Duncan had supported her, given her money and a place to stay, and I thought at first *Oh yes he was trying to fuck you* but apparently he never laid a finger on her. It was hard for me to believe that she was speaking about the same Duncan – our Duncan with the workman's cap and blog and affected accent – looking after her in the way she described, taking her in, paying for everything, asking for nothing back. I just couldn't picture it, that man with his fifty thousand Twitter followers.

'I've been hard on him,' I said.

'No, George. You've been fine. You're fine with all of them.'

There was love in her voice. It made me want to tell her how I felt about Laurie, that I'd let her down again. The riot was in my mind so often then, I don't know why, making me angrier and more desperate, and Helena was the only one I'd ever considered telling what happened. I was ready to pass the burden on, so ready, even if it wasn't her business and she didn't deserve to carry what I'd carried and what was gradually eating me up. I was thinking about it when she said: 'Actually I'm considering moving back.'

'To London?'

'Duncan's dad has arranged an interview for me at the campaign office there.'

'You've gone pro.'

'Indeed I have.'

A space opened for me to congratulate her but before I could she asked: 'Have you seen Laurie?'

I told her I hadn't. 'Not since that time. She's gone off the map.'

'She hasn't. I saw her last week. She was outside my house.'

'Christ.'

'I wasn't in, I got back late. She was in the launderette opposite, sitting by the window. She came out and spoke to me on the doorstep. She asked if she could come in but I said no.'

'Was she upset?'

'I think so. It looked like she was trying not to cry.'

An old man skidded past on a bicycle with a collie attached. A little mud jumped up onto Helena's tights. Calm fled me instantly – it happened more often then.

'Fuck's sake.'

Helena pulled her satchel towards her. I didn't want her to see my mood swing. Maybe she already understood. 'We took a walk. She was quite erratic. She was trying to apologise, I think, but she kept going off on these tangents about stuff I really didn't want to talk about.'

Gingerly, I asked her what.

'Political stuff. Kurdistan. I don't know what she's been watching.'

I could only imagine. Helena had never been into the fiery judgement thing, even against the worst of them. She was never angry in the same way Laurie was.

She went on: 'I told her I was thinking of moving back to London but she didn't take that very well. She's obviously struggling to cope. Which is odd because really this is what she wanted. She was never content.' She ran her fingers through her hair. 'It would be much better if she left me alone though.'

Perhaps she was asking me to do something about it, perhaps not.

'What can I do?' I said. 'She's an idiot.'

Too loud, too sharp for a quiet village. Helena was patient. Finally she asked me about Antonio.

'Jesus,' I said, 'what *about* Antonio? Everyone is asking me about Antonio.'

She said nothing.

I wiped the tiredness from my eyes. 'I'm sorry. Carlos, my manager – he was asking about him yesterday. I've been trying to put him out of my mind.'

I told her about his visit to Lewes and that since he'd met 'Reginald' all the life had left him. He was like a whole different person. I told her about the incident on the New Road, with Queenie and the landlady and the man who drowned in the *aldgy*. I went on, but she just listened. When I'd finished, she seemed to hesitate before answering me. A newspaper blew up against my leg – ELECTION DEBATE SPECIAL, some bollocks.

'I saw him,' she said. 'Same day I saw Laurie, actually.'

'You did?'

'Yes, I saw him at the Clock Tower. I was volunteering.'

I'd seen Helena there many times, serving hot food from fold-down tables. There were always people in the queue and many more eating on the steps in all weather. I had volunteered there myself, just once, on Helena's invitation. But I took a sadness from it that she apparently didn't, and I couldn't do it again. In that sense she was stronger than all of us.

I asked her if Antonio was working with her.

She shook her head. 'No, he wasn't volunteering.'

'Oh. I see.'

I pictured him in the queue for food, even pictured his smart trousers and the Spanish-English dictionary under his arm. I knew that most of the people who ate there did so every week, some of them had for years. Some of them were the same men I'd seen Antonio with on the New Road benches – the men who drank and chatted and pressed strangers for cigarettes. Antonio had not belonged there, not really, and even less in the queue for food. He was far too senselessly proud to take something for nothing. I'd thought he would rather starve. That kind of pride.

I lowered my head in shame. *So so tired*. Helena put her arm around me.

'You need to see him. He needs you.'

I nodded but I couldn't look her in the eye. 'What am I supposed to say to him?'

'Honestly?' She waited for me to lift my head. 'I think you need to tell him to go back to Spain.'

This had occurred to me already but I couldn't imagine how I would go about bringing it up. He had come here to forge a new life. I would be telling him to accept that he had failed.

Helena rubbed my shoulder, let me go.

I pulled myself up. 'I'll think about it.'

I should have wished her good luck for the election next week but it slipped my mind. When she returned to her canvassing I decided to walk at least as far as Lewes, and when I was alone immediately started stomping around the countryside. My thoughts returned to me then, blackened by the image of Antonio at the Clock Tower.

Fucking idiot – that's what I thought. All the energy I'd expended on him in the past year. *Idiot, absolute idiot.* The frustration burst out of my mouth. *Fucking idiot, fucking—* I swore under my breath, then louder, speaking-volume, then called out the words to the trees, the grass, the wildlife. I imagined him in the queue for food, drinking Special Brew on the benches at New Road, my stupid hands lifted above my head at the riot in London. He was a forty-year-old man for Christ's sake, how could he not take care of himself? *Total idiot.* And after all his bravado and his quixotic little crusades. How was he going to sit down and give up? No sense at all. Only when I looked across an open field at a man with a dog, standing across a stile, both simply staring at me, did I realise I was lost.

I shouted: 'What are you looking at?'
He shook his head as he walked away.

I regained the main road at Malling, kicked my shoes against a flint wall until the bus arrived, joined the top deck. It was empty. I watched the clouds blow over Brighton. The swearing in my mind receded with it until only the sympathy for Helena's situation was left. I swung like that then. It was as natural and predictable as the splash of mud from a bicycle, or the gentle gathering of clouds.

I scrolled through my phone and read the digits of Antonio's number over and over till I could remember them. When I got home, I called.

I was relieved when the phone rang on to nothing.

I stood by the door of the bar toilets with the sharp smell of piss in my nostrils, rattling my change bucket. The queue of people hobbling from one foot to the other stretched all the way down the corridor to the fire exit. Beyond them I could see more people joining from the street, all pissed up and desperate. Beside me was the door to the bar area, locked now. Through the little diamond window I could see Carlos and his husband from behind, serving bottled beer from a table that barricaded the front entrance, their arms reaching in and out of a dustbin filled with water and ice. Sending bottle tops flying. Dropping money into a little strongbox at their feet.

That year Carlos decided to make a special effort for Pride, since the bar had been so quiet all year. He painted the banner himself – a huge thing strung above the entrance, harnessed to two chairs propped up at adjacent windows.

ICE COLD BEER £2
TOILET £1

Underneath it, just to the right of the doorframe, a hired speaker stack played queasy dub songs on shuffle. Bass that you felt in your stomach. I'd offered to run the beer table, but Carlos told me I'd probably scare people off with my *poor glum face*. He was probably right. Catching sight of my faint reflection in the diamond window of the door, totally at odds with the upchuck of reggae guitar, my face was pale and limp and undeniably *glum*. But at least I was out of the way.

*

Since Ringmer I'd carried my anger with me everywhere. Everything exasperated it then, even the Tories snatching the snap election, which I told myself I didn't give two shits about but that no one seemed to want to let go. I'd think about Laurie and Antonio alternately and every time I pictured them their stupidity was compounded in my mind, these two adults who couldn't look after themselves, who I had no idea how to help. What could I do for two people who'd spent their whole lives in opposition to the world, and were now suffering for their lack of fitting in? I'd spent my whole life being aware, unbearably aware, of the waves I was making – surely they could have a crack at it for once. Instead of upsetting everyone else and themselves.

I'd been sweating in the corridor all morning and most of the afternoon. Occasionally between customers I'd go in and throw a bit of bleach into the toilet bowl but it was a token gesture. Several hours of sustained use had turned the place into a mess of wet paper, plastic cups and empty baggies. At one point a middle-aged man with glittery fairy wings complained about the lack of toilet roll but I wasn't sure what I was supposed to say. I gave him the blue roll I'd been using to wipe things down, and he took it gingerly like I'd offered him a dirty cloth. I held my temper until the toilet door closed behind him.

'Bloody fairy,' I muttered. A couple of people in the queue stared at me. 'Not like that.'

My phone pinged. A message from Marta and a missed call from a non-UK number. I'd had a few of those over the past two days. I never answered.

I read:

George are you there?

but then the fairy guy came out and shoved the blue roll into my stomach so hard it winded me.

'Disgusting,' he said, and the people in the queue moved back to let him through, staring at me as if I was going to do something. He never even paid his quid.

An hour passed, during which I got another call from a non-UK number. I went to answer – I was really in the mood to tell someone, anyone, to fuck off – but I was interrupted by an old man's voice.

'Excuse me, thank you.'

The couple at the head of the queue were naked except for their thongs and bumbags and mirrored sunglasses. My brain took in the love handles, the folds, the mess of pubes. The men were brown and leathery and the hair across their chests was silver and moist, and for one brief moment of horror I thought I could smell the sweat that glistened on their shoulders. They squeezed past me and headed into the toilet together.

'No, one at a time, please,' I said.

One of them gave me a wry look. 'Spoilsport.'

He came back out and paid with a twenty – I swallowed my anger but I'm sure he could see it. He stood there counting his change while he waited for his partner. It was so hard not to look at the leather of his skin that I was actually grateful when my phone pinged again.

It was Marta.

Answer if you can

For God's sake. They were having a party at her old flat, same place we'd been kicked out of one year before. Perhaps she wanted me to swing by. Though that wasn't going to happen.

Another hour passed, another hour of sweat, thirst and toilet smells. Two men in leather joined the back of the queue, one leading the other by a lead. I caught eyes with the little guy, the one with the spiky collar round his neck, and felt suddenly like going back there and asking whether he was happy, truly happy in himself, being led around town like that. It was cynical and irrelevant but something about the whole thing angered me, something inherent in the swollen creatine muscles and proud butch face of the man holding the lead. I felt reactionary and silly, like parts of the Shoulder of Mutton were casting their shadow on me. Which upset me even more.

My phone pinged again and I swore. This one was from Helena, a long one. I read it carefully and then shook my head and read it again from the beginning. The last words of Helena's message, her first invitation since Ringmer, in a desperate tone I'd never once heard from her:

Come quickly if you can

I unlocked the door through to the bar, locked it behind me. The bass from the speakers outside was so loud it made my heart murmur. I tapped Carlos on the shoulder but he didn't turn. I leant right over the table and shouted in his ear.

'I have to go.'

'What?' He was still handing out change, someone else was asking for beer.

'I have to go, right now.'

'No, George, Jesus.'

His husband turned. 'What's wrong?'

I guess he'd have to take over at the toilets, but I had to go.

'I'm sorry,' I said, and dropped my bucket of money.

Carlos tried to grab me as I crawled under the table but I slipped through his fingers. I straightened out in front of the small crowd clamouring for beer and the sun hit my eyes – so hot and white and alive. I tried to squeeze through the bodies, shoving, apologising.

Carlos' husband called out to me: 'You can't just run off like this and expect to—'

But the rest of it disappeared into the noise of King Tubby and the crowd.

I ran down Kingsway towards the pier, through the smashed plastic cups, the broken bottles and faded glowsticks. The Old Steine was covered in people, mostly horizontal or else leaning in various states against the fences, lamp posts, trees. Dozens of couples clung to each other in the dusk, their painted bodies faintly ridiculous against the failing light. Odd casualties lay strewn among the small groups of revellers, lying in crumpled heaps like swatted flies. I passed a boy with *All You Need is Love* painted on his chest, hanging backwards from a bench with his hair trailing into an empty pitcher. All bacchanalia has its casualties. Normally I might have stopped to see if he was alright but I was running now, running and tripping like I was being chased.

On Grand Parade, the damage escalated. Everyone's skin

was red and blistered, and the combination of alcohol and sunshine had turned several groups of young straight men into charging, cawing seagulls. I passed a few of these groups, walking purposefully down the middle of the road with their jaws roaming from side to side – athletic boys with their shirts off. I jogged through the middle of a group of them, expecting trouble, but they paid me no notice. It was Pride and they'd seen it all already.

At Preston Circus I caught my breath in the middle of the intersection where at any other time of the year you'd be knocked down and killed. I looked around at the people sitting with their backs against the shutters of the fire station and coughed over the black smoke that blew from a metal drum outside the Jamaican takeaway. Everywhere I saw people smoking and drinking – legs dangled from rooftops, dancers shuffled in lit windows as I'd once seen in Amsterdam. I felt unsafe around these people, alone and struggling for breath.

I stood outside Marta's old flat, panting. Lungs rattling, head spinning, mouth dry, throat sore. Nothing had passed my lips all day. My first thought was that I needed a drink, and not water, *fuck water*. Then I saw her. She was standing outside the house on the opposite side of the street, just as Helena had told me in her message. She wore all black – she must have been the only secular gay person in the whole city wearing all black – except for the old denim jacket, which I baulked at the sight of. She stood straight and tall, with the old familiar posture that meant *I'm here for business*. I hated that way she stood. All around her, happier people drank, smoked, danced, blew bubbles, but she just stood there, alone, with a sober, serious look on her face, staring at the house. I could see people dancing on the rooftop, and Marta herself at the edge by the chimney, looking down.

Laurie noticed me approach but didn't say anything. I grabbed her by the sleeve of her jacket. She didn't react.

'What are you doing here?' I said.

When she spoke, her voice was so flat it infuriated me. 'I want to speak to Helena.'

'Well, she doesn't want to speak to you. So let's get out of here.'

I should have known better than to try to move her physically. She just stood perfectly still with her taut sleeve in my hand.

'I've asked her to come down. So now I'm waiting.'

'For Christ's sake, Laurie, she's not coming down. You're making a fool of yourself.'

She shrugged and said nothing. I could see Duncan on the roof now, holding Marta's arm, trying to look at us without being noticed.

'Come on, Laurie, let's have a drink.'

That was all I wanted, just to be away from here with a bottle in my hand. No fights, no arguments – just peace and a stomach full of wine. *Why shouldn't I?* That's what everyone deserves, this one day a year. She held up the back of her hand – a black cross was drawn in thick ink, so thick it was turning the skin around it blue. I recognised the symbol from some punks I'd met in Italy. No alcohol, no smoking, no drugs. *How predictable*, I thought.

'Fine,' I snapped. 'So let's go do something else.'

Still she kept her eyes on the house. I looked around desperately for something to distract her but all I could see was drink. On the roof, Duncan had a drink, and from a lower window I could see people drinking. Even the twelve-year-old girls stumbling down the street had a fucking drink.

I was tempted to leave, until Helena came out of the house. She walked carefully through the people on the front steps and waited while a boy reached across her way to offer a girl white powder on a key. Laurie's posture never changed but suddenly it looked as if it was taking every inch of effort to keep her body from moving. Helena reached us, all glitter and rainbows, but touched neither of us. She looked like she'd been crying but her face was stern and purposeful.

'Hello, George,' she said, and then immediately: 'Laurie, what are you doing here?'

'So you are leaving Brighton,' she said.

I tried to back away. 'I'll let you talk.'

'Please, George.' Helena looked me in the eye. I couldn't go.

Laurie was waiting for an answer.

'Yes,' Helena said, 'I've taken the job in London.'

Still, Laurie's posture didn't change. Straight and tall and unmoving. She looked like she was strapped to a gurney receiving lethal injection.

'With Duncan's dad?'

'It doesn't matter.' Helena gritted her teeth. I'd never seen her like that. 'Actually, it's none of your business.'

'When are you going?'

Laurie's voice faltered when she said that. It was the first chink in her armour.

'I start work in September. If you must know. I'll be moving out in two weeks' time.'

Laurie remained silent and I could see the pain

overwhelming her, the simple pain of loving somebody who can't love you back. I was sure she was going to say *I love you*, I was absolutely sure she was going to say it. Everything in her face said *But I love you* and I think that Helena was already bracing herself for her to say it. But then Laurie's face changed and she hardened again, and said in an accent as Sussex as I've ever heard her: 'That's fine. I'm going away as well.'

'Right,' Helena said, and took a step back.

I was shocked though. 'What? Where?'

She looked at Helena while she spoke. 'I want to volunteer with the YPJ.'

'What on earth is the YPJ?' I said. My head was spinning again.

'The Women's Protection Units in Rojava. The Kurdish volunteer army.'

The words were all jumbled in my head. 'What are you talking about?'

'I want to join the YPJ in Rojava.'

I thought *Is she really fucking saying this shit?* I might have said it aloud.

She went on: 'I've read a lot about it and I think it's the right thing to do. It's my cause, it's all our cause.'

Bullshit. What utter bullshit. Helena stayed there while we argued but she said nothing.

I scoffed. 'I think you've made this up right now.'

'Listen, George.' Laurie's voice got magnanimous, I wanted to push her as hard as I could. 'You know I want to participate in the world. You always *told* me I needed to participate. That's what I want to do. Rojava is our generation's Spain.'

I glanced up at the roof. Marta was there, standing with her hands up to her cheeks, and even from the ground I could see the sadness and fatigue on her face. Laurie was wrecking everything. Again.

'You don't know shit,' I said. 'How is this like Spain?'

'The Spanish Civil War, I mean.'

'Spare me.'

'You should know, you're always banging on about Spain. You and your mate. Well, before he ditched you.'

When she said the word *ditched*, Helena sighed and turned back towards the house. Laurie called after her but I moved into her way and she tripped. Raised voices from the roof. Mouth dry, rashes burning. People on the street backing away. When she stood the fire was in her eyes. Then she was shouting and I was shouting too.

'What's this got to do with Antonio?' I shouted.

Antonio, Christ. There was a voice in my head screaming: *You've abandoned him, how could you abandon him.* An image of him on the benches at New Road. *Fuck – off – George.* I tried to shut it out.

Laurie's voice faltered. 'You used to give a shit, George.' It looked like a nearby group of men were deciding whether to intervene. Maybe they thought I was going to hit her. Her words were bringing tears to my eyes. 'You used to be so strong.'

'What are you talking about?'

'You used to care about things. Now all you care about is yourself. You're worse than Dad.'

I shook my head. 'Don't be a bitch.'

'When did you give up, George? I mean, you saved my life. You got down on your knees and dragged me through those policemen—'

But she never finished. I stepped forward and my face was up against hers and I was saying as clearly as I could though my voice was shaking: 'That – wasn't – me.'

The facade vanished from her face then, all the strength she'd put up against me. She just looked confused. 'What?'

'I didn't pull you through the line that time. It was just some other cunt with a denim jacket. Jesus Christ, you're thick.'

She was still confused, looking between me and the rooftop and searching me for answers while the truth dawned on her slowly and my image shattered in her eye. I tried to hold her gaze but I was still so angry. That was all I could take.

'Anyway,' she looked flustered. 'I've already given up my flat. So.'

At those words I leapt on her, no thoughts, no plan. My fingers found the creases of her jacket and I pulled. She struggled against me but I flailed around with the denim between my fingers. Then, the sound of tearing, so loud and definite it was like the ground under our feet was being torn, and I stumbled back. I held the front panel of her jacket in my hand. Two feet away, though it may as well have been a hundred miles, a thousand miles, Laurie stared down at the empty hole as if it were a bullet wound.

I stopped to catch my breath, noticed two policemen walking towards us. Their hats were garlanded with rainbows, though their eyes were blank.

I remember the sound Laurie's fist made against my face. A hollow crack, like the sound of the baton that struck the first boy at the riot, that whole lifetime ago. I heard that sound before I felt it, before I fell backwards onto the ground. Then the noise of the crowd, bursting into action, the scream of the city, the grinding gears of the carousel spinning and spinning like the earth on its axis, and Laurie's voice, wavering, as she was pulled out of my reach.

A policeman made a grab for me like *okay, sir, are you okay*, but I slid away and by then Laurie was already tussling with the other one and the crowd were cheering and booing, cheering and booing. She freed herself from one but then the other was on her, pushing her awkwardly to the ground while people on the rooftop shouted down at us. She caught my eye from the pavement, looking up at me with a red bruise already formed on her cheek – I didn't know if I'd given it to her or they had. Instinctively I started to back away.

'George!' she shouted. 'Come back here!'

I backed away and her face flickered from spite to fear and back to spite. The policemen were tying her hands behind her back and I could hear her raging voice chasing me: 'That's right, just run away, fucking coward,' and I could hear people gasping and asking what was happening.

Fucking coward, is what she said. *Coward.*

I looked over my shoulder, just once as I ran off. Some men from the street were standing around her and she had her arms behind her back, ready to be led away. People on the roof shouted down at her and she just took it, blank-faced, not even watching me run.

I turned away from it all.

Fucking coward.

I rushed through the streets but they were still loud and covered in people. Everyone that was going to the festival in the park had already gone, so that now the streets belonged to the people who had no intention of going home. I passed under the bridge where some boys were blocking the way for a couple of older men holding hands. The echo of the bridge distorted the shouting but I thought I heard the word 'poof' and the rising bubble of a collective *Ohhhhhhh*. The boys let the old men through and they walked evenly, unhurried, shaking their heads.

I caught my breath at Seven Dials and then carried on until I found the turning for Antonio's street. A group of ravers in fluorescent body paint was blaring jungle music on the corner. They took my attempt to squeeze through as an invitation to dance. *No, sorry, can't, no.* They protested and the chatter of senseless, garbled vocals from the speakers chased me down the street.

When I finally reached the front door of the bedsit, Antonio's window was wide open. I could see the drawn curtains moving gently in the breeze. He never had a doorbell so I called up to him.

'Antonio!'

The curtains remained drawn.

'Antonio! *¡Venga!*'

Still nothing.

'Antonio…' My voice cracked. 'It's me.' And I tried to say *It's Jorge* through my tears but the guttural sound of it caught in my throat. I felt like I was crawling back to him, now I needed him. And I did need him. I was lying to myself if I said anything but that I needed him. I felt like he was the only one who might understand. The curtains fluttered wildly so that I could see the light inside his room, but then fell closed again. He didn't appear.

I slumped down onto the pavement. I could feel my pulse throbbing around my eye where Laurie's fist had landed. Through a gap in the buildings I watched the observation tower making its descent. *Pointless ugly thing, fucking pointless ugly thing.* The graffiti from Antonio's building was gone – the little quip about rent – though over the new paint someone had written THE WORLD IS A FARM FOR HUMAN MEAT. Infuriating shit. I sat down beside the wall, wheezing uncontrollably, my thighs burning, head thumping. Too sober to block out my thoughts. *I need you, Antonio, for God's sake I need you.* Then a voice called my name.

Antonio's sister stood in the open window, palms resting on the windowsill, with the curtains open around her. From the ground I could just about make out the deep red around her eyes.

'Alejandra?' I said.

Her voice was hoarse. 'I've been calling you.'

It took me a moment to remember the phone calls. 'That was you?'

She didn't answer for a second. Then I knew something was horribly wrong.

When she called down to me it was coldly and curtly and without one scrap of human feeling.

'You'd better come up.'

4

THAT KIND OF PRIDE

When I was growing up I tried to think dispassionately about things, to consult the facts. This didn't come from Dad or Laurie, who never knew how to do that, and really I'm not sure where it came from, other than from the books I read and the teachers I had and the fact that I knew I was different from my father and sister, no matter how much I loved them. If we were watching the news and passions flared, I tried to be the one to take the middle ground. If something bad happened – if I was beaten up at school or a family pet passed on – I tried to blot out the tears and think of the wider context.

Causes, effects, reasons, facts. I never quite understood it but I knew it had something to do with being English. No matter how strongly you feel about something, take a step back and look at the whole picture. Today, yesterday, tomorrow. That's the English way – taking a step back, bottling up, getting perspective.

Looking at the facts.

Antonio Javier Gutiérrez Jimenez died on Wednesday 2 August 2017, and was buried in Guadalupe, Spain, four feet above the ground. A niche lay open for him – a black square of empty space set into a wall of grey polished stone. Around it on every side were sealed slabs memorialising other *Guadalupenses* – mothers, fathers, sons, daughters – with their names and dates, and crosses or images of the Virgin, and flowers in stone vases. Three graves high and several dozen across. Antonio ended up on the middle tier, circled by eight bunches of other people's flowers.

The funeral crowd was large – thirty or forty people from the village. Some wore formal black, others came in simple dark clothes or the hunting gear Antonio had told me they wore all year round. Some sobbed, some stood with their heads lowered. Most of them simply waited with their hands folded in front of them. There were no children at all and, it seemed to me, no one else from outside the area, at least no one who looked out of place. Just *Guadalupenses* – people from the *pueblo*.

At the front, Alejandra stood quietly as the priest passed in front of her and made the sign of the cross. Her mourning dress fluttered around the shape of her as she bowed. Beside her, an old woman in a wheelchair sat gently rocking. Then there was me, the only one who understood nothing at all of what was being said. A space formed around me and I felt I could see myself standing in it, in the same suit I'd borrowed for New Year's, which felt baggy now and ridiculous, hanging off me in the heat of the early morning. And on my face the yellow bruise Laurie had given me, ringed around my eye. I remember looking around at the craggy hills, the branches of olive trees that looked malformed and grey, the crenellated outline of the monastery towering over the village – but not at the niche, not for too long. I remember trying to fill my mind with the lyrics of Antonio's song – *Ay Carmela Ay Carmela Ay Carmela Ay Carmela*, that favourite of his – until the loop of it brought my panic up. I remember pushing it down and exhaling the emptiness, that old trick.

Trying to stick to the facts.

It was Alejandra who had gathered me from the bus stop the night before the funeral – just her, an hour after the sun went down. I'd been travelling since early morning – Gatwick to Madrid and via coach through the hills to Guadalupe – so that by then the quivering mess who'd struggled to get through Passport Control was now broken and still, like a dying animal. I'd tried to calm myself by picturing Alejandra's stony face, which I was sure I would never see crying, but that had the opposite effect. I thought about her as the bus wound through the mountains, sitting at the back, shaking in my chair. I put her out of my mind and puffed on my inhaler and tried to think about the puzzle picture that hung on the back of Antonio's door – the white horses, green grass, blue sky – until my breathing settled down. That was how the panic of it gave way to that particular fatigue you get after pain, when all you want to do is sleep and feel nothing.

I felt that way when the bus pulled into Guadalupe, with the bright stars beautifully visible over the sierras, when I saw Alejandra, looking so much like Antonio it should have broken me. I alighted in a daze and in the glow of the lamp post I looked over her skin, the same deep olive brown as his, deepened further by summer, and her hair, the same glossy black. She was a mirror of him, before the decay set in. She took my bag without embracing me – I tried to hold on to it but the straps just slipped gently from my fingers.

'*Buenas tardes*. Please come with me.'

Her voice – cold, calm and emotionless as it always was, even then – matched the void in me perfectly. She led me in my numbness through the *pueblo* and the stars over the sierra disappeared into a blur. I walked like a sleepwalker being led back to his bed. Really I remember hardly anything of that walk – though it must have been twenty minutes at least –

except for a series of empty streets and a fountain I'd seen before, in a photograph somewhere, and then a doorway and an empty room and a clean white bed that I fell onto with the light still burning.

I do remember the last thoughts flickering through my mind as I fell asleep. Just that finally, in spite of everything, I was in Spain.

The funeral felt distended – it moved languidly through the hot morning. The priest spoke for a while, reading from his Bible in Spanish, and as I began to feel the heat prickling the skin under my suit, my mind began to thaw.

I thought *If I can work out anything he's saying that'll keep my mind occupied*. Because I didn't want to look at the empty niche that might compromise my numbness. *And I won't look at Alejandra who isn't crying I don't think and I won't cry until she does*. Which was another point of futility, I suppose, but one that was so built into my English sensibilities I never even questioned it.

I couldn't work out a word the priest was saying and as my mind woke further it frustrated me that *For fuck's sake I never even bothered to learn his language*, but then again it was hard to concentrate, trying not to look at the niche or Alejandra and trying not to think of Antonio, the pain of it. I knew if my mind continued running it would arrive at places I didn't want it to, not here, where I wanted my grief to be hidden, where I was too tired to allow anything but the facts, just the facts.

I focused on the priest's black cassock and the cross around his neck that hung not freely but pinned up to one button so that the chain formed a swinging letter W across his chest. The woman in the wheelchair took Alejandra's hand and her shoulders broadened out like she was filling with strength. She seemed still and composed and as if she might not cry at all – no, I was convinced she wouldn't. I wondered if her mind was wandering like mine, except in its own language and through its own niches of memory. The morning so hot so early. I watched her hand close around the woman's beside her. White knuckles on black.

White knuckles, green hills, blue sky. And the facts.

We had stood together in Antonio's bedsit room, she and I, among the debris of his life, with the empty bottle that might have done it still on the floor and Alejandra's own soiled goalkeeping glove waving at us from the bedpost. It was a mess but the police were done with it and now it was her task to clear it out. There were used condoms in the bin, I noticed, which turned my stomach. She was busy putting his documents in order – letters that Antonio had annotated with translations in blue ink. A lease agreement, a bank statement, a final notice letter, and then the yellow folder holding pages and pages of handwritten notes – everything Antonio had discovered about his *bisabuelo* and had shared with no one. She handled them methodically, dispassionately, as if they were a diary of his appointments. It frightened me, her composure.

She slipped the folder into her briefcase with the letters. It was my impression then that those papers would disappear forever. She spoke to me quite formally, as if I'd been invited to help with the practicalities, and I want to remember her exact words, which were so precise, and the way she spoke, but I can't. I never could. She told me, of course, what had happened, but the words shook me too much. Only the details remain — Antonio's body already repatriated, a death certificate from a doctor at the Royal Sussex, a post-mortem, *no foul play*, an insurance company, a funeral director, a transport coffin sealed with zinc, two days in Madrid, a mortuary in the basement of a hospital in Cáceres, waiting to be taken back to Guadalupe. The facts.

I couldn't stop picturing his body inside a coffin and wondering if they would set him on fire or carry him around the village or whatever it was Catholics did in Spain — baseless thoughts, my imagination was burning. Like an idiot I asked if she wanted a drink. She told me she was pregnant, and I tried to say *Felicidades* but stuttered all over it.

What I remember most clearly is the softening of her voice, which brought water to my eyes. 'I want you to take Antonio's books.' She showed me the boxes with my name already on them in plain sloping letters.

I agreed and felt suddenly like I might be sick.

She turned back to her files. 'He admired you very much.'

I wanted to cry from the shame of it and I knew she could see I wanted to, but she wasn't crying so I bottled it up. Pointless, maybe, to bottle it, but how could I cry if his sister, standing right there in front of me, wasn't crying herself? That's what went through my mind then, the thought of crying in front of this woman, this cold, practical woman who had much more right to let herself go than I did. I wanted to reach out and touch her and make her cry — not for her sake but for mine. I wanted to share it with someone. But I didn't reach out and touch her because I was too afraid. I just looked down and felt ashamed.

She handed me a piece of paper – an invitation, an instruction. I read it without saying anything. That was how I accepted.

After that she put me and the books in a taxi, and the next day I followed the instructions in her perfect handwriting and looked for flights. They were just about affordable. I booked them and only afterwards picked up the phone to tell Carlos I was going to Spain, though we hadn't spoken since Pride and I didn't even know if I had a job anymore. I didn't ask his permission and he didn't mention it. He asked only, quite simply and calmly: 'What for?'

The words formed on my lips before I understood what they meant. It was like they came out in a different language – an old language that's been forgotten too long to translate, something already long buried. 'Because he's dead,' I said, and then turned my phone off as if for good.

I was trying not to think of that moment, actually just of the words *What for* and the swell I felt as he said it, while six men pushed Antonio's coffin into the niche. A few sobs came from behind me – old women. The sound got under my skin, rose slowly like a flush with the heat, and I looked to see if Alejandra was struggling but she wasn't. I breathed deeply and looked again at the gold W of the priest's chain, the roll of the sierra, the monastery walls, and then at the ashy, crippled-over olive trees twisting in agony on the hillside, but the soft sound of sobbing cut through everything so that I thought *Not now, please not just now* and I looked again at Alejandra but still she wasn't crying and I thought *God she's cold* but of course she wasn't that. She was still gripping the old woman's hand and my mind wandered to the idea that this was a woman's hand and *where's the father of her baby* but *God they're not going to seal it in front of us are they* and two men bent down and picked up the slab that was leaning against the polished wall – it looked heavy, they were sweating, so was I. They lifted it up and placed it in front of the niche and the blackness disappeared behind the grey stone. Alejandra lowered her head and I read the slab and choked on the thought of his body behind it. *Antonio Javier Gutiérrez Jimenez* with his dates and the phrase *SIEMPRE ESTAREIS CON NOSOSTROS*. You will always be with us.

The facts of his name and his dates and the fact he was no longer here in any sense, the facts that could no longer hold me together. Though I tried.

Antonio Javier Gutiérrez Jimenez died on Wednesday 2 August 2017 – yes, that's the truth, three days before Pride when I rushed to his building. *The Argus* printed a brief account of his death, which I didn't see until the day I was leaving for Spain. It delivered the police statement and the testimony of the bouncer who'd called the coastguard. It mentioned the rescue attempt and the vodka in his stomach and that he'd been pulled out naked. *Fucking newspapers with their gory details*. His things were found further down the beach – work shirt and trousers neatly folded, his wallet stowed in a pair of smart black Oxfords, no towel.

The article must have fallen out of my pocket or maybe simply out of my limp fingers because I never saw it again. But most of the facts were there in my mind – I'd read them, they'd never leave me – and it didn't take long to piece together the rest.

I bought a half-bottle of Glen's and walked with it down the seafront until it was finished, and then threw it on the ground and went up to Antonio's building, an hour or so before my train to Gatwick. The same route he must have taken in his best clothes after he'd finished his litre of vodka – a strange choice, the vodka, it was never his favourite. I pressed all the buzzers until a neighbour came down to meet me, a Spanish woman I'd met before. She told me she'd knocked on Antonio's door that day because she'd been bothered by a song playing on full volume over and over for several hours. It was a song she recognised – '*¡Ay Carmela!*', of course it was. She didn't have much more to tell me so I left her there clutching her dressing gown and forgot all about her, about everyone.

I kept the song on repeat throughout the flight, thought about Antonio singing it as I had often heard him do, with the folk songs and the anti-Franco songs and the songs he never explained.

Ay Carmela Ay Carmela Ay Carmela Ay Carmela.

It was that, finally, that broke me.

The words galloped through my head *Ay Carmela Ay Carmela* as the slab was sealed and the priest read once more from the Bible and everyone made the sign of the cross like *Godspeed, que sera,* that whole thing. My hands gripped the lining of my pockets, wet with sweat, the heat of the morning turning to the heat of day, boiling heat, no hat and the words running through my mind. *Ay Carmela Ay Carmela* over and over but I could feel my lip trembling now and my hands were shaking and people were starting to leave. When Alejandra turned towards me, I saw the tears spilling down in black lines over her cheeks. She passed right by without seeing me and the old woman beside her let her go and was wheeled away by someone else. I looked back at the stone and read the words *Siempre estareis con nosostros siempre estareis con nosostros siempre estareis con nosostros* and in my head the sound of singing and chanting *Ay Carmela Ay Carmela Ay Carmela you will always be with us you will always be with us you will always be with us* and someone bumped into me as they passed *No Pasarán No Pasarán* and knocked the tears out of my eyes. I felt suddenly the violent release as if a long arm was pulling my body out through my throat and all the breath in my lungs with it and my shaking hands came up to my face in claws and I wept thoroughly, thoroughly and without shame. The sound of his voice was in me then like *Franco, Franco, que tiene el culo blanco* and the anger and pity and fatigue *que tiene el culo blanco* though it wasn't any of these things, not individually, it was grief, only grief, that pounded in my ears *No Pasarán* and twisted my vision of Antonio into the ashy olive trees on the hillside *No Pasarán*. And then I was living in a world without facts without the one true crucial fact that I loved Antonio and he was gone and I was here, in the place of his birth where he belonged forever and I would ultimately leave *Ay Carmela Ay Carmela*, never together. Never his tears his laughter his eyes on mine our faces turned up to the blue sky over Brighton to the green grass at Hove Lawns to the white Spanish horses in Guadalupe in Sussex in a time where nothing else mattered, not really. All these thoughts coming out now, in the cemetery outside the *pueblo*, the sound of *¡Ay Carmela!*, which had not gone through my mind until now, until it was far, far too late.

As if the sky had been rolled away without me ever once looking up.

I was another kind of broken, soaked with sweat and tears, when the funeral finished up and the *Guadalupenses* walked in a quiet procession back up towards the village.

Siempre estareis con nosostros

With Alejandra's black shape walking away slowly and her head up, shoulders back.

You will always be with us

And then Antonio walking into the waves and the white surf splashing around his bare legs in the darkness, and his smart clothes folded up neatly behind him on the shoreline.

The dinner table sat ten. Antonio's family spoke vociferously – uncles, aunts, cousins, a debate across the whole length of the table, a couple bickering, stories being told. It blurred in my ears like white noise. The family were emotional, certainly – most of them looked as though they'd been crying all day – but they brought more than just their pain to the table. There was laughter, shouting, exasperation, pity. A gallery of gestures and expressions. The only one who didn't speak was the elderly woman from the funeral who sat at the corner of the table being fed with a spoon. I glanced across at her several times but her eyes never rose from her lap. She and I were the only silent ones.

I sat opposite Alejandra, who quickly introduced me to everyone and then left me to it. Underneath the table, I twiddled the tablecloth in my fingers. These were the people Antonio had wanted me to meet, I supposed, when he invited me to Spain. All the people that loved him, under what had once been his mother's roof and was now assumedly his sister's. Memories of his invitations kept coming to me, insistently, like the first images of a dream breaking through. I regretted that I hadn't tried to sleep that afternoon like everybody else. My tears had just kept coming, along with the words in my head, sounding cruelly in the voice of my sister. *Why are you so upset? You weren't even that close.*

Alejandra tipped red wine into my glass and pushed it towards me by the stem.

'Thank you,' I said, '*gracias.*'

Perhaps she knew I'd had a drink in the spare room while the others were resting – she probably did. She must have noticed my rashes and the red look I couldn't wash off my face. Everyone must have noticed. So I picked up my wine carefully and drank the tiniest sip I could feasibly draw – a timid, English sip. Alejandra watched me from across the table, and when she saw I was trying not to catch her eye, she leant over and whispered to me.

'Relax, George.'

'Yes.' A couple of her aunties glanced at us. 'Sorry. I'm fine.'

I wanted to relax, I really did – the last thing I wanted was to make a scene. I tried to hold my head up to show I wasn't struggling, but then all I could see were the dozens of photographs hanging above Alejandra's head in the dim light of the dining room. They covered every wall – photographs of various sizes, in various wooden and plastic and gilded frames, all jostling for space. I only had one photo of my whole family, the one of us four in front of the Shoulder of Mutton, though I put that out of my mind. I recognised Alejandra and Antonio and their parents, at different ages in different places, on family holidays or at birthday parties or in smart, dated clothes. They posed among a great crowd of strangers – a ring of Spanish spectators smiling statically all around me. One particular photograph caught my eye. It was Antonio, standing in front of the sea, his chin raised proudly so that his nose stuck out, just like Arthur John Martín. When I squinted I could make out the black skeleton of the West Pier in the background, a piece of Brighton history broken off, suspended in time. 23 June 2016, a Thursday. I even remembered the day of the week.

It was like being punched in the stomach. I wanted so desperately to get up and remove that picture from the wall and run away with it – the picture I had taken, on our spot of beach, on our day. A picture so clear it looked like you could jump right into it. The tears came to my eyes again but Alejandra was watching me so I hid behind my wine glass. She must have hung that picture, since it was taken after their mother's death. He must have sent it to her and spoken about me, him and me, and she must have hung it when she moved from Madrid. How much more had happened, how much more than I'd seen? Sisters and aunties and cousins and friends. Photographs and phone calls. All the stuff that may have involved me but that I hadn't been a part of. The way he spoke about me when I wasn't there. The thought of it swept over me like a wave.

Alejandra cleared her throat and pointed me to a platter on the table. The prawns looked up at me, four hundred kilometres from the sea. Cold and beady. I took one and sat it on my plate and knew I wouldn't be able to eat it – the waves were still crashing all around me, with the incomprehensible Spanish in my ears and everyone's eyes on me, that's how it felt, everyone looking and wondering *¿Quien es este realmente? Who is this really?*, this man with the bruise around his eye. There was nothing I could do about it but try to eat.

The prawn looked up at me accusingly, as fish do when you see them dying out of water. Gasping for oxygen above the noise of the waves.

I went pretty much unnoticed for at least an hour, with the family deep in discussion and no one confronting me on how little I'd eaten or said. I thought maybe I could keep my head down for the duration, and then they would go and I could sneak back up to the spare room without even talking to Alejandra. After sleeping maybe my mind would be clearer.

It was only when I tried to stop a sickly old man in hunting gear from spooning more *lentejas* onto my plate that an uncle at the far end of the table pointed at me openly and spoke. A hush came over the family as the old man buried my plate in lentils. I reached for my glass instinctively – my throat closed up as I tried to swallow so I had to hold the wine in my mouth, warm and spitty. Alejandra stared at me as she translated. This would be her role, it seemed, whether it was a burden to her or not. As ever, her voice was calm and stern.

'Manolo would like to know what part of the UK you're from.'

I wasn't sure whether to address my answer to him or her. I picked a spot somewhere on the wall between them, where another photo of Antonio happened to be. A young man in a bright white uniform. He looked so healthy.

'I'm from a village in Sussex, about fifty miles south of London. But I don't live there anymore.'

Manolo seemed to wait for me to meet his eye, and when I did I saw he was looking over his milk-bottle glasses with his eyebrows raised and his lips turned down. It felt like he was staring at my black eye, sussing me out. He held a prawn in his hand but hadn't yet undressed it. It dripped red.

He wanted to know why I'd left my hometown. Even in Alejandra's translation, it was that direct.

'I don't know, really. I studied at university, in Wales, and after that I went abroad for a while... When I got back my sister was living in Brighton and—' There were murmurs of recognition around the word Brighton. 'That's where I met Antonio, of course.'

I could hear the scraping of cutlery against china – it was as if it scraped at the lining of my stomach. That's where the grief was sitting, now I'd pushed it down. One of the cousins, a young man with a crew cut, spat a few words through a mouthful of food, stabbed at me with his fork. He looked like he belonged in the Shoulder of Mutton. I gripped the tablecloth and caught the sudden horrifying notion that I was sat in Antonio's chair. But the family laughed politely, even Uncle Manolo.

'He says you look like an English teacher,' said Alejandra. She rolled her eyes. 'He says you should take my job when I go on maternity leave.'

I laughed, too loudly. It knocked everyone else's laughter out of kilter. *So English.*

'Where do you work?' she said.

'I work in a bar.' Though I wasn't sure if I still did or not.

'Ah yes, you are still at the bar. You are a manager, is that right?'

'Oh. No.' I waited but the silence never passed.

'So what are you?'

'I'm bar staff.'

'*George es el camarero.*'

Again my throat closed as I drank so I was left holding wine in my mouth, willing myself to swallow. I thought *Don't fucking spit it out* and then saw another photograph of Antonio with a beer in his hand. Perhaps they imagined me getting pissed with him, doing shots together. Did they know he died drunk? Assumedly they have their own word for 'enabler'. Someone asked if I had children.

'Me? No. I've never been married.'

Again, the hush.

'And you have a sister?'

'Yes. Laurie.' Who still hadn't called, hadn't even messaged, though she must have known, surely she must have. I pushed the food around on my plate, sitting in the silence of the people who loved Antonio most. I blurted: 'My mum lives in France,' and it sounded so sad and self-pitying it made me feel ill.

My cutlery felt hot and wet in my hands. I wanted to cry again, for myself now, just for myself, so I took more wine to wash it down. Uncle Manolo said something quite gruffly under his breath. The only word I thought I recognised was *hombres* – 'men' – but no one picked him up on it. I wanted so desperately to get down from the table that my chair had already started drifting back. A bubble rose up in my stomach like my heart pushing its way back upwards, the desperation. I thought about excusing myself for the bathroom but I wasn't sure if that was appropriate and it couldn't be done in this silence anyway. I tried to put down my wine glass but it met the edge of my spoon and almost tipped over. There was a clatter of cutlery and glass and I knew Uncle Manolo was staring at me but I didn't look up. I just coupled my knife and fork on my plate before any more food could be put there, with the lentils that the sickly old man had given me uneaten at the edge. *Is that rude?* I thought. *Maybe I should ask for more?* But I didn't want any more. *How could anyone eat any more than this?* No, if I forced down another mouthful it would all come back up.

Eventually the cousin with the crew cut offered to take my plate, still covered in food.

I'd barely eaten a thing.

Only at the end of the evening, when the wine was drying up and the family looked exhausted did the conversation turn back towards me. Everybody stood and prepared to leave, and I found myself near the door shaking hands with people. I said *I'm sorry for your loss*, in English, and felt utterly stupid doing it. I wanted to go up to the spare room so that people couldn't see the shame on my face. I wanted to get out of the room filled with photographs. I shook their hands. It'd be over soon.

Manolo gripped my hand so firmly it hurt, so did the boy with the crew cut and the old man in hunting gear. There was understanding in these men's eyes, some kind of camaraderie, even for the wheezy Englishman. One of the last to leave was the old woman in the wheelchair. Her carer stopped her in front of me so we could speak. I bent down and caught the smell of lavender and fish.

'*¿Has salido ya a dar un paseo por la montaña?*'

I was surprised by her voice. Beyond the rasp and the lisp of her toothlessness, her voice was even and dignified. But not free of pain.

Her carer replied to whatever she'd said but Alejandra translated for me anyway. Her voice matched the old woman's quiet: 'Abuela Mirasol wants to know if you have been up in the mountains yet.' Antonio's paternal grandmother, a woman he'd loved but rarely mentioned. Eclipsed, I think, along with his father, by the image of Arthur John Martín.

I leant across the table to answer but the old woman wasn't looking. Still, I knew she was waiting. 'I haven't been yet, no.'

The old woman rasped again.

'*Bien, Abuela – lo hare.*' Alejandra stared at me. 'She is telling me to take you up there, before you go.'

'Oh. That's very kind. But I can go myself, if that's the... if that's the done thing.'

Uncle Manolo paused in the doorway and the others seemed to chastise him as he spoke vigorously at great length. I thought I must have said something wrong and hoped to God the evening was over since all I wanted to do was go upstairs and break down. The old lady spoke once more in the silence, slowly but firmly. I tried to look receptive – I was, I was just half drunk, more than half. Alejandra said *Si, entiendo* repeatedly until she'd finished. When she did the old woman lifted her tiny hand with the black sleeve trailing from her wrist, and took my own hand and pressed it. Her skin was as soft and white as poached egg. I flinched instinctively like an idiot.

Alejandra said coldly: 'Abuela Mirasol says she's extremely grateful for everything you did for my brother. She says you're a good person. She will pray for you.'

I had to say something to the old woman, anything at all, but suddenly there was no breath in my body and I thought I was going to fall. I turned my back on her and the others so no one could see my face, and drifted back to the table as if I'd forgotten something.

There were murmurs in Spanish but no one came after me. I took up someone else's glass and tried to drink down the dark wine, which was thick like blood. I looked again at the photograph of Antonio on the beach, his face so proud and confident and sure in being alive. We were supposed to come to Spain together. He was supposed to be here with me but he wasn't because I was the kind of person who turned their back when people needed him. I was the kind of person who simply *backed away* when things got tough – with Antonio, with Laurie, with everyone. And more than that I was still, even with all the images of Antonio crashing in my mind, thinking of myself.

Behind me, I heard the last of the voices fade away and the door shut and lock. I didn't want to turn and face Alejandra so I moved down the table. Then I heard the sound of crockery being cleared and I forced a dead look onto my face. The pain was twisting up my insides but all I had to do was make it out of this room, then I could let it go. I just had to make it past his sister, without letting it spill out onto her.

I turned. I even tried to smile. She slammed down a couple of plates.

'George,' she said, with genuine anger in her voice, 'you should have said *Buenas noches* to Abuela Mirasol.'

Please, I thought, *please let me go.*

'I'm sorry.' *Please let me go.* 'I suddenly felt sick.'

She looked at the wine glass in my hand and her tongue rolled over her teeth. 'It was rude.'

She cleared away the dishes in silence. I stepped forward to help.

'No,' she said forcefully. 'You're too drunk.'

My heart pounded in my chest. I wanted to tell her I wasn't that drunk, and that all I wanted to do was help, and that *For God's sake I loved your brother, can't you see that? Maybe not in*

242

the same way he loved me, but please. Though I knew if I said anything at all I would break down. I'd done enough damage already.

The sound of clattering crockery followed me up the staircase to the spare bedroom. I shut out the noise and felt the grief rushing up inside me, rushing up and filling my throat and lungs like seawater. Antonio's image in my mind – his proud look on the beach at Brighton, waves crashing, his clothes folded up neatly, the very same spot.

I took out my phone and scrolled down to the picture of my family. Mum, Dad, and Laurie reaching up her fragile little hands to grab at my cotton shoes.

Then the sweats came, and I held my head over the en suite toilet to throw up a bellyful of blood-red wine.

I woke up in the spare room fully clothed with the shutters down and the lights on. I reached for my phone but it was dead, and only then felt the drums beating in my brain. A full glass of water sat on the dresser beside me. The house was silent and all I could hear was birdsong coming softly through the shutters.

The spare room was clean and plainly decorated except for a shelf of football trophies above the dresser, perfectly polished. I staggered into the en suite to wash my face – the white light made me look anaemic in the mirror. My rashes were burning but the people at Gatwick had taken away my cream – I'd fought them for all 150 ml of it fruitlessly. I splashed myself with water, dried myself, tried to raise the shutters. They wouldn't move. I picked up the remote control and the shutters jerked upwards with a loud clatter of metal. I winced. No sunlight came in through the crack, just the faint glow of dawn, soft blue.

A firm knock at the door. It made me jump. I shoved my shirttails into my trousers in a panic thinking *Shit, I've woken her up.* When I opened the door Alejandra was already fully dressed with a backpack on and sturdy boots yellow with dust. Her white T-shirt hugged the bump of her belly. I'd almost forgotten, throughout all of this, that she was pregnant.

'Good morning,' she said, full speaking volume.

I straightened my clothes. '*Buenas dias*, good morning, Alejandra.'

She waited.

'I'm sorry for the noise,' I said. 'I didn't realise—'

'Give me the control.'

She took it. Other than her change of clothes, she might have been up all night. Maybe she'd been doing the dishes or cleaning the house or looking after her relatives, while I'd been dribbling pink goo onto the pillow.

The shutters rose. The clatter echoed around my head as the Jimenezes' garden came into view – a covered pool down by the patio, an old kennel with no roof, a garage with a dusty tyre track, an olive tree, chamois-yellow ground draped over an open hillside separated off by a wicker fence. Beautiful in a broken, rustic way, but lifeless.

'Do you have good shoes?' she asked.

'Well, I—'

She picked up my smart shoes. The stitches were coming apart at the brogue – perhaps I should have fetched some others from the village before I flew. Though that would have meant seeing Dad, Laurie.

I noticed the time on Alejandra's watch. Five a.m.

'Put them on,' she said. 'Let's go.'

She led me in silence through the empty cobbled streets, which were slippery with the morning, past shuttered houses and overgrown gardens and identical signs on the broken fences – *SE VENDE*, *For Sale*. The hens were awake and so were the dogs but there were no people at all until we reached the edge of the village, where a man in overalls stood digging up an empty plot. He didn't look up.

Alejandra walked quickly with her elbows high, metres ahead of me, never looking back. I jogged a little to come alongside her but she didn't slow down. After we passed the last of the farms a main road appeared, empty of cars, and she strode across it barely looking. The valley rose up ahead of us, densely green in the morning light. When I stepped onto the road a truck almost knocked me down. Alejandra stretched her thigh muscles as she waited for me. I skipped across and asked through shallow breaths where we were going.

'The path we're taking will give you a good view of the village.'

So we were going for a walk.

'You needn't have worried about me.' I was panting already.

'Later it will be too hot. Besides, then you'd be in the house alone.'

'Oh, I wouldn't have minded.' Though really I think she meant that I was a stranger in her home.

She checked her watch. 'Better like this.'

We met the valley and began to climb – a rough path, partially overgrown. The way she led me made me think it was more of a punishment than a treat. She strode over the sharp stones and tree roots, and actually picked up speed when the gradient increased. I fell behind her further and further until she disappeared at every bend, and then if there were trees I'd have to jog a little, and then see her going round the next one, and jog again. I sweated profusely even before the sun was up. Already, after just a short climb, I could have begged her for a rest. But she didn't stop. She pressed on relentlessly up the side of the mountain, never slowing, never turning her head. Whenever I stopped, even for a second, the spins of the night before returned to me. I felt the bare, exposed texture of my teeth with my tongue – the too-clean feeling that follows a night of vomiting. My bruised eye throbbed. The sweat bound my collar to my neck and I pushed on again to try to catch Alejandra and ask for water. But she pushed on further.

She did stop eventually, at the foot of a steep bank where the path narrowed. At the top, I could see the trees open out into clear blue sky. The sun had risen on the other side of the mountain.

She drew a flask of water from her backpack and offered it to me first.

'No, please.' I could barely speak. 'You first.'

She unscrewed the cap and poured a little on my head, swearing in Spanish. She pushed the flask into my hands. 'Drink.'

I choked on the water but I was grateful for it. I rubbed my eyes with my shirt, sighed openly. She took back the flask and strode up the bank with big, even steps, never looking back. I said *Fuck my life* out loud and started off again but pain was starting to bloom in my thighs and back. My face and neck burned where the rashes were — sweat always aggravated them. At the top of the path we hit the sunlight and suddenly everything was much hotter, but then I could see the valley behind the village and the path smoothing out and winding back towards the main road. I could hear cars now — brief, infrequent rushes like waves of nausea. I followed the path with my limbs turning to jelly, far behind Alejandra, until we reached the corner.

I wasn't sure how long we'd been walking. Less than an hour, probably, though now that seemed interminably long. From the corner I could see how high we'd come. We looked down on the whole of the village, spilling down the hillside as if the houses were pieces of broken masonry falling from the monastery at the top. The valley curved around and disappeared behind the mountain. Among the canopy there were no houses, no buildings at all, just trees and one small opening with a dark lake in the shade of a cliff. The water was almost black – a deep, cool black in a perfect circle.

The heat and sweat were sharp on my skin. I wanted to throw myself into the water – not to dive in gracefully but to hurl my body against the surface, then to sink and be surrounded by the cold of it. I felt as if I'd never been cold, never been wet except for with the thick, hot dampness of sweat. I felt like I'd never had saliva, never had a brain that didn't knock sensitively against the inside of my skull. When Alejandra gave me the flask it took every inch of my stupid Englishness to take only one polite sip and nothing more. I held it back out to her and she huffed and pulled out another. She drank from hers freely, letting it tip everywhere, and I panted like a dog and did the same.

The water made my stomach ache but I didn't care. I just sat down on the ground beside her and tried not to look dead. 'What's that water over there?'

'A reservoir. Antonio used to swim there.'

It was the first time she'd used his name since I'd arrived, at least to me. It sounded just as formal and abstract as the rest of her vocabulary, like a word exercise in one of her English classes. It sounded especially cold in a sentence about him swimming, as if she'd asked me to identify the verbs in *My brother died while swimming*. I thought perhaps she was gearing up to talk about him, so I stayed quiet and tried to think of a respectful question. But the moment passed. I wondered if he swam there at night.

Eventually I said: 'Can you see the house?'

She pointed at arm's length. It could have been anywhere.

'Have you lived there all your life?' I asked.

'No, you know I haven't. I told you I lived in Madrid when we met.' She stared at the village. 'Your memory's not so good.'

'No.' Nervous again. 'It's never been great.'

'I would have stayed in Madrid. I only returned now because of the baby.' She bit into an apple, spoke while chewing: 'I would have aborted it but I've had two abortions already. It's too risky.'

Everything in my being wanted to say *I'm sorry*. I resisted. Even through the fatigue and the pounding headache I thought *God, I'm so squeamish it hurts.*

She went on: 'The house was Antonio's but he didn't want it. It's been empty since my mother died.'

This I didn't know. 'Did he inherit it?'

With a crunch on her apple: 'What do you care?'

I wasn't sure why she wanted to punish me by dragging me over the mountains at daybreak like some kind of cadet, but I could hardly ask her. Perhaps she was still angry at my behaviour the night before, or maybe she'd never expected me to come to Spain, maybe regretted giving me her instructions in Antonio's bedsit that night. Though she didn't seem like one for regrets.

'The house has been in my family since the war – it was given to my great-grandmother when she moved from

Madrigueras. When my father was dying he made Mama promise that Antonio would take the house, but even when she was very sick he would not agree to go on living there. She didn't push him. She knew he wanted to go to England.'

'So you took the house instead?'

'No. No, I sign the papers for it next week.'

I wanted desperately to ask if she was alright, but the way she stared so fixedly out over the village made my question seem absurd, even obscene, like an invasion of her privacy.

'It's a beautiful house,' I said.

She pulled out a hunk of bread, split it for us, and we ate in silence looking over the village. When the bread and water was gone, she stood up quickly.

'You're here for one more day,' she said. 'Don't get drunk again.'

'I'm sorry. I didn't mean to.'

'Just wait till you get home.' She was angry again. I think not being able to hide it frustrated her. 'Then you can get drunk all the time.'

'Okay.'

I stayed sitting down with my legs crossed and I thought Alejandra might drop it but she didn't. 'Antonio had many problems when he lived here.' Huffing like she was trying to reiterate something I already knew. 'He was in the navy, you know.'

'Yes, he mentioned it sometimes.'

'Not too often, I bet.' She looked out at the hillside. 'He was dishonourably discharged, did you know that?'

'Yes. No. I don't know.'

'After less than a year. Something to do with another

seaman – a boy, I mean. When he came back he drank a lot more than he used to. He had many friends like you who would drink with him.' She spoke spitefully. 'He would entertain them, too.'

My knees drew instinctively to my chest. I pictured him with his friends on New Road, the way he spoke with them, the performative way he crushed his can of Special Brew the day he told me to fuck off. I don't know why it was that, in particular, but suddenly after all the struggle of the night before I knew that I was about to cry.

'I only wanted to help him,' I said, wavering against my will.

'Oh, for God's sake—'

We looked out over the village and I felt the tears forming in my eyes. I felt them physically, before the emotion of it hit. It was like feeling the sudden cool on your skin, standing in the shadow of a tidal wave.

'My brother was sick. Don't pity yourself. You couldn't have helped him.'

I lowered my head onto my knees and began to weep. I wept gently, trying and failing not to make a sound, until the pain shook my whole body. Then the sound was too hard to suppress and the sobs broke from me in sharp pieces that shook me even harder. It was not the way I'd cried at the funeral, or the way I'd cried alone in the spare room. It was the crying of a man in a tube carriage, at a bus stop, in a pub toilet. The shameful kind of crying, the worst kind of shame. I hid my face but I could feel Alejandra watching me, surely with disgust.

I flinched when her hand fell on my shoulder. The first time she ever touched me. Her fingers gripped me gently and I thought she was going to comfort me but then she pushed me, hard, so that I rolled onto the ground in a cloud of dust. It shocked the tears out of me. I scrambled back.

She stood over me. 'For God's sake! Look at yourself.'

And then all my fears were coming true. His sister was looking down on me, the rage in her face reserved for me, pointing a finger in my face, shouting at me directly in full-blooded Spanish, with no attempt to hide her hatred of me. The kind of confrontation you have nightmares about. Like the nightmares I had about Laurie doing the very same thing. I saw myself down on the ground, with the dust sticking to my skin, while the sun rose from behind the mountain and spread its heat all over me. The shame of it.

'You're just like all the others,' she said, though I wasn't sure who she meant. 'You don't understand a thing.'

I was confused and my head was roaring but still I managed to say: 'He was my friend.' I scrambled to my feet, she turned to fetch her backpack. 'Alejandra.'

'Antonio didn't *have* any friends,' she said over her shoulder.

'No,' I said. 'I think you're wrong about that.'

She stared at me for just a second, and then huffed and turned away. She started to walk off in the direction of the path, paused there, heaving, turned back to me. 'Are you coming or not?'

'Alejandra—'

'Are you coming or not, George? Time to make your mind up.'

There was a crack in her anger where the grief was starting

to show. I wanted to reach out to her and tell her how I felt about her brother, and how if she really looked at it we were both the same, he and I, or at least the same kind of people. Or perhaps we weren't but we were still something, even if she didn't understand it.

Either way my old shame and frustration rose up in me and I walked straight past her towards the path. It split in two and without thinking I took the one that seemed to lead down to the reservoir, without looking back at Alejandra, just walking away from her and her words and the village, scuffling down the path in a cloud of dust.

I never turned back and I never heard her say anything. Whether she watched me or not I have no idea.

I stumbled and tripped down the path until the stones got larger and the thorny bushes denser and I had to kick my way through. Descending into the valley it seemed to get quieter and quieter until I was aware of the sound of my own breathing like a hunted animal. It didn't take long to reach the end of the path, which opened out naturally onto a small jetty where the wooden posts were covered in a thin film of algae.

From the edge of the reservoir, the water still looked black and cool in the shadow of the cliff overhead. There were reeds surrounding the edge and a couple of other jetties, empty but for the Spanish signs I couldn't read and a rubbish bin on the opposite side – a fishing spot, maybe. There was no birdsong or even the sound of insects or the rustle of wind through the trees. Just the thick quiet of a Spanish morning.

I looked down into the water with Alejandra's words ringing in my head – *just like all the others*, more than anything else she said, that injustice. Like the others who had *used him*, was her implication, as if I'd *used him, used him up, done him over*. I began to remove my sodden clothes. *How could I have used him, this man who was so much older than I was, who'd needed my help to get a job and a flat and a National Insurance number?* My T-shirt clung to me as I peeled it off and made a tidy splat when it hit the jetty. *I mean, for Christ's sake.* I took off my shoes, socks, shorts, underwear, and then stood there completely naked, glistening with sweat and half asleep from the crying, looking down at the water.

Jump right in, I thought. *That's what a person of character would do – jump right in.* I thought of Antonio crashing into the sea as he always did, usually with a *¡Venga!* or *¡Geronimo!*, and even if that wasn't my style I understood what he meant now, facing the still, black unknown of the water with a kind of battle cry. It must have been what it's like being on the edge of the cliffs at Beachy Head, like the end of *Quadrophenia*, except all that was so noisy and dramatic and this was quiet, so quiet, as swimming at night must have been for Antonio, that last time. So I didn't make a sound when I went right in. I just did it.

Without a thought in my head I hopped off the edge of the jetty with both feet together and my arms by my sides, holding my breath, scrunching up my eyes. I braced my feet for the impact of the reservoir floor – rocks perhaps or cool mud. But my feet found nothing. I just plunged all the way under and the water swallowed my body, and I disappeared.

It's quieter underwater than even in the basin of a quiet valley. It's a different kind of quiet – not the calm, clean quiet of a lonely morning, but the muggy quiet that seems to give way to the sounds inside your body. The sound of your blood moving around, the pressure on your lungs as your body realises it can't breathe. The sound of your useless legs kicking through the water, your heart smashing against your chest. That sound in your ears that is the pressure of water trying to rush into you, to fill you up and replace you. The sound you hear when you're becoming part of the lake, the river, the sea.

That was what I heard, that kind of quiet, as my body sank like a smooth, pointless stone.

I never told anyone about how I nearly drowned in the reservoir outside Guadalupe. Even as I lay on the jetty, coughing up lungfuls of water onto my clothes, I knew I wasn't going to tell anyone. I was lucky that my hands found the wooden posts, so that I could hold on to them while my legs kicked me upwards until I was spat out among the reeds, but if I told anyone about it I'd have to explain why I'd done it in the first place, and how could I ever justify nearly drowning there, in Spain, outside Antonio's village one day after his funeral? The problem is that in order to explain I would have to understand it myself, and already, while lying on the jetty like a caught fish, I knew that I didn't want to. So I just pulled on my clothes and started my slow ascent back up to the corner where Alejandra left me, where the marks of our scuffle were still alive in the dirt, and then made my way back to the village.

All I understood was that the voice in my head – the voice that had driven me to the edge of the jetty – was silent, and I was no longer hungover.

It took about two hours to find my way back and when I did there was a note on the kitchen table reading *Siesta*. I was tired – tired in a new way, not the way that led to pity or anger or anything else, just tired, so I was happy to fall facedown on the bed and sleep. When I woke, my phone was charged and I had a message from Dad that I could see started Quick msg I'm just @ pub with... but I didn't read it. I peeked round the doorframe into the house, guessed Alejandra might be waiting for me somewhere. The lights were off on the landing and everything was dim. My legs ached and I could still hear water trapped in my ear. It must have been early evening at least.

Downstairs there was no one. I passed through into the dining room and said *Hello?* and then more uncertainly *¿Hola?* which I cringed at the sound of. There was no one in the kitchen either. A stone arch led through to the garden, some old remnant of an original building. It looked like a piece of a ruined abbey – something from a school trip to Bramber Castle – except that a modern wooden doorframe had been fitted into it. Through the little square window on the door, the twilit garden looked like a framed photograph of another time.

It was warmer outside – I could feel the heat still tingling in the arid ground. The chatter of crickets came from the fields and around my ear the buzz of mosquitoes. This felt like the kind of place where it never rains, where there's only one season all year round. My movement triggered a lamp that lit the cover over the swimming pool. It glowed sickly green like the traces of algae that floated above me as I'd sunk into the reservoir.

There was a light on in the garage. I stopped moving and in the quiet I could hear the sound of indistinct music and a faint hum, like a car trundling along the fields behind the garage with its radio on. I walked towards it along the tyre track, kicking up dust. I stopped again and heard the music, the engine running. A car engine, for definite, running inside the garage.

Alejandra.

I ran. The pain burnt up my thighs. No images in my mind, no daydreams. Just the panic of realising, at some unconscious level, that somewhere within reach someone was doing something terrible to themselves. I smashed against the side of the garage, pulled open the door. But there was no smoke, no hosepipes, nothing much at all. Just a room full of paint pots and tools under a layer of oily grime, and a woman sitting in an old sports car with her hands on the steering wheel, crying into her lap.

I recognised the car and the music – the yellow Seat that had belonged to Antonio, the spirited Civil War music. When Alejandra saw me she popped out the cassette and spoke without rolling down the window. Her sleeves smeared the black around her eyes. 'Come round. Get in.'

There were loose cigarettes on the passenger seat. She brushed them away to let me sit. 'Don't worry. I thought I might smoke but I won't.'

I looked automatically, quite pointlessly, for her pregnancy bump, but her lap was covered in folders and papers. She moved them on to the dashboard and there it was, the little hillock with the new life inside.

We sat in silence for a while and my first thought was that maybe, somehow, she knew about what'd happened at the reservoir. Though that was absurd, of course. Then I was sure she would say something about herself, now I'd seen her crying, but she didn't do that either. She just sat there in the quiet while her watch ticked off the minutes. I looked around at the shelves covered in drill parts and black rags, the rusty spanners displayed horizontally on a cork board like bones in a museum. It reminded me of the shed round the back of the Shoulder of Mutton, where Laurie had once caught me sniffing aerosols and slapped the can out of my hand. A very manly kind of place, though this one was rusted over and finished.

Alejandra stared into her lap. I suggested she put the music back on so she pushed the tape back in and a male choir sang 'Jarama Valley' in English. Antonio had played different versions of it for me many times.

'You can smoke if you like.' She pushed a gnarled pen into her mouth. 'I don't mind.'

'Thank you, I don't.'

'Did Antonio smoke when he was in Brighton?'

'Not often. He did at the end.'

Idiot phrases – 'at the end'. I couldn't stop using them. I hadn't even seen him 'at the end', unless his end had already begun, the last time I saw him, on the benches. In Spain it felt as if everything I said about him, even the tone with which I said it, was either too crass or too sentimental, too simplistic or too grand. But I was here in the car with her now, and I think we were both so desperate to talk that to have just sat there and listened to the music would have been impossible. The silence between songs confirmed this. It shouted profanely as if in a chapel.

'Can I ask you something personal?' It was me who said this but either of us could have opened that way. Actually when I said it, it sounded like someone else's voice.

'Okay.' Though she didn't seem sure. Perhaps she was still angry.

'When will it be born? I mean, when will *they* be born – he or she?'

'He, she or it will be born in October.'

'Are you going to have the baby here?'

She scoffed. 'In the house?'

'In Guadalupe, I mean.' Though I had meant the house.

'In Cáceres. But yes, we will live together here.'

I asked if she'd continue working, and whether her family would chip in – all questions I could have guessed the answer to, but I was just rambling. I noticed a torn picture of a black Madonna as I was talking, pasted to the wall of the garage. The *Virgen de Guadalupe*, some kind of local Catholic icon – Antonio had shown me her picture once or twice when describing his *pueblo*. She was adorned in gold and there was a little black Baby Jesus pinned to her chest like a brooch. Her eyes looked somehow glazed, somehow determined. I couldn't tell which.

'How do you feel about your trip?' Alejandra, direct as always. She shoved her papers onto the dashboard and rested her hands on the wheel. The car Antonio had wanted to drive us around in.

'I think it's been a disaster.'

'Explain.'

'I've never felt so out of place in my whole life. Not because of you, or your family. You've been very kind – far too kind, actually. That's part of the problem. I feel like a complete burden, I feel like a child.'

I looked down at her stomach with the baby inside and then hid my face in my hands, pretending to rub the tiredness from my eyes. She waited a moment while the song changed. 'The Internationale' – I knew that one too.

'I'm sorry,' she said. 'To give you that impression. If I

thought you'd be a burden, I wouldn't have invited you. Actually, it gave me something to do. Taking care of you.'

I kept my head in my hands. I couldn't think about my words anymore. 'I feel so guilty.'

She wanted to know why.

'Your family treated me as though I was good to Antonio,' I said. 'I really wasn't. I really wasn't there for him at all.'

Quiet again. The tune of 'The Internationale'. She waited until I looked out from behind my hands. She was relaxed at the wheel, as if driving down a familiar street. But the crack in her voice betrayed her.

'I don't know what there was between you and my brother. I only know what he told me, and I know he didn't tell me everything. It was just unfortunate you met him at the time you did. Whoever he'd been around, I'm convinced this was to be the last year of his life.'

The *Virgen* on the garage wall was watching us now, calm and blank and more than human. She looked motherly, in the way you see mothers take on far more than they can handle but just do it anyway, just handle it. I thought maybe that Alejandra meant what she said about her brother as an admission to fate, as something Catholics might understand innately but that didn't feel right to me at all. I didn't know.

'I could have helped him,' I said. 'Or somebody could have.'

The tape popped out at the slap of her hand. She turned towards me and I pulled back. The cool of the window shocked my bare skin.

'No. It was unfortunate for you. My brother only went to England because our mother was dead, only to find out about our great-grandfather. If my mother were alive he wouldn't have found out about him, and he wouldn't have had the money to look for him. Our mother should simply have told him, whatever it was. That's all.'

I sensed she'd rehearsed this logic many times but I still didn't understand it perfectly. She stared at the folders on the dashboard. I recognised them now – Antonio's notes.

'He seemed to take it hard,' I said. 'Whatever it was.'

'He took it very hard.'

'Did he tell you about it?'

'No,' she said. I think she was just as surprised that I knew nothing either.

'He told me he was a Civil War hero,' I prompted.

'There was a photograph that my mother kept of her grandfather. Antonio saw it when he was a teenager, I think he asked to keep it. Mama kept it in a drawer and sometimes Antonio would take it out and look at it, but she only let him keep it at the end. I couldn't find it in his apartment.'

My God. I'd forgotten completely.

'I have it.' *Though Christ where was it exactly, what had I done with it*. I had no idea.

'You do? It makes sense he would give it to you. I didn't see it until the day of Mama's funeral. He showed it to me here, in the car, actually. And again in Brighton, after you gave him the family tree. Not a great idea on your part.' She idly dismantled a cigarette, tipped the flakes out of the window. 'Anyway, I'm not sure what conversations took place between Mama and my brother but whatever was said made him curious. My great-grandfather was part of the International Brigades – you know that, of course – but we didn't know anything else about him.

I didn't care, Antonio did. Maybe just because he was a boy. It would have been better for him to let it go.'

'I'm sorry.' I remembered the day of his birthday, her clipped voice and the way she looked afterwards. The scolding cold of her gaze, unmoving like the eyes of the icon on the wall. 'I thought I was helping him.'

I looked again at the *Virgen*, at her face that was in the end simply full of purpose, the cold purpose of committing her life to one person, the little baby pinned to her chest. It was almost as if her gaze was pushing me to break down as I had on the hillside with Alejandra, and then my mind was wandering again and a thought was trying to come into being, something important. Now wasn't the time.

Alejandra put her hand on me, left it there.

'George. He was grateful for your help. You didn't speak to him after he found out, did you?'

'No. Yes, I did speak to him, but he never told me what he'd found out.'

'When Antonio called to tell me, he was extremely upset, very drunk. His Spanish was awful, like an English person's. In the end he told me nothing at all. Though obviously he didn't like what he found out.' She took her hand off me and withdrew a single sheet of paper from the folder on the dashboard. 'I've translated this note for you, go ahead and read it.'

'Oh.' A mess of blue and black ink, English and Spanish. '"Arthur John Martín, first infantryman—"'

'In your head is fine.'

The translation was written neatly in block capitals above Antonio's handwriting, for my benefit. It read: ARTHUR JOHN MARTÍN, FIRST INFANTRYMAN IN THE [UNKNOWN]

REGIMENT, BORN 1 SEPTEMBER 1919 IN LEWES, EAST, and then after a summary of his race, height, education, achievements: FOUGHT IN THE BATTLE OF JARAMA JANUARY 1937.

She'd taken it from Antonio's room with the rest of his documents.

'I see.' But I didn't. I still didn't really understand what they were supposed to tell me. Just that Antonio's idea of his great-grandfather, whatever heroic image he'd dreamt up, did not correlate to the life in these pages. *My grey gran-father was a* cabrón, he'd said.

I offered back the paper. She refused.

'There's nothing here,' she said. 'Just a few details. The rest of his notes were made in the books I left with you. Obviously he didn't find what he expected to find. But that's all the more reason.'

'All the more reason for what?'

She softened then. 'You can be very obtuse, George. Sometimes I think you're putting it on.'

I moved to apologise, stopped myself.

'Just have a look for me,' she said. 'I want to know what happened.'

She tried to hide the eagerness in her voice but it didn't work. I remembered Antonio sitting on the beach in front of the West Pier and telling me with his fist held to his chest, in almost the very same voice: *I want understand.* I pictured the boxes with Antonio's books inside, sitting on the floor of my bedsit in Brighton, all sealed up. So many memories clamouring for my attention. And now I understood why she'd written my name on those boxes, why she had invited me to Spain at all. If it was just that.

'I'll read them,' was all I said.

She didn't hug me as Antonio would have done, or even thank me. She just sat back in her seat and pushed the tape back in. 'The Internationale' — *¡Borrad el rastro del pasado!* — still playing, still playing.

'You are lost, aren't you, George? So obviously lost.'

There was no comfort in it. No attempt at sympathy. Just the truth.

'I am lost,' I said.

'Will you return to Brighton?'

'I don't know.'

'I mean will you continue to live there?'

'I don't know.'

I hadn't even considered the option of leaving. I'd already stood on the end of the pier more than once that summer, looking down at the forty-foot drop and daydreaming that if you were a swimmer you could just swim away from Brighton, straight out, and probably reach France by morning. If you were brave enough to leave when the time came. If you were a swimmer.

Alejandra threw her chewed-up pen into the glove box. She reached into her pocket and pulled something out. A little white tube, 100 ml.

'Take this.'

She pushed it into my hand. I couldn't recognise the words in Spanish or the ingredients. I twisted off the cap and sniffed at it. It smelt of nothing.

'For your rashes. They will go,' she clicked, 'like that.'

'Oh.' It surprised me. 'Thank you.'

'Do you have anyone who can help you?' she said.

I scratched my neck. 'I think I'll manage.'

'Not for your rashes, George.'

'Oh.' This was a conversation I didn't want and hadn't been expecting. I wasn't sure whether to say it but I did: 'I'm not an alcoholic.' It sounded childish in my voice.

'I know that.' She took apart another cigarette. 'You're just play-acting.'

I wanted to take offence but that didn't seem to make sense in the passenger seat of Antonio's car, with his sister who could say things so simply and clearly. It was like she'd watched me jump into the reservoir, and seen me pull myself out by the jetty – unharmed, really, when it came down to it. Like she already knew what I was coming to realise. I caught sight of my black eye in the mirror, beginning to heal.

'Yes,' I said, 'I know what you mean.'

'I mean, do you have someone at home? Someone you trust? Or no – not even that. Someone you can commit yourself to.' Which were the exact words that had been running through my head. 'Not in a romantic way. Just someone you're invested in, who's invested in you.'

I thought of her baby and the two of them in the house, in this car. There was a future there, for these two at least, even without Antonio in it. Even if that future was Spanish skinheads and riots and whatever else lay ahead for that place. I don't remember exactly what was going through my head when I muttered my agreements and then said: 'Do you need help with the baby?'

She could have taken this as an idle question – like *Will you get a nanny?* – but she took it the absurd way I meant it, as an offer of help. That was the first time I heard her laugh, loudly and wholeheartedly and quite beautifully, over the Civil War music and my own awkward silence. She flicked off the music again.

'George. You won't find what you're looking for in other people's problems.'

Then I said again what I'd been saying for so many years, which never sounded so untrue until just then, in the passenger seat of Antonio's car. 'I haven't done enough.'

'No one can ever do enough.'

I looked at the folders on my lap. I remembered Laurie outside the house at Pride – *you told me to participate in the world*, which I'd told her once way back in the Shoulder of Mutton, the night she came out and I announced my plans to leave Sussex. I urged her to go out and try to change the world – a world made up of people like Marta with her music and Alejandra with her baby and Duncan with his placards and blog posts and tatty paperbacks. All already carving out their own niches, all kinds of niches. And never ashamed of it.

Alejandra gathered up the folders and turned to me once more before getting out of the car. She didn't touch me, didn't even smile. She just spoke.

'Go home, George. Don't be lost.'

5
THE *BISABUELO*

I had never grieved before, not beyond the thoughts of what life might have been like had Mum stayed. I never knew my grandparents and the only funeral I'd been to before Antonio's was for a boy at my primary school who'd died of leukaemia, I can't even remember his name. I didn't know how grief was supposed to work, and the constant confusion of being absolutely clear-headed one minute and in pieces the next took me completely by surprise. I knew I was supposed to talk to people but the prospect of ringing anyone without a definite idea of how the conversation was going to go terrified me. Carlos rang several times, and then left a long, confused voicemail explaining I was fired. At first the only messages I replied to were Alejandra's, simply to tell her *Yes*, I was back in Brighton, *Yes*, I was using her cream, *No*, I wasn't drinking too much. Some of this was true, some of it wasn't.

I sat there and watched my phone ping with her messages. *Ping ping ping*, and nothing, not a single word, from Laurie. One whole month. Not one word. I sat on that pain like an overfull suitcase, and when I couldn't sit on it any longer, I stretched out on my bed and tried to sleep.

It was Alejandra who told me, in that direct, impersonal way of hers that I tried to resent but couldn't, that it would be a good step to commemorate Antonio's birthday in some way. She told me she planned to take his car up into the Sierra de Villuercas, to a spot where he'd enjoyed taking people to show them where a battle had been fought. She wanted to pour out a beer for him while his music played. But I had no ideas of my own. I hadn't even looked at his books in the few weeks I'd been back, it was just too painful. I resisted the thought for as long as I could, until his birthday came and I picked up my shoes from the mess of crumpled cans and crisp packets on the floor of my room, and headed out against my instincts. In a panic I bought a bouquet of supermarket flowers – cheap yellow ones, the last in the bucket. If someone dies in a car crash people put flowers at the site of the accident. Where do people put flowers for those who've drowned?

I took them to the seafront, walked west from Brighton to Shoreham with the crash of the waves in my ears, and back via the bowls green and the Lawns all littered in dogshit. I thought about going down to the shingle at Hove Lawns, where Antonio and I used to sit, but I couldn't face going down to that patch where he'd folded up his clothes and entered the sea. I walked on past the basketball court where we used to stop to watch the games, and on to the carousel, which was going round and round as always with no one on it. I looked across at the pier with its flashing lights, brighter than usual against the grey sky in September. I thought about the dark space underneath but nothing in the world could have made me go under there. Something in me said that if I'd gone with him to Spain, if I'd just bitten the bullet and gone, he'd still be alive. There were so many ifs, and when any one of them managed to sink into my mind, heavy and unexpected, I felt the guilt ripple through me.

As soon as I saw the fishing boat I knew this was the place to lay my flowers. I sat with my feet among the beer cans and ice cream wrappers in the hull, looking out at the rough grey sea. I must have sat there a long time because I remember running through everything Antonio and I had spoken about in the boat, that day when he got the keys to his flat. I remembered how he pretended to row, and said *¡España! ¡España!* which I took for a joke until he started to cry. I'd marvelled at this, but of course he cried, that man who'd just lost his mother and who was alone in a country where he couldn't speak the language – a country that didn't even seem to want him. I'd taken him for a knight errant, though maybe he was more like an orphan.

A couple walked past me hand in hand and then another who stared at me openly, and then a woman close by the boat, with lank hair tinted blonde. She wore a big coat with the hood up and rainbow patches stitched to both shoulders like epaulettes, an oversized guitar case on her back. She stopped and peered down at me and I worried with dread that I was going to have to use my voice. Her eyes crinkled in a smile.

'Is that you under there, George?'

Maybe she meant under my mess of hair, or under the black cloud above my head, I don't know. My voice cracked with disuse. 'Yes, I think it is.'

Marta clambered in and sat opposite me at the bow, facing me with her legs folded as if I was rowing her across a boating lake – she wouldn't have looked out of place with a parasol. I hadn't seen a single one of them since Antonio had passed and I hadn't prepared in my head what I might say. I noticed her septum piercing was gone. *Maybe I should mention that*, I thought. Her eyes were kind, like they always were. She was looking at the flowers on the bench.

'I was sorry to hear about Antonio,' she said. There was no skirting round it.

'It's his birthday. His sister said I should do something.' Drops of rain slid down the plastic around the flowers. 'I wasn't really sure what.'

I knew she could see I wanted to leave.

'I'm sorry I never replied to your messages,' I said. There had been many over the past month, from her and Helena and others, from Dad, too, though he never mentioned Antonio, but I ignored them all. It took a lot of effort to make sure I didn't bump into any of them around town either. But I managed.

'You went to the funeral, didn't you?'

'Yes, I did.'

She asked how I was coping. I wanted to say I had no idea, since I'd never been bereaved before — if that's what I was — and really I didn't know if I was doing well or if I was right on the edge. I wanted to tell her about Antonio's books and how I couldn't bear to read them because the sight of his handwriting brought out the fear in me. They were waiting for me in the flat like a dangerous animal waiting to be fed. Out at sea I saw the tour boat making its journey towards the West Pier.

'I'm sorry, Marta.' I played up my wheezing. 'I have to go.'

'Wait.' She held my arm, again it surprised me. I'd forgotten this was a changed Marta, a Marta who was willing to grab you if you needed her to. 'George, don't go,' her voice honest and unembarrassed.

I slumped back into the hull and she shuffled down the edge to put her arm around me. I thought she might try to talk about something light, which I couldn't bear, but instead she looked seriously into my eyes.

'Have you spoken to Helena?'

'No,' I said.

'She's gone.'

'Yes. She's in London, isn't she?'

'That's right.'

'Good for her.'

I should have found comfort in that, since she seemed so ready to move up in the world. I pictured her in her suit, marching down the corridors of the Houses of Parliament with a clipboard under her arm, ready to take some jowly backbencher to task. A life in London, doing something, being somebody. Everyone getting on and doing something.

'And me and Duncan... Well, we got our place. In Hanover. That was a few weeks ago now. He had a thing in *The Guardian* last week, did you hear? Opinion piece...'

I knew what was coming next.

'How is Laurie?'

'I don't know.'

'Jesus, George. You haven't spoken to your sister?'

I shook my head. 'She hasn't called. Can you believe that? She hasn't called.'

It was Dad who explained what happened, after I eventually replied to his messages. Laurie had been arrested, of course she had, and now she was back home putting in shifts at the Shoulder of Mutton. So at least she hadn't gone off to Syria, *Christ's sake* – she was just around the villages again, probably causing trouble. I was angry at how stupid that made me feel for worrying about her going off somewhere. She hadn't messaged me, even though she must have known about Antonio, surely she must. So I wasn't going to message her. That was that.

'You should call her,' said Marta. 'You have to.'

'No. God, no. It's been a month. I really can't believe she hasn't called.'

'She's just in pain, George.'

But I didn't want to talk about it.

'You've spoken to your dad though?' she said.

'Yes. He told me he came down to bail Laurie out.'

When I thought about it, it made me laugh with pity. I could picture Dad in a police station quite easily, but not picking up his daughter and bailing her out. *God, how ridiculous.*

'He took her back home,' I said, scoffing.

The fact that she was back in the village pricked me as much as anything else, thinking about her back there, back behind the bar. Exactly where I had been when I got back from travelling and she came up to collect me and drag me down to Brighton. There was mocking laughter in my head, an image of her posture, her strongwoman performance behind the bar. The way she made people feel small, even when she thought she was fighting the good fight. I told myself I didn't care, and if she felt any different now she knew about the riot, well, fuck her. She'd behaved like a bitch for too long.

Marta took my hand again. 'Try not to be too angry, George.'

I huffed. 'Sure.'

'And what about you? How are you doing?'

I sighed. What was I supposed to say? I told her I'd gone on the dole and that I could only scrape my rent for another month, possibly two, if I didn't get work. I told her I'd been glossing jobs websites for weeks but there was something wrong with all of them, something I couldn't yet articulate. All I knew was that every time I applied for a job in Brighton, I felt like I was wasting time when I was supposed to be doing something else. I even told her about how when I needed food I took the bus out to the Sainsbury's in Portslade, just to make sure I never bumped into anyone I knew.

'Whatever you need to do,' she said with my hands in hers, 'if you show me I'll help you.'

She rubbed my cold fingers and it seemed to me she wasn't offering to help because it would *take her out of herself*, the way I'd once thought of her kindness, but simply because she was there and she felt I needed it. I thought again of Alejandra waiting for me alone in that house in Guadalupe – waiting for me to call and put this *bisabuelo* thing to rest.

I think I knew already that I was going to leave Brighton – I knew it as soon as I'd found out that Laurie was no longer there – but I needed Marta's help, more than I needed a job or money or anything else.

I stood and placed the flowers into the hull of the boat. 'Will you come with me?'

She lifted her guitar case to follow.

I took her back to the flat without explaining, rifled through my drawers, books, boxes. I huffed and swore until I eventually found what I was looking for. I felt ashamed when I pulled Arthur John Martín's photograph out from under the sink, where it had got wet and crinkled. How could I have kept it under there, in the damp and dark, like a dirty secret?

I showed it to Marta and then reached into the boxes marked *GEORGE* and arranged every single book in front of us on the bed. There were dozens of them, maybe sixty or seventy – hardbacks, paperbacks, textbooks, pamphlets, their pages dog-eared and sand-coloured, falling apart. Some had prices written in pencil on the title page, others were stamped WITHDRAWN and dated with a library stamp – September 1992, July 1980, March 1965. Among the military history and memoirs were manifestoes, novels, even books of poetry, all with the musk of matured paper that made my room smell like a second-hand bookshop. And then there was Antonio's dictionary, which I couldn't look at without welling up.

Marta looked through them fondly, quite lovingly, as if at some piece of childhood nostalgia recovered from a flood. She squinted at Antonio's annotations, so dense that the margins were grey with pencil. He'd underlined whole pages – not passages of profundity or poignancy, just information, selected with no discernible pattern. Other passages were crossed out and sidled with exclamation marks in groups of two – outrage and alarm. The lines wavered like loose thread, I pictured his hands shaking with drink or the lack of it. Before he gave up on the books entirely.

'What *are* these?' Marta asked finally.

I told her about Alejandra, the boxes, my trip to Guadalupe and the funeral. I explained about the dinner, the mountain and the little yellow sports car with the Civil War music playing – everything except for my dip in the reservoir. It poured out of me desperately with no restraint or cogency and no logic at all – just an overflow of raw information and emotion. She listened patiently. I hadn't told anyone else. She took up a book and flicked through and said nothing. Just got started.

She scanned through the books with me, picking out notes she thought might be useful, explaining some of the recurrent Spanish words. The process of translating these notes into English was daunting, and I thought that even twenty years earlier this might have been impossible without someone like Marta present. I remember translating the first one – a loose page stuffed into an André Malraux novel, with Antonio's handwriting crawling over the paper, his curlicues cut through with firm strokes, a kind of flamenco. I laboriously typed each Spanish word, and then watched my slow computer display the word *Translating...* Marta read it with me.

training in madrigueras, where british volunteers with the expectation they will immediately engage field combat without training – political zeal or chance to become man, to demonstrate manhood, much courageous

His voice came through clearly even through the broken syntax – the passion and flair, so consistent as to become almost cartoonish. I heard his voice as it was when he first saw his great-grandfather's real name, under the pier one year ago, on the last birthday of his life. His voice like a man from history. *He died without bleeding*, I thought. He can't have wanted that.

Marta put her arm round me. She knew I needed it, I think, though there was more to it than that. She explained briefly about her grandparents who were born in Revolutionary Catalonia during the war – Loyalists like Arthur – and afterwards how her family had been persecuted by the Falangists, forced to speak Castilian Spanish, bullied and beaten. Though they never spoke bitterly about it, so she said.

'They had a hard time of it, well into the 1970s. Until Franco died.'

I wanted to ask if she'd introduced Duncan to her parents when he went to Barcelona, what had happened there, why she'd taken him back. I wanted to ask properly, sensitively, but in the end I just blurted *What happened with Duncan* while setting down her cup of tea. She was sympathetic to it.

'You mean in Barcelona?'

'Yes.'

She held her cup in both palms. 'He just showed up, I didn't know he was coming until he was there. I got a message saying he was waiting for me outside La Pedrera. He didn't even have anywhere to stay.'

'Did he ask you to come back to Brighton?'

'Yes. I know how he can be, with you and the others, but he can also be very sincere. Very sweet.'

As Helena had suggested on the bench at Ringmer. Though still I couldn't picture it. 'What swayed you?'

'Nothing. Nothing dramatic, I mean. We met on and off for about a week and then I found out he didn't have a return ticket. He asked me to forgive him and I could tell that he meant it. I'd felt so much like I didn't belong here, after the vote, I mean. He was the only one who put that right in my mind. I spoke with my parents and my friends and in the end, I forgave him. I'm sorry but it's that simple.'

I tossed aside one of Antonio's books. 'But he was such an arse.'

Again she smiled, knowingly now, as if she'd expected to tell me the story and expected me to miss the point. She stroked my agitated face. 'That's how forgiveness works, George.' And then returned to the books.

We carried on talking and drinking tea and pouring through Antonio's notes, each one bringing the history to life. By midnight I was exhausted. I'd been typing out a long note in the back of *The Battle for Spain*, which was so full of annotations it was hard to read the original text, when I noticed Marta rubbing her eyes. She had several books open in front of her and was looking blearily between them all.

'Okay,' I said. 'I suppose it's getting late. I want you to know how much I—'

I froze when she picked up the dictionary. I felt like she was touching something special, like I needed to grab it from her. Though I didn't. The tears were coming.

'His dictionary,' I said. 'He used to carry it around.'

She flicked idly to the back flyleaf. Stopped with her finger over something. 'Look at this.'

I moved around to look. In among Antonio's handwriting, with his frustrated strikethroughs and circles where he'd warmed the ink from the pen, was a barely legible word repeated half a dozen times.

'Does it say Reginald?' I said.

'I think so.'

She handed me the book, a big unwieldy hardback with loose stitching. There on the flyleaf, in new words written in scratchy biro, was Antonio's inscription.

Reginald Miller

25121939

As soon as I saw it the weight of the past month collapsed onto me and I started to cry, loudly and uncontrollably, until I was shaking in Marta's arms. She held me there and I cried at the sight of his handwriting and only when I was completely exhausted did she let me go.

'That's the man he went to meet?' she asked.

'Yes. Yes, that's him.' I squinted at the numbers. 'Is that a service number, maybe?'

Marta followed the numbers with her finger. 'Twenty-five, twelve, nineteen thirty-nine.'

'My God...' I wiped the tears from my eyes and as soon as Marta saw them she was laughing, and I was back in her arms.

Reginald Miller. Born Christmas Day, 1939.

A detail from another world.

I climbed Albion Hill while on the phone to Alejandra. It was a mistake – the road is so steep it's impossible to breathe properly while walking it – so I asked her about the baby and hoped she'd talk at length.

'This thing is so heavy now you wouldn't believe…'

She told me she was as big as a house and I wished her luck with her final trimester though I didn't know the first thing about that whole business. Laurie always hated the idea of having kids, said she'd never consider it, *fuck that*. I paused by a lamp post to catch my breath. I knew by the open-ended way Alejandra was speaking she knew I'd called with a purpose.

'I think we've found the name of your uncle,' I said. 'Your great-uncle, I mean.'

I explained about the name – Miller, he must not have taken his father's – and how I'd looked in the directories for Lewes but couldn't find a number for him.

'I'm not giving up,' I said. I checked my watch. Twelve p.m., running late.

'I'm grateful for that,' she said. 'What are you doing?'

I set off again. 'I'm walking up the Travelator.'

'What's a Travelator?'

'Never mind.'

The house at the top of Albion Hill had hanging baskets on the outside, a front porch with an ornately filigreed bench and a plaque that said a music hall star had lived there for eighteen months. In the shallow bay window hung the familiar Hanover drapery – heavy open curtains and a blue poster for the NHS.

It was Marta who answered the door. She wore a summer dress with cornflower print and her hair was cropped short.

'*Benvingut*,' she said, the Catalan warm to my ears.

I think she was surprised I'd accepted her invitation. Truthfully, I was only there because she'd called to ask me, and then called again, and again, and then sent me pictures of the dessert she was making, and then sent me videos of her with the dessert, singing her insistence from behind her guitar. With her beautiful singing voice restored to confidence. In the end I simply couldn't find an excuse she'd accept.

I noticed she was shoeless so I slipped mine off in the corridor. Duncan waited for us in the living room, in an armchair by the empty hearth, with a book on his lap. With his glasses on, which I'd never him seen wear, he looked almost like someone who would actually read a book instead of just talk about it. He removed them, saying nothing, and stood. His face had gained a thin beard and the tuck of his shirt revealed a rounder shape, the beginnings of a masculine belly. I expected him to look like a fish out of water in this new, domestic environment, so far from the old school. But his body looked at peace.

'Am I in the wrong house?' I said.

He smiled. 'Good to see you, comrade.'

His voice was untouched. Still the same false bounce, the smoothing of its upper middle-class edges. Marta brought in crisps made of vegetables and some elderflower wine that I had to work hard to refuse. It surprised Duncan but he let it go. They'd been in the house for over a month, and there was no sign of any unpacked boxes, but still I noticed just a handful of his collectibles around the room, including his *Coal Not Dole* poster. His books were missing, the shelves sparse and orderly. There was a photograph of him and Marta in the corridor of the school with the EU flags limp above their heads. The night Antonio entered my life. I stared at it until Duncan's hand came down suddenly on my knee.

'Your rashes have gone.'

I told him a friend was sending me cream, but in reality it had less to do with Alejandra's medication than with her phone calls – once, twice a week – when she asked me every single time what I'd been doing and how much I'd had to drink, and never came down on me unless I lied. I didn't want to talk about it with Duncan. Maybe I should have accepted the wine.

'Tell me,' he said, 'is Big Sis still knocking around?'

I was amazed he mentioned her so readily, and with absolutely no sign that I might chastise him for the way he'd treated her. *Big Sis*. It was almost as if he'd forgotten all that had happened between them, or simply didn't consider it important. I wanted to want to snap at him. But I didn't. It was possible that in some odd way he thought Laurie was his friend, despite everything. Marta watched me over her wine glass.

'She's back in Sussex, actually,' I said.

'Is she? How's she getting on?'

'I haven't seen her. You know, I don't—'

Marta hurried out. Duncan's eyes lingered on the doorframe, and after a few seconds he said: 'Have you seen Helena?' The question was chipper but his voice was lower.

'No, not since summer.' The memory of Pride dangled

again between us – he'd been watching us from the roof – but I cut it off. 'She's still full-time for the party, is she?'

He was pleased to tell me she was working for his *pappy* in London, or rather not for him but with him or alongside him, or whatever. Though I already knew. 'She wears a suit,' he said. 'She's gone pro.'

I laughed. 'That's just what I said.'

Marta came back with more hors d'oeuvres, returned to the kitchen. She seemed comfortable in that role – she looked in control of the place. As Duncan leant across for some crudités, and I saw the little belly he'd earned spill over his belt, I realised how quiet it was. Duncan's record player wasn't there in the living room, neither were his LPs. There wasn't even a radio.

'Don't you still have your records?' I asked as Marta came back.

His eyebrows waggled up and down. She sighed openly. Then he jumped to his feet and marched through to the kitchen.

'You'd better go with him,' she said, and she smiled sympathetically as if to say *Yes, George, I know, but just go anyway.*

I followed him into the corridor and through the kitchen to the back garden, which was small and concrete with real grapes growing from the trestle and a plump Buddha squatting in the flowerpot, and on into Duncan's shed.

I ducked under the sign above the door.

THE BUNKER.

For God's sake.

*

Inside were his records, his books and his postcards, jumbled together on shelves with wonky brackets, intact but musty and disorderly. Even then there was much less of it than before, less than half. I wondered if his mahogany desk was somewhere in the house or whether he'd since realised – or maybe Marta had told him – that he only ever used it for snorting drugs off anyway. We sat in dilapidated armchairs, looking at the record player.

'The needle broke last week,' he said, and then fished around in a wooden box for a pipe and some loose shag to crumble into it. Through the curtains of smoke in the light of the plastic window, I watched him cross his legs comfortably, and yes, he looked like a dickhead, but he also looked something like a great writer, or perhaps just a book collector.

I asked him about the house.

'Well, we have a cancerous mortgage. But it's turned out cheaper than your average rent.' He picked up a paperback, flicked through it, tossed it. 'Actually I'm selling off all this old junk.'

I left a space open for him to tell me all about it, how he was selling off his trinkets to help pay for a studio for Marta, a room in the house for her to record her music. I'd been surprised when she told me how excited he was about it, especially that it'd been his idea. He was thinking about that, I think, after he said *old junk*. But he chose not to mention it.

'When did you leave the old school?' I asked.

'Oh, you know me. I've always been old school.'

I suspected that whatever issues had led to his eviction were problems long since left at Marta's feet. I caught a hint that maybe Marta had *taken him in* when she took him back, on the promise that he'd behave – even for his own good – and that was probably what he wanted and needed. This was all speculation, and I never asked, but things had changed, that I could see. There was a feeling that things were settling.

The playful, alert look he had at his best was on his face then, just for an instant, before he tweaked the position of his Lenin statuette and relaxed back into his armchair. He put a hand on my arm and said: 'I'm glad you came, I wanted to talk to you.' For a moment the affectation evaporated from his voice. In its wake was gentleness and sobriety. 'I'm sorry, very sorry about what happened between us.'

I saw an opportunity to punish him. 'What did happen between us?' But it wasn't convincing.

'About Antonio, I mean. I feel so stupid.'

'What for?'

'For hitting him that time. I was in a bad place then.'

'He's dead, you know.' I hadn't expected to say it like that.

'Yes, I heard. I'm sorry. You went to the funeral, didn't you?'

'That's right.'

It hurt to say but I didn't show it, not to Duncan who I would never, under any circumstances, show my pain to. He slumped a little in his chair.

'I mean it when I say I was in a bad place. I was just confused, I was lashing out…'

I didn't much want to take his confession but I could hardly walk out.

'…Marta saved me, she really did.'

'What do you mean?'

'I was groping around in the dark. I just didn't know where I was going.' He ran his fingers through his beard. 'I never slept with any of those women, I mean it. I haven't slept with anyone else since I first met Marta. She pulled me back and gave me meaning. I know I need someone to look after me, and she needs someone to look after her. And ultimately that's how it works for us. I had to swallow my pride...'

He sat there and thought for a moment and then shocked me by leaning right over and placing his hands on my arms. Then his face was in my face and I could see the forks of red in his eyes. It was so out of character it frightened me. It was like he'd been body-snatched, swapped for someone else, someone dangerously human.

'George—'

'Jesus, Duncan.' I was surprised by how strong his grip was.

He held me there for just a second, staring with his wild eyes, before he let me go and fell back into his chair. When he sat, the space between his buttonholes dilated so that I could see the belly hair underneath his shirt. He picked up his pipe slowly and the matches rattled around inside the box in his hand. I settled back into my chair, brushed myself off.

'I'm sorry,' he said. 'That's all.'

'Don't worry.'

He spoke quietly. 'Marta told me I can be a prick. I know I can.'

'Well, we're all pricks sometimes.'

He lifted his head and I thought he might be crying but he wasn't. All my desire to punish him, which I'd held for months now, fled completely. I remembered what Helena had told me about how he'd supported her in London, something I still couldn't actually picture, until now. It was as though he, like Marta and Helena and everyone else, was doing good things just out of sight. As if goodness ran through the centre of them, like the word BRIGHTON in Brighton rock, so that wherever you bite through it's always there.

'I saw your thing in *The Guardian*,' I said. 'Congratulations.'

'Thanks,' he said. His phone pinged. He'd got his blue tick, too, on Twitter. A verified pundit.

'No, really. I mean it. I'm genuinely proud.' And I was.

He held my eye, wanted to believe me. I think he did. 'Thank you, George.'

'You're welcome.'

I stood and considered telling him I'd decided to leave Brighton, though really my decision had only been finalised there, just then, in Duncan's shed. Instead I shook his hand.

'Anyway. We're all as bad as each other, aren't we?'

Then Marta's voice called us from the house.

We spoke over lunch – she'd made vegan lasagne, which I couldn't get enough of – and they told me about their jobs, which I'd forgotten all about, impossible as it was to visualise Duncan working anywhere at all. I could feel my attention failing, and then when he told me about their planned trip to Barcombe Mills my mind wandered to the reservoir outside Guadalupe while my head kept nodding. I'd felt for so long like a spectator, and even now at the dinner table and in Duncan's Bunker I felt like a spectator, but when I thought of my naked body piercing the water of the reservoir, that didn't quite ring true. I wondered idly how close I'd really been to drowning, and when I started paying attention again Duncan was talking about Virginia Woolf and then cut himself off mid-sentence. I felt the hole open out where he meant to say *We're going down to where she drowned*, but I closed it with a shrug.

'It's lovely there,' I said, and put the reservoir out of my mind.

At the end of the meal Duncan asked how I was getting on with my search for Reginald Miller. Before that afternoon I wouldn't have dreamt of discussing it with him. Then again there wasn't much to tell.

'We've hit a wall,' I said.

Marta mentioned the note we'd found in the dictionary. 'George can't find a number for him. So all we have is his name, which I suppose might not even be his real name, and his date of birth.'

'Fascinating,' Duncan mused. 'What's his date of birth?'

Marta and I answered together: '25 December 1939.'

Duncan muttered *Christmas Day...*, sat back in his chair, put his fingers together. All the old affectations were back now, but what he said next was so sincerely warm it surprised me. 'That's the year my grandmother was born.'

This was the first time Duncan had ever mentioned anything about his family, other than his dad's job. I wondered if this was a new thing for him, something he was maturing into. I was curious – I asked where she lived.

'Oh,' he said, 'well, she's getting on for eighty, you know. She's in a care home.'

I looked at Marta and she looked at me. Duncan was speaking about his grandmother but I couldn't listen. I stood and prepared to leave.

'I'm sorry. I have to go.'

'George!' Marta stood but I was already backing away.

'I'm sorry.'

'What's wrong?'

'Nothing.' I struggled to unlock my phone, laughed about it. 'Honestly. The lasagne was lovely, really lovely.'

Duncan stayed sitting, trying to look unfazed, and I turned and went through into the corridor. I already had my browser open by the time Marta managed to stop me.

'George, do you want me to—'

I leant in and kissed her – *smack* – on the cheek.

'George, I'll call you—'

But I didn't hear what she said. I didn't hear a thing.

By the time I got to the bottom of the hill, I'd already found a directory on my phone for all the nursing homes in Lewes. There were twenty-two in total, running alphabetically down the list. I started with the first.

The phone rang, I asked for Reginald Miller, there was no Reginald Miller, I hung up. By the time I reached my street I'd called six of them. Then on the seventh attempt, when the sun was just going down over Brighton, I got through to a care home with an address somewhere on the way to Malling. A deep Caribbean voice answered the phone.

I hadn't worked out what to say. 'I need to speak to Reginald Miller, please.'

There was a protracted pause. The voice came back with bristles on it. 'We don't bring residents to the phone, sir.'

'Oh.' My nerves bloomed.

'Perhaps you could call him on his mobile?'

'Well…' I rattled my key in the door, pushed my way into my flat. 'I don't have his number.'

'Are you friend or family?' She asked it offhand but it still unnerved me.

'I'm family,' I said, squirming. I could never lie well.

'Oh? What relation?'

'I'm his grandson.'

I stood in the middle of my room, surrounded by Antonio's books, my heart thrashing in my chest.

The nurse sounded satisfied. 'I see. Well, why not come in person? Residents usually appreciate a visit.'

'Oh.' I said. 'Okay.'

She said goodbye and as the phone went dead, I lowered it to my side and let the anxious beeping rattle on.

I looked around at Antonio's books, his handwriting splashed across the lot of them, and the definitive note at the back of the dictionary – *Reginald Miller, 25121939*. I hadn't actually thought about how it would be to go and see him. An old man. Dying even? And I'd never been in a care home in my life. *Should I bring flowers? I mean, it's not a hospital…*

I called Marta while I was pacing up and down, up and down. Her soft voice interrupted the tone.

'George, what's happening?'

'Marta. Fuck. Sorry. Hi.' I filled my lungs with air. 'I need you again.'

We sat on the top deck of the bus, Marta and I, facing each other on opposite seats with our backs to the windows. I felt none of the calm I felt last time I'd made this trip, getting out of town for the first time in months to join Helena in Ringmer. I had images of the old man shooing us away, or being comatose or having died suddenly or dying while we were there. Maybe I should have rung again, but then the woman on the phone had told me a visit would be best. Did they just let anyone in? Maybe I should have brought him flowers, if that's the done thing, or chocolates or books. What if he had dementia and thought I was his grandson, or a nurse came to change his sheets or his bedpan, or whatever it was that happened in old people's homes?

'Maybe I should have thought this through,' I muttered aloud.

The bus stopped by the high walls of HMP Lewes. I watched a woman in a black suit walking towards the far gate, traipsing, heavy-footed. A lawyer, maybe, or just someone visiting their spouse. Dressed like she was heading to a funeral.

'Duncan says you two had a nice chat in his "bunker",' said Marta.

'Yes. He was really,' I struggled for the word, 'sincere.'

She laughed and told me he could be like that when he wanted to be. I asked if he missed all his stuff and maybe she was fibbing but she said he didn't. She'd told me already how little all that bric-a-brac had really meant to him, which astonished me, and how he'd been happy to part with it for the sake of her studio. *He just loves culture*, she told me, really loved culture of all kinds — not just as a collector but as a passionate supporter, a kind of old-fashioned patron.

Truthfully, I didn't know what to believe but instinctively I trusted her. The new strength in her voice was matched by the unwavering way she took in the world around her. Even when we alighted at Lewes and a local lad who looked too drunk for that time of day knocked into her on the pavement, she looked that way. Calm and sure of herself.

She said *Excuse me* and stepped aside for him. And he said *Mind out, Spanish* before stumbling through the open doors of The Volunteer.

I asked if she was okay and she hooked me by the elbow. 'Try not to worry.'

We crossed the bridge and passed down the cobbled high street with the little antique shops and posh tea rooms and eventually found the nursing home, tucked away on a quiet residential road under the cliffs. It was small and tidy with red brick and a gravel drive lined with carnations.

Marta said: 'Are you sure you're ready to do this?'

I looked up at the building, the old English style of it. I couldn't imagine Antonio doing this alone, coming out here without even the proper means to communicate, not with the carers or with the old man who might not even have known that Antonio existed. But he had done it, somehow, and it had damaged him irreparably. I'd been telling myself that all this was for Alejandra. But that was only part of the truth.

I nodded to Marta. I'd come this far. She took my hand and led me in.

The reception was decorated with marigold wallpaper and a thin carpet in conference-room grey. The smell of lavender was strong enough to make you gag, and underneath that was a sharp hint of disinfectant. At the counter sat a woman in a powder-blue smock scratching furious notes into a folder. She was in her sixties, maybe, with strong shoulders and tight curls. I was in no doubt this was the woman I'd spoken to on the phone – she was exactly how I'd imagined her, even down to the thick glasses on the end of her nose.

I read her name badge. 'Good morning, Beatrice.'

'Good morning.'

Her accent, which had sounded so severe on the phone, was softened by the kind look on her face. I said *Good morning* again, realised I was freezing up.

Marta's voice was gentle. 'We're here to see Reginald Miller.' This is what I needed her for.

'Sign in, please.'

I'd expected some trouble walking into a care home, with all these elderly, vulnerable people, but Beatrice didn't seem concerned about us. I passed her desk, rushing into the corridor, but Marta didn't follow.

'Thank you,' she said. 'Remind us which room he's in?' Like she'd really forgotten.

'Twenty-five, dear.'

We followed the grey carpet through the corridors down to Room 25, where the door was ajar. I could hear a television on inside, Hollywood voices. I recognised the timbre of them against the tinny orchestral music and the old-fashioned gunshot sounds that sounded faintly like slamming doors. I turned to Marta. 'It's okay. I'll go in alone.'

I knocked on the door but no one answered. I could see the light from the telly flickering onto the bedsheets. Without thinking I drew out the photograph of Arthur John Martín from my pocket and held it tightly.

'Go on,' said Marta. 'I'll be right outside.'

It was a small room – just slightly smaller than Antonio's bedsit – and dark. The lights were off and the drawn curtains so thick you couldn't tell if it was day or night. The only light came from the half-open door behind me and from the television, casting its pale flicker onto the bed, where a man's body lay under the covers. Humphrey Bogart was on the screen, dancing with Ingrid Bergman under a slow-spinning disco ball, and for the moment that was the only thing I could think about – that the old man was watching *Casablanca* of all films, which I love.

The body in the bed was short and straight and looked stiff as a board with his arms by his sides – skinny, too, under the thin white duvet. His face was blotchy with liver spots and bruises and his eyelids only lightly closed so that I could see just a sliver of his eyes. He might have been watching the film, though it looked more like he was asleep or dead. Suddenly I felt like I was in the presence of a corpse and fear rushed into my body. I pulled Marta into the room and she looked down at the man in the bed, who seemed to me now like he wasn't even breathing. But she wasn't fazed.

She half closed the door behind her and said: 'Reginald? Mr Miller?' quite gently. She shrugged. 'He's asleep.'

'Maybe we should go—'

'No, come on.' She held my arm. 'Let's wait a moment.'

She pulled out a chair for me and took the spongy-looking

armchair beside the bed for herself. I still had Arthur John Martín's photograph in my hand.

She smiled at what was on the TV. 'This is one of yours, isn't it?'

Onscreen, Rick and Ilsa were sitting on the banquette in Paris, and she was telling him that yes, there had been another man, and that he was dead, which of course he wasn't. That short scene in which we see what the two of them had shared, before the invasion and the fade back to the bar in Casablanca, 'As Time Goes By', et cetera et cetera.

Marta settled into the armchair, and I glanced between her and Bogart and the man in the bed, and we watched TV together like a family.

I remember bragging to my schoolteachers about how much I liked *Casablanca* back in Media Studies, when I thought it set me against the grain – this sentimental, black-and-white film at a time when all the kids were watching superhero movies. I even brought Laurie into my room to watch it, since she loved seeing Nazis getting a kicking, though *Inglourious Basterds* was more her speed. As I watched it again, with Marta who told me she'd never seen it, I wondered what she thought of these characters – about Rick and Captain Renault and Signor Ferrari. I wondered how she felt about the woman who cries at the bar when they sing 'La Marseillaise' – the one who'd been sleeping with the Nazis but was probably, like everybody else, just praying to escape. I glanced at the old man in the bed with no idea whether he was watching too, or whether he knew we were there or not. Perhaps it was wrong that we were even there, with whatever we'd come to drag up, and as the film went on I had to accept that we might not leave with what we came for. In which case, it was all over.

We watched it for half an hour maybe, right up until Victor is arrested, before someone rapped on the door. I panicked, I thought we were going to get chucked out – two strangers in this man's room, not even relatives. *Watching his telly*, of all things. One of the carers nudged open the door and pushed in a trolley full of cleaning things. Not cleaning things for the room, things for a person's body. She smiled warmly.

'Asleep is he?' she said. Her voice had the same soft edge as Marta's. 'Bless.'

I whispered: 'Is he like this all the time?' That care home, hospital ward, funeral parlour whisper.

'Usually, yes. Dr Miller does get tired.'

He murmured then, a deep, vague, guttural murmur, and I jumped out of my skin. Instinctively I shoved Arthur John Martín's photograph into my pocket.

The carer patted his forehead. 'Oh, you are awake, Dr Miller. He doesn't often get visitors.'

Nothing moved in the old man's face. Again I hoped he was simply asleep, and not listening to every word we said, wanting to join in, to affirm his existence. His eyes were still just fractionally open, pointed at the television, never moving. I was struck again by the horror of it, though neither Marta or the carer even seemed to notice.

'He used to be a lot more chatty,' said the carer.

She began to draw out the things from her trolley – implements, wipes. Things I didn't really want to see.

'Do you know much about him?' asked Marta.

'Oh, not too much. Dr Miller keeps to himself now, don't you Dr Miller?'

His still face, no murmurs.

'Today's a bad day,' she said.

'Do you know anything about where he came from?' I asked. The anxiety in my voice was beginning to show.

'Oh, not so much, dear. He was a lecturer, I know that.'

She explained briefly that he'd taught English at one of the local universities – Brighton or Sussex. She didn't know much more than that.

'You'll have to excuse me now,' she said, drawing out a long cloth, 'if you would.'

'Oh.' I looked down at him, willing him to snap out of it. 'Yes, of course.'

The emotion was rising within me but it had nowhere to go. I walked slowly towards the door with Humphrey Bogart's drawl following me out, until Marta spoke.

'We were only hoping to find out about his upbringing,' she said, bold as anything. 'Did you know his father fought in the Spanish Civil War?'

The carer laid down her cloth, reached for something else. 'Oh, the Spanish Civil War. He used to go on about that all the time.'

I turned back. 'He did?'

She leant over the still body, it gave another murmur. Horrifying. 'Excuse me, Dr Miller,' opening the drawer underneath the television. 'He won't mind me showing you this, he was always flinging it about. Weren't you, Doctor?'

She reached into the drawer and withdrew a small case in purple felt. I knew what it was before she opened it but still I couldn't believe what I was seeing. I thought Reginald Miller twitched when she prised open the lid, maybe I imagined it. There was no life in him, not really, just the flicker of telly light across his face.

She held out the case to show us the little red medal with the soldier's head and the protruding sword hilts and the words that read: REPUBLICA ESPANOL. Seeing it there in the case, it was smaller than it looked on Arthur John Martín's chest – just a dainty little thing like a child's prop. It looked almost worthless in itself, something you might see in the window of one of those trophy shops that are forever closed. Except it wasn't worthless, at least not to Antonio who would've given his right arm to see this object, to hold it, to wear it. He would've cleared out every piece of crap from his room for a look at this thing. This little thing that he may or may not have seen when he came to visit Reginald, that time, and who he left with an empty heart.

I didn't draw it out or ask to hold the case, I just nodded and said *How interesting* until the carer put it back in the drawer, and we thanked her, and it seemed suddenly time to leave. Reginald was out cold, and I suspected that however he'd been with Antonio that time he was always out, and so would never be able to give me the answers I was looking for. Maybe I should have shown him the photograph of his father, or left it there with the medal, but for whatever reason I hung on to it. You could almost see him in Reginald's face, the line of the nose. Almost but not quite.

We said goodbye at the door and I turned once more to see Reginald Miller's face, still no idea whether he knew what was going on around him or not. No more murmurs, just his eyes on the television where 'As Time Goes By' was playing and the story was carrying on, all that peril and excitement and grand romance. *Yes, maybe I should leave the photograph behind*, I thought. But then we were heading down the corridor and through the reception, the photograph still in my pocket.

Before we left the carer said casually: 'I suppose you've read Dr Miller's book?'

I froze by the reception desk. 'Pardon?'

'Dr Miller. He wrote about his life in a book.'

'He did?' A torrent of noise washed through me. 'Well, where is it?'

'I'm afraid we don't have it anymore. He donated his copy to the library.'

I held Marta close to me. 'Well, Christ, what's the name of it?'

The carer shrugged and smiled once again, that warm oblivious smile. 'I'm sorry. I don't remember.'

I ran down the high street and across the bridge with Marta following behind me. I ran up the hill from the bus station, ten or fifteen metres, and then realised I couldn't remember where the library was. Marta found it for us on her phone and I followed her with my lungs puffing strongly, again past the pubs and charity shops and down the road. We rounded a corner and the library stood there on the slope with its big glass windows reflecting the clouds. Its lights were off.

The locked door clanked in my hands and I swore loudly enough to bother an old lady in the car park. Marta typed something into her phone and held it up for me. The words *reginald miller* were in the search box for the library catalogue.

Sorry, your search for Anywhere: reginald miller (keywords) did not find any records.

'But the nurse said he wrote a book!'

'Wait.'

She typed something else in and then paused. My hands were shaking with the nerves.

'Look at this.'

She held up her phone again. A grey box with a cross in it stood in place of a book cover, but the title was clear. *Stories from the Spanish Civil War, ed. Derek Hill*. And beneath it a list of contributors, at the bottom of which were the words: *Prof Reggie Miller*.

'That's it, that's it.' I ran up the steps to check when the library was next open. 'Tomorrow morning.'

Marta was shaking her head. 'George.'

'Nine o'clock. So that means we can—'

'George!' She pinched me by the neck. It bothered me.

'Christ's sake, Marta,' wriggling away.

She held up her phone again. *Shelf status: Missing [since April 2017]*

I felt the world collapse into my lungs.

'I'm sorry, George—'

But I was already rushing off, I knew where I needed to be. She yanked me back by the arm. 'Christ, wait a minute.'

I turned to grab her. 'We've got to get a taxi back.'

It took almost an hour to get home and before I did I made sure to drop Marta back in Hanover. She insisted on coming with me – we even argued about it on the back seat – but I told her I needed to deal with this alone. The taxi dropped me off and charged me a fortune. I remembered how little money I had in the bank, nowhere near enough to make it to the end of the month. *Fuck it.* My keys jammed in the lock and by the time I made it upstairs I was out of breath again and my head was spinning and the noise inside it was so loud it was like being behind a waterfall.

I scrabbled through the books on the bed, then through the others I'd put back in the boxes. I thought how stupid I'd been not even to look at every single volume. I tipped out the boxes until everything was on the bed, a whole mess of scrappy hardbacks and paperbacks. I picked them up one by one and threw them onto the floor. Then, after a few minutes searching, I saw a thin paperback resting upside down on my pillow. A cheap cover with a warped photograph of a war memorial on it. I picked it up carefully and turned it round.

Stories of the Spanish Civil War, edited by Derek Hill.

I pulled it open and saw the sheet of withdrawals and the stamp – April 2017. I could just imagine Antonio taking it to the desk to demand a stamp. The pages were cheap and white and starched into a wave by some encounter with water. I flicked to the contents. The chapters were all by different authors, Englishmen the editor probably knew in person. I read from the bottom of the page – the title of one of the final chapters, page 107 of a book I'd had with me, in my room, since August. The words left my lungs like the last bubbles of air from a drowning man.

To Find and Not to Yield: The Story of my Father, the Soldier, by Professor Reggie Miller.

George Grocott
<george_grocott@gmail.com>   Thurs 19 Sept at 02:57

To: Alejandra GJ

Dear Alejandra,

Hey, sorry, know you're busy. Tomorrow I will get to the library
and scan all this in but I've found it, here's the important bits.
There's a lot about the guy's childhood growing up in Sussex etc.
and stuff about his real dad, seems like he didn't know about your
great-granddad until he was a teenager. Also stuff about him
looking for him etc. and all that, won't bore you with it, will send
tomorrow. Tried to take photographs but you can't really make out
the words, shit phone. Just thought I'd better type up the
important bits now, since anyway I can't sleep, not sure I'm going
to sleep. So yeah yadda yadda you'll see it all tomorrow but here's
this, I hope you pick it up, hope it makes sense. He's just tracked
him down at a pub in the East End (London). Fuck I've read it like
ten times already.

> He told me with clear pride that he was born into a
> shipbuilding family in the East End, under appallingly
> sooty conditions (naturally I pictured Dickens), and
> was moved to Worthing during the Great War that
> killed my grandfather at Ypres. The boy was raised by
> his mother alone, who seems to have instilled him with

the industrial values of the East End because Arthur, as soon as he was old enough to enter work, paid his immediate dues for membership to the Sussex branch of the Communist Party of Great Britain.

My father's relationship with the party, so I surmised, was an ambiguous one. He was intelligent and loved Tressell, but his approach to good and evil was instinctive and probably never fully backed by the pamphlets he used to hand out as a teenager on Montague Street. In reality, I suspect he was more motivated by his fierce hatred of the Sussex landowners and their prop policemen (or of Mosley and his Blackshirts who had taken a drubbing in Worthing in 1934) than by anything handed down to him from the Party. When his mother challenged him on Party doctrine (so he said), he had almost nothing to say, just that it was obvious that the world (that being the world of the early 1930s, truly a bad decade for good people) was being split down the middle by the arrival of that black menace Fascism, and it was time to choose sides. That choice came to him in an epiphany moment in July 1936, after seeing pictures of the gargantuan swastikas fluttering over Jesse Owens' winning dash. It was just a few months after this that he heard the call of his ancestral homeland.

More stuff here about Spain, Spanishness, he visited at some point. I'll include it tomorrow.

Sometime in the new year 1937, he handed in his overalls at the cucumber farm and travelled up to the

Communist Party offices at Covent Garden to sign his name on the dotted line. Naturally he identified with the cause of Spain, and debriefing me in the pub in Bethnal Green, he actually urged me to visit Spain myself, which he said flowed through my blood and all male Martíns' blood much more thickly than the tepid springs of England. He explained at length the joy he felt in lying to the policemen who questioned him as he waited to depart from Victoria Station, the excitement of his sojourn through Dunkirk, Paris and via the Quai d'Orsay to Marseilles, and the eventual triumph of evading the border patrols of the Pyrenees and crossing into Spain. He complained about his five weeks' training at Madrigueras, but only about the poor sanitation and the 'dirty queer element' he found running through the British ranks ('disgusting', he said, 'buggers everywhere', with unashamed malice). Otherwise he spoke proudly, even boastfully, of the booze, the foreign food, the beautiful girl who 'comforted him' (his descriptions were more explicit) in his billet and who apparently waved him off to the front in showers of tears and handkerchiefs. But this is where his pride came to an end.

The Battle of Jarama was, on paper, a victory for the 600 British volunteers who served under Tom Wintringham in the XV Brigade, but not for my father. I would call his decision to flee the destruction at 'Suicide Hill' a shrewd one, and though I *have* been softened by a lifetime in tweed I feel I would have scarpered like the rest. Despite his Spanish blood he was still an Englishman, and he must have known that he was in mortal danger and risking never seeing Albion again. For that thought, which for him came in a vision of green fields of cucumber, I am grateful since without it I might never have been born.

Again, stuff about his family, man who raised him, etc.

The facts preceding are clear. The morning of the battle he had decided to fill his water bottle with *vino tinto*, to which he (like the other poor Brits and Irish) was seldom accustomed. After ascending Suicide Hill half-cut and finally facing, for the first time, the hordes of vicious Army of Africa troops advancing across the valley, he underwent a severe and unexpected attack of drunken panic. I can't fully picture the scene, and he never properly described it, but one should imagine whizzing bullets, crashing artillery, swathes of Moroccan soldiers. Whilst his comrades fell all about him, he threw down his rifle and his helmet, and simply ran away. He ran blind, screaming for his mother, until he was hit by a Rebel bullet, which did him damage in the manner of Dr Watson. He was pulled to safety by a young Spanish infantryman, who managed to drag him to the now-infamous *white house* where the rest of Bert Overton's No. 4 Company were sheltering. But there, shining bright white in the sunshine like an Aylesbury duck on the hillside, the farmhouse was prime for the shelling. The infantryman who had saved my father, crouched with his rifle, was blown up by artillery fire. The pieces of him spattered Arthur's face. With the bombs exploding all around him, he covered himself with the cadaver of his Spanish comrade and lay there weeping, waiting for death. That is where he was found, after the smell of blood had brought all the *vino* up from his stomach, at nightfall when the Republican machine guns had finally been assembled – broken, buried and sober as a judge.

He was treated by the BMU at Villarejo de Salvanés before being despatched to hospital and eventually back to Albacete as a *mutilado*. After he was repatriated, the Communist Party of Sussex threw a bash in his honour to thank him for his service. It was at this event that he gave in his Party membership card, swapping it for the bottle that was to sustain him the rest of his life.

little bit about Reginald's own problems, alcohol, etc.

He told me about his visit to Brighton and about my mother, who was so beautiful it made him want to cry, which he did as he explained it. He told me that it was with deep remorse (but not regret) that he had fixed not to be a part of my life, seen as he was (since his return from Spain) a roving alcoholic, womaniser and in his own words a terror to children. This I accepted with good grace, as I had no other choice, and I asked him whether at any time, perhaps when he was fighting in the subsequent war, he had considered seeking me out at our home in Ringmer and making contact with me.

It was only here that the pathetic nature of his story became apparent.

My father was excused from fighting in the Second World War due to the injury he received in Spain (and no doubt because he had been a card-carrying Communist, marked conspicuously on one of Special Branch's special lists). He told me that whilst at the time he begged to be sent to Normandy, in reality he was so terrified by the prospect of facing the enemy that he thanked God regularly for the smiting he'd received. It seemed this thankfulness was twisted up painfully with the thought that he was ultimately a Lord Jim, someone who turned their back to save their own skin. This was made especially bitter by Franco's victory, which he seemed to take personal responsibility for. At his most inebriated, he told of the guilt he had felt after acquiring his medal in London in 1938, and seeing recently returned volunteers gathering at Victoria Station to march on Downing Street against the appeasement of Hitler, which he was too ashamed to join, and afterwards of the way he used his reputation as a hero to seduce women like my mother. He cried when he mentioned that, and admitted just once that he had not earned his medal but bought it for a song from a veteran who had heard Juan Negrín's farewell speech at Barcelona. He wept more as he listed hopelessly the names of the Englishmen and women whom he had seen die at Jarama, and impressed their memory so firmly onto me it was as if he were seeing visions of their ghosts float across the bar. Amongst descriptions of these people the words 'heroes', 'champions', 'warriors' and the like were repeated so often as to become meaningless. Conversely, when he described himself, his vocabulary was stunted to just one word, which he repeated with all the different shades of malice, disappointment, despair and self-pity available to him. He lived his life by that word; he sieved every last idea in his head through that word, along with every nuance of his being and all that he projected onto the world from it. He lived by that word and in the end he died by it. That word was 'coward'.

My father returned to the hospital in which he was born, Mile End Hospital on Bancroft Road, London, fifty-five years after the event, to die. I didn't hear about this until many years afterwards when I was passing the pub where we had met together that first time, when I was just a young man, and resolved to pop my head around the door to see if he was still in the old chair they kept for him beside the fireplace. The pub was wholly altered in character, this being the late 1980s, as was I, but the same landlord slouched behind the bar and it was he who passed on the medal my father had given him for want of anyone else. In the end he went the way of Toulouse-Lautrec, though with much less talent and a much bigger coffin. Perhaps I shouldn't joke about it, since despite everything Arthur John Martín was still my flesh and blood, but to say he was my father is only to say he was the *semilla de clavel* ('carnation seed') to my mother's English garden. I never felt pity for him, even when seeing him weep at the bar, bloated and blue like something fished out of the North Sea, and I never felt anything like the love I felt for Dad, a teetotaller brave enough to face a lifetime of beer brewing just to keep me smeared in purple lollipop goo. Yet when I think of Arthur John Martín and his deep unhappiness I think of the things that Spain had given him and the things it had taken away. I think of a man like any other, who was shown his true self reflected in the face of death, and saw not the strong, impassioned man he had believed himself to be, but a little boy who has wandered too far from his mummy.

At his grave in Bethnal Green I have more than once left *claveles rojos*, red carnations: the national flower of Spain. It reminds me that his was Spanish blood, wherever he happened to be born, and that his name belongs on the list of casualties that made the International Brigades' Roll of Honour, even if he died much later, having never returned to the place he fought, carrying Spain in his heart.

I'm sorry Alejandra. I don't know if that's a lot to take in or what but whenever you want to talk about it I'm here. Just call. Anyway I'll scan the original tomorrow and send it on.

I hope everything is alright with you and the bump and everything. You're in my thoughts.

Best wishes,

George

6

A BAD DECADE
FOR GOOD PEOPLE

Brighton Station was unusually busy. The commuters were there as always, though that day their usual sleepy confidence had been replaced with open chagrin at being squished in with the hundreds of protestors also heading for London. That day there would be no quiet carriage.

Across the station, the energy of the protestors was upbeat and sociable, as if they were on route to a carnival. Actually, except for the lack of rainbows and open bottles, the atmosphere reminded me of Pride – that same sense of history, identity, a confidence in their hope for change. There were people in costume – portentous Hazmat suits and others dressed as ghosts – and others with Guy Fawkes masks and face paint. They held placards with bold, all-caps slogans on them like WE CAN'T EAT MONEY. It made me feel like the boy who had pinned up anti-army posters at school, like the person I was before we'd been let down by our failed protests and was only now beginning to emerge from the dark lonely box I'd shut him in since then. Marta had noticed something of that already that morning. She and Duncan were heading to Barcombe Mills, and waiting there for him to come out of M&S she noticed how admiringly I looked at the crowds. The jolly swell of them.

'You look different, George,' she said, though I didn't answer, just hugged her and told her I'd see her as soon as I could and passed through the gates before Duncan returned.

I could see it was a bad day to travel but for once I didn't mind the crowds, noticed myself not minding, enjoyed the feeling. Actually there was something comforting about them, as if the city council had gathered them together to see me off. I took out my phone and brought up the picture of the red, squished-up baby with the blue blanket around his head – he looked like ET but I never said that aloud. Alejandra had told me he was ugly – *ugly as his father, hopefully not as stupid* – but I still didn't think it a good idea to agree.

When she didn't reply to my email with Reginald Miller's story attached, I'd decided to message her – *¿Todo bien?* – and sat in my flat waiting with no other plans at all. Just waiting, with Antonio's books back in their boxes, 'sober as a judge' as Reginald put it. Her reply came eventually in the middle of the following night – *Baby coming*. I messaged back immediately and again the next morning when I woke up, but she didn't reply. I pictured her giving birth – the sweat, the screaming, a bloody mess on the dining room floor. Watched by the bullring of photographs that hung on every wall. For some reason I couldn't get the image of her having it at home out of my head, though she'd already said she would go to the hospital at Cáceres. Would she drive herself? Surely not. Maybe the baby had been born by now, or something worse had happened. *Maybe I should message again*, I thought, and then, *Maybe I shouldn't push her...*

She named him Pablo Antonio Gutiérrez Jimenez, and I supposed his middle name was for Antonio though I'm still not sure how Spanish names work. He was born via caesarean on 21 October 2017 in Cáceres, Spain, the same day the country stripped Catalonia of its autonomous power, so Marta had explained to me. Those were the facts. What kind of world Pablo was born into was more difficult to say.

*

All the way to London the protestors chatted excitedly, and when we arrived at London Bridge I hung back to let the bulk of them wander off towards Whitehall without me, and then trailed behind them so I didn't have to rush. I went straight down to the riverbank to see the Thames. I weaved through the tourists and their selfie sticks just as I did on the seafront in Brighton, wondering why people gravitate naturally towards large bodies of water. Maybe it's psychological, something innate that social scientists are still trying to understand, something primordial. Antonio had felt that draw, I think, to be part of something vast and historical, and there is something about the Thames that makes it feel like you're seeing a chunk of history that has slivered out from the past. The oldest thing in London. Someone bumped into me from behind, a man with a briefcase who scowled as he passed. I said *Charming*, but he walked off without replying. I held on to the railings. It was too busy here.

I ducked into the Tate Modern – one of the many places in London that always feels exactly the same – and left as soon as I'd seen the Beuys room with the clay turds all over the floor. It was busy in there, too, a Saturday morning. I carried on idly past the OXO Tower, past the National Theatre, not thinking at all now, just avoiding the crowded spots around the singers, dancers, magicians, contortionists. I stopped at the stalls under Waterloo Bridge to flick through the books. I picked up a copy of Tony Blair's autobiography – a chunky hardback with a frayed dust jacket, the same book Laurie had torn up in front of the librarian in her last year of school, 718 pages, heavy as a murder weapon. *Man, she must have been strong.* A mass of steel hung above my head – the bridge that led to the LSE where I'd fled my interview and beyond that to the square where Laurie had faced up to the police and the police, that day, had won. Where the baton had opened up a vessel of strength in her that had only after seven years bled out to nothing.

I followed the flow of tourists down the river until I came to the London Eye and then, completely without thought, joined the queue. I stood there daydreaming about the Thames until someone asked me to move forward, and I suddenly realised where I was and turned into Jubilee Gardens where I was expected – looking at my phone – round about now.

I stood in front of the statue, the one I was looking for. When I'd looked it up on the map I was amazed it was in so prominent a place, right by the London Eye, somewhere I must have been before but that I'd never seen or never noticed. A tall black statue, tucked away in the heart of London, for the International Brigades.

The monument is made up of a black marble plinth with two bronze hands lifted towards the sky – one closed in a fist, the other an open palm. In the curve between them, four figures without faces follow the movement of the hands and form a tangle of limbs that could be a bull's head and horns, a horseshoe, the oarlock of a rowing boat, a wine glass. All of it is held up by something like a sexless torso, sunk into the marble like a terminator. The whole Picassoey mess reminded me of the olive trees at Guadalupe, twisting painfully on the hillside, though I'm not sure it's meant to evoke physical pain at all. It is modernist and tangled and difficult to interpret, but the words on the plinth are clear:

IN HONOUR OF OVER 2100 MEN &
WOMEN VOLUNTEERS WHO LEFT
THESE SHORES TO FIGHT SIDE
BY SIDE WITH THE SPANISH PEOPLE
IN THEIR HEROIC STRUGGLE
AGAINST FASCISM 1936-1939
MANY WERE WOUNDED AND
MAIMED 526 WERE KILLED
THEIR EXAMPLE INSPIRED
THE WORLD

It was cool to the touch. I took out the picture of Arthur John Martín, though it was hard to look at him now without seeing him leaning against the bar with his face bloated and blue. Was this statue for him? If I'd read his story independently of Antonio, without ever having known him, I would have thought Arthur John Martín was just a man who threw himself into a conflict that wasn't his, and was chased home at the tip of a bayonet. But Antonio had seen something different. Perhaps Antonio, with whatever sense of valour he'd inherited from his Civil War stories, would have said no, this monument wasn't for him, it wasn't for those who ran away. But instinctively I felt differently. It was for those who fought and those who ran away indiscriminately. It was simply for those who had the strength to raise their hands in the first place.

I laid the photograph down at the foot of the statue, and then rose and looked at the river and thought of Antonio. Someone tapped me on the shoulder and my daydream evaporated.

Helena's smile was open and bright and at odds with her smart suit and polished shoes, so I thought. She hugged me and while she did I looked at the statue and promised myself I would come back here regularly, once I got set up in London. That decision, by now, was made.

'I see you've become a bigwig,' I said.

'That's right, Georgie.' She took my elbow. 'The biggest of wigs.' And then stopped as if remembering something. 'Do you want to stay here?'

I think she meant where it was quiet.

'No,' I said. 'Let me walk you to the site.'

Assumedly the photograph sat there a while on the stone, perhaps handled by a tourist and placed back or taken and slipped into a scrapbook somewhere. Or else pecked at by a pigeon, flipped around, trodden into the pavement, kicked into a drain. Or – which is what I like to imagine, though it's sentimental and false – lifted by the October breeze and swept into the river to float along the Thames, under the bridges and out to sea.

We walked together slowly down the South Bank. People of all kinds rushed around us, pedestrians and cyclists and grown men on little scooters. It's sometimes easy to forget in the bubble of Brighton that there are all kinds of people in the world, with all kinds of cultures and beliefs and idiosyncrasies. Losing myself among them, I felt the thrill of London again. Being lost in something vast but still feeling the rush of moving forward, moving forward safely and with purpose. This is what I wanted.

'Do you have a plan for world domination?' I asked Helena.

'Someone has to fill the role.'

I could picture her at a lectern with half a dozen microphones poking towards her, speaking to the cameras and impressing even the hardened journalists with that honest, unashamed way she spoke. She would be great on TV. I asked her about her job – she told me it was busy as hell but she'd managed to take a day's holiday to join the protest. She was helping to coordinate it. From the few modest things she said I deduced that she was a much bigger wig even than she'd suggested. Actually she was the first person I knew who had a genuinely significant job – I mean someone who impacted on the world professionally. Not that Marta or the rest didn't impact on the world – they did in their own ways, Duncan too of course – but being with Helena was like being with someone who you might see on *Question Time* one night while flicking through the channels. I was sure that was her destination – *Question Time* and select committees and all the rest – though more than that she was destined for great things. For actual *great things*.

She asked me about Brighton and my joblessness and Professor Reggie Miller, which Duncan had told her all about, and mentioned the dinner party in September.

'Yes,' I said. 'I saw them at the house. Just once.'

'Duncan has invited me down to visit. To see his shed.'

'Of course. "The Bunker". Will you go?'

'Not at the moment. When I have time.'

We approached Westminster Bridge quietly and the memory of the confrontation at the Cowley Club, the last time the four of us had been in the same room, passed between us. Or maybe it was only me who still thought about it. Though then I thought of Laurie, languishing in the villages, doing whatever she was doing, and knew that wasn't true.

Helena stopped me by the steps. 'He told me you two spoke.'

'Me and Duncan? Yes, we spoke.' I said it abruptly. I guess I still had strong feelings about him, even if I'd told him I forgave him. From the riverbank I noticed a couple of protestor's flags on the bridge. A blue-and-green icon of the planet Earth.

'You know how good he was to me in London.' She looked down at her feet. 'I don't think I would have been alright without him.'

'Yes, I remember. I never told anyone about it.'

'Not even your sister?'

'No. Perhaps I should have done.'

'No,' she said. 'No, that wouldn't have mattered.'

She led us up the steps to Westminster Bridge and we joined the procession shuffling down the pavement in the direction of the Abbey. Thousands of people were gathering with their flags and placards and chants about fossil fuels and the polar icecaps. Helena kept us as best she could to the edges of the throng – I think she guessed I was nervous. But I wasn't, not really. I looked up at Big Ben against the grey sky, and listened to the sound of people marching, and thought suddenly that there was nothing more British in the world, which was a new thought for me entirely. Somehow I'd never reconciled our country's backwards island mentality, the kind that keeps the toffs in power, with the long history of protest that Duncan celebrated in his postcards and posters – Kett's Rebellion, the Levellers, Peterloo, the General Strike, Women's Suffrage, the

Jarrow March, Kinder Scout, the Bristol bus boycott, the very first Brighton Pride in 1972, the miner's strike, the Poll Tax riots, the marches against Iraq, the student protests that had set everything off for Laurie and I and where I'd lost my faith. All that had been a part of British history, and these protests were part of that same endlessly rejuvenating history. Brighton stood with that – I could see that now. Even with all its blind faith in itself and its bacchanalia.

It was a new thought, all of this, and all I really understood was that it made me feel safe among these people who were working for change.

We moved with them north towards Whitehall, right past the Cenotaph, which I realised I'd never seen, and when they veered off towards Downing Street we stood among them on Parliament Street, right in the thick of it. It was the same route the Spanish volunteers took when they got back in 1938, the procession that Arthur John Martín had been too ashamed to join. Today there were people all around, jostling us as the street filled out. Helena asked again if I'd like to talk somewhere else – *away from the fray* – but I told her it was fine. Still, she led me to the side and we stood up against a low wall. She looked at me as she had on the village green at Ringmer, eager to talk.

'Have you seen Laurie?' she asked.

'I haven't spoken to her since Pride.'

'George. That's a long time.'

'I know. I know. But she hasn't called.'

'So she doesn't know you're coming?'

'No. I haven't told Dad either. I only decided this morning.' I poked at the wall, some loose masonry crumbled off. 'I really thought she'd call me – after I got back from Spain, I mean – but she never even bothered. I mean, she hasn't said a word.'

Helena put her hand on my shoulder. 'Maybe she doesn't feel up to it.'

'What does that mean? She obviously knows what happened to Antonio. Why couldn't she call?'

'Maybe she's ashamed.'

'Bollocks.'

I was losing my temper just as I'd done on the village green at Ringmer – not with Helena but with her rationale, her reasonableness. For whatever reason, the story of the man who drowned in the *aldgy* popped into my head. And after that the reservoir, the shoreline at the West Pier, the rubber brick at the bottom of the swimming pool that I'd nearly drowned trying to retrieve. The noise was rising – whistles and air horns. Someone beat a drum.

'I used to go to things like this all the time…' I said, as much to myself as to her.

Two police officers passed us on the pavement, their extendable batons swinging from their belts. The polite face of it all that I'd been so scared of for so long.

'You know Laurie's scar?' I said it without thinking, and then I realised I was about to dredge up what had happened all that time ago. Had I held on to it for that long?

'Yes, the one from the riot, you mean. I know all about it.'

'Not all about it.'

I watched the policemen walking away and a few protestors step aside and let them pass. It looked like they were sharing a joke – they were all laughing as they passed each other.

'George.'

Helena's hand was back on my shoulder and she was smiling. That warm, genuine smile that made all her struggle to improve things make sense. I tried to match it – failed, I think. And then I simply told her.

The train, the crowds, the flags. The boy beside us having his head struck. The swell, the violence, the police, the stranger. Whitechapel. It came out of me quickly, all jumbled and inarticulate, and as I spoke it felt like I was confessing something from my childhood, something silly that should have long been forgotten. It all sounded so unimportant. The whole story passed within just a few minutes. Less.

She answered softly. 'Is that it?'

'Well. Yes.'

'George. You have nothing to be ashamed of.'

'But I lied to her. I mean, I blurted it out at Pride, but I lied to her for years.'

She smiled. 'Everybody lies.'

'I just let her go on thinking I was someone I wasn't.'

Someone official-looking appeared and called for Helena. She turned and held up a finger and they waited for her there. The professional.

She wasn't smiling when she said: 'If you want to make it right with her, do it now.'

I just want to make it right. That's what I'd told her the night she came to the Shoulder of Mutton to pull me out of my rut and drag me to Brighton, when I was thinking how we were already different people even if we weren't. I'd let so much time pass.

Helena held my eye. 'She's your sister. She loves you, George – so do I. We all love you very much.'

I looked at her standing there among the people and I saw her for what she was. The strength of her, shed of all the people who would slow her down. I thought again of Laurie and how I had tried to keep us afloat, as Helena had tried. *Those who fought and those who ran away indiscriminately. Those who had the strength to raise their hands.*

I was welling up again. It was becoming a thing. 'You will answer my calls, won't you? When you're Prime Minister.'

The official reminded her she had to go.

'Of course I will.' She smiled. 'Are you tempted to stick around?'

'I can't. I have to be at London Bridge for three.'

'I mean in general.'

She looked at me then as if she understood that this is where I was meant to be, or at least that I wasn't meant to be in Brighton, on the dole, waiting to find another bar job or whatever else. She offered to help set me up when I got to London, if I wanted to come. She had a sofa, and knew a bunch of people who might be able to help. That was who she was.

'Anyway, you'll have to excuse me,' she said, checking her watch. 'Can't stand on the sidelines forever.' And then she hugged me and ran her fingers up the back of my neck before she turned away.

She left me there with the people chanting *Who are you? The people!* and I thought of 'Jarama Valley' and the songs Alejandra played in the yellow sports car. I had no idea what would happen with this new movement of theirs – I'd missed that whole thing really – but whatever happened I sensed these people would keep fighting, that people like Helena will always be here. In Brighton or London or in the villages that feel so much like the middle of nowhere. Laurie was one of those people, for all her faults. Those people are everywhere.

I thought of her and how she might at that moment have been putting in a shift at the Shoulder of Mutton, miserable and defeated and probably seething under Dad's roof, poor girl. Poor woman. I thought of her here at the protest, where she should have been, only without the petty teenage frustration that got her nowhere, and without the grand visions that she thought would take her to Syria and put a rifle in her hand. I'd been angry with her myself now for many months, still was. But she remained the one person I was *committed to*, Alejandra's words. Even if I didn't see it until now.

I left the protestors at Whitehall, hollering on the PM's doorstep, and walked back through the crowds towards the river.

The Shoulder of Mutton never changes. Those things that had always been there were still there when I returned – the black beams, the sagging ceiling, the frosted light, the crude doodles on the tables, all of that. Dad would never change the pictures on the wall or get the smell of hops out of the ancient carpet. Getting rid of a single one of these things would be like removing a vital organ, and once it had been removed the place would die quickly and naturally to no one's surprise. Whether you loved it or hated it, this was the way it had to be. I saw Dad at the bar, passing little mixer bottles to someone under the counter, stains down the front of his Ben Sherman, face as pink as bacon. When he'd finished Laurie stood and brushed herself down and neither of them noticed me come in, nobody did. I looked over them like a stranger – the farmers, the factory workers, the alcoholics who'd been propping up the bar since I worked there and long before. I watched the kids by the window in hoodies for their prospective universities, lit suddenly by a car pulling up outside. For a moment their happy, chattering faces shone coldly in the white light.

I'd rehearsed my lines on the walk down but now I was inside they disappeared into the din from the jukebox – *This is England*-style music, Bad Manners or something like it. My nerves rose gently. *Rumba la, rumba la, rumba la...* Dad dipped into the backroom. Laurie's eyes glanced over the pub and found me finally at the door. She saw me but her face didn't change. So that was where we were. I walked across to greet her but then neither of us moved for a hug or a handshake. She just said *Hi* and I said *Hi* and then the moment for touching each other quickly passed and left us in that quiet space where the rules had changed.

'Do you want a drink?' she said. 'I won't charge you.'

And again things didn't feel like they were going to plan. 'IPA, please.'

When Laurie pulled the pump I noticed the black-ink cross was gone from her hand. She wore a shirt I'd never seen before, a polo shirt like Dad might have worn. I thought it looked expensive. I waited in silence with a new thought sweeping over me, that perhaps I'd made an awful mistake in coming here, here to this place specifically, with no invitation. She set my pint down.

'Will you have a break soon?' I asked, but before she could answer Dad appeared from the backroom and his face lit up at the sight of me.

'Georgie!' He slapped Laurie on the back and then leant over the bar to clap me one across the shoulder. 'Grab an apron, you can do me a shift.'

He laughed, I laughed, Laurie didn't. 'Great to see you, Dad.'

Laurie whispered in his ear and then poured herself a half. Then I knew for sure that the whole straight edge thing was over, maybe for good. She led us to a table just off the end of the bar, where the old carpet was worn white around the line of the oche, right where Dad once took a dart to the foot.

'It's good to see you,' I told her.

'Yes.' Her voice was tired, maybe just from work. 'Long time.'

I wanted to ask so many things but instead I just said: 'How's work?' like *How is the old place*.

'It's alright. As long as I get everything done he stays off my back.'

Though instinctively I disbelieved her.

'How is he?' I asked, thinking it would force the truth out of her. I braced for the tirade.

'He's fine. I give him shit but he's alright.'

In the three months since she'd returned, Laurie's accent had already relaxed some way back into the light Sussex drawl that had always been more prominent in her than me. I imagined her hearing a recording of the sharper voice she'd used in Brighton, the city voice that so many people develop when they move down. Maybe it would have made her wince, though I think it was, in its own way, just as genuine as her village voice. She had loved Helena – really loved her and I'm sure still did – so she had to forgive herself for wanting to impress her. If she was able to.

She looked flushed out when she said: 'So you're moving back to London,' and sipped her half. Dad must have told her. I wondered how much they spoke about me.

'I might be. I have an interview next month. I'm a bit apprehensive, actually.'

'You love it.' She meant London, I guessed, or city life. 'I know you do.'

'Well, it feels like the right time.'

A rising, masculine *weyyyyy* lifted from the pool table. The belly of a middle-aged man hung over the cushion as he broke.

'How have you found being back here?' I said. But I couldn't hold her eye.

'I like it.'

'Laurie—'

'What do you expect me to say?' A false energy, not quite enough for genuine anger. 'I like being back. I'm sorry if that's hard to believe.'

'I do believe you. Why wouldn't I?'

'You thought I'd be miserable. Well, I'm not.'

'Good.' I fell back in my seat, my own anger rising. 'Good for you.'

She turned her head and I saw the scar above her eye and wondered if it would be her or me that brought up what had happened at Pride. Or neither of us.

'I saw Helena,' I said, 'in London. I wasn't sure if I should mention it.'

'That's fine. How is she?'

'Seems very busy.'

'I can imagine.'

She failed to look fine. She'd never called Helena as far as I knew, never sent a message, even on her birthday. I'm sure that fact hung over her. I had so many questions and with every one I asked the night seemed to get further and further from how I'd rehearsed it in my mind.

'I'm going to Spain at some point,' I said. 'For a holiday. Once I've got a job sorted.'

'To Guadalupe?'

She must have remembered the name from ages ago, whenever Antonio had first mentioned it to her. I was surprised it stuck in her head.

'That's right. Antonio's sister has just had a baby.'

She looked away and her tongue ran anxiously over her lip,

just for a second. She cleared her throat. 'I was sorry to hear about Antonio.'

I put my glass down and pushed it away from me. This, more than anything, was what I should have prepared for. But I hadn't found the strength to do it. 'You could have rung.'

'Yes, I should have done.'

'But you didn't.'

She wouldn't look at me. 'I'm sorry.'

And then it was coming out. 'You knew Antonio had died but you didn't ring.' This was the last way I wanted this to go but the words came out of me before I could stop them. At least I was saying something.

'You humiliated me,' she said.

'That was a mistake, and anyway you were being a bitch. It doesn't justify you not being there for me.'

Her fingers balled into a fist. 'I'm not a child, George.' She spoke through her teeth. 'You don't need to punish me.'

I moved to scold her about that whole Kurdish fantasy of hers and the way she'd called me a coward and everything else but then a hand appeared on her shoulder. It was Dad, swaying on his feet, with the smell of hash blowing from his jacket, the same old smell. He looked tired now like his daughter. His face was turning from red to blue – you could see the booze in his skin, drawing the colour to the surface. I'd have to help with that at some point too, if I could.

'Back at the bar, lazy arse. Foster's needs changing.'

He pulled Laurie's shoulder. I was surprised when she let him – maybe she was that tired, maybe she'd given up completely. Dad's voice was low and slurred. He aimed it at me. 'She's moody but she can lift a barrel.' He straightened out with difficulty, seemed to realise he was missing something, tottered off to serve someone at the bar.

Laurie stood and took her empty glass with her.

'I'm not going home yet,' I said, arms folded, petulant.

'Fine.' Her face was cold and still. 'You can keep drinking till closing.'

So I sat there in the corner, just waiting, glancing occasionally at the picture still hanging behind the bar. Me, Laurie, Dad, Mum. Skewed now at an angle, as if someone had knocked it.

The bell rang at midnight. At the bar, one of the young lads was leaning over the counter and Dad was prising his fingers from one of the pumps. The kid fell back and knocked the WKD out of a teenage girl's hand. Laurie acknowledged none of this – she just carried on wiping down the bar as if nothing was happening. People were slow to leave and Dad was slow to shut everything down and cash up, just like always. I offered to help but Laurie wouldn't let me, so I just watched her getting on with the old routine that had for a brief stint been my job, setting everything down, cleaning, preparing to lock up. When she'd finished she took a jacket from the peg, a black donkey jacket with leather shoulders, and walked out of the door. I followed.

A light mist covered the muddy Land Rovers and derestricted scooters that the kids from the villages still used. Dad's Mini was there, the same old one with the chequered roof and the bumper sticker on the back that read SKA'D FOR LIFE. We stood in the car park with the night air cool on my face.

Dad stumbled out, fell onto the door of the Mini, fumbled with his keys. Laurie walked over to him as if she was going to hit him.

'Give me the keys, Dad.'

'What? I'm fine.' He slipped on a puddle of black leaves and bashed his knee.

'I'll drive, just give me the keys.'

'Bugger off.'

He slipped again and Laurie held him up. She took the keys out of his hand and held them out for me.

'I can't drive,' I said.

She pushed them into my hand and told me to unlock the car. It was difficult dragging Dad into the back and after he was shut inside I could hear him groaning.

We sat in the Mini with the silly boy-racer interior. When Laurie started the engine the subwoofers came on with a ska song I remembered from barbecues in the pub garden. Dad's voice came sloppily from the back. 'Skinhead Love Affair', in the same awful karaoke slur he'd always sung it in.

I looked across at Laurie. Perhaps she wanted to be angry but she couldn't hold a straight face. We laughed as she pulled away and Dad laughed too.

It wasn't possible to sit in the car without saying anything but we couldn't speak freely with Dad in the back, no matter how pissed he was. So we spoke about my interview for the job in London, which I realised by then I desperately wanted, though I didn't say that. We spoke about the government, just briefly. Laurie was pessimistic, more deeply pessimistic than I ever remembered her, and when she had to say one of their names

– Johnson, Rees-Mogg, Gove – she lost even more energy, so much so that for the first time in our lives I could see she didn't want to talk politics. We stayed off that, and off Brighton and Helena and most of all Antonio, so that all we really had was small talk – mundane stuff like how she'd finally gotten a driving licence – which pained us both. We spoke to each other like old school friends who'd bumped into each other by accident, catching up after a long absence, ready to part casually for another few years. I wouldn't let things stay like that.

The houses in our cul-de-sac are identical in every way but for the little brass numbers underneath the doorbells. Laurie pulled Dad out of the car and opened the front door for him. In the dark hallway I could see a mess of muddy boots and unopened catalogues. Dad tried to dribble out an apology and Laurie whispered: 'It's alright, Dad, it's alright'. Laurie hustled him into the house, muttered something I couldn't make out and shut Dad in the living room. I pictured myself in that state. It had been a while.

'Come on,' said Laurie. She gathered the collar of her donkey jacket around her neck. 'Let's go down to the end of the drive. Otherwise Dad will never let us talk.'

The night was cold and the streetlights were off. We set off in silence towards the main road, walking soberly in the light of her torch. There were no stars in the sky, you couldn't see them for the clouds. Opportunities to say how I felt came and went. And then we were quiet again.

In search of something to say, anything that might lead us back to something important, I told her about Antonio's *bisabuelo*. I told her about the books and the visit to the care home, and about how I felt when I typed up Reginald's chapter for Alejandra.

'To be honest, I was tempted not to send it at all.'

She asked me why. We were stood so far apart.

'I don't know,' I said. 'It did Antonio that much damage.'

'You shouldn't put that much faith in people.'

I wasn't sure if she meant me or herself or everyone. 'No, I suppose you shouldn't.'

We stood there in the dark and only eventually, when the tension became too great, did Laurie say: 'I'm sorry I didn't call after he died. I am.'

As soon as she said it, all the anger I'd felt against her in the past few months slipped away. I was tired and full of love and my voice was quiet and unsure. But I was ready.

'What happened with the police?'

She sniffed. 'Nothing. A caution.'

I thought again about the riot and that *if the policeman's baton had found Laurie half an inch lower she would be blind in one eye*, that old thought. I remembered the stitching and the gooey rivets and the halo of yellow bruising. All that, and the thought that *if things had been even just slightly different, she would be stood here now with a patch over one eye and it would all be my fault*. Time was bearing down on me, I could feel it now. The whole weight of the decade that neither of us had been able to shrug off. I gathered strength. 'Can we talk about what I said? About the riot, I mean.'

She ran her finger over her scar but she didn't answer. I pictured the man who had pulled her through the line, a man whose face I never saw at the time. For whatever reason I pictured him with Antonio's face, that blank sort of look he had sometimes. Like he was from another world.

Laurie stopped under a lamp post and shoved her hands in

her pockets. 'Look. Did you come back just to talk shit or what?'

I stopped and mustered myself. Helena's voice came to me then, simple and clear. *We all love you very much.*

'No.' The night air was in my lungs but I had to stay firm. 'I just want to—'

'George.' Her voice was still stern. An adult's voice. 'I'm here, I'm happy. Why are you bringing me this shit now?'

'Because I don't believe you.'

'I'm fine.'

'You hate it here, I know you do.'

'I don't hate it here.'

'Laurie—'

'I fucked up. I thought I could be smart like you and go out and make a difference. But obviously the world doesn't want that.'

'That's not true.'

'Why did you encourage me at all? If you were going to pack it all in yourself?'

'I just got confused.'

'I could have stayed here and carved out a life for myself.'

'But you're not happy here!'

'So what?' She lifted her boot over the low branch of a tree. 'Who's – fucking – happy?'

On the word *happy* her boot came down and the branch split. I could see the white insides that looked alive and vulnerable beneath the bark. And then Laurie was sitting down beside it holding her knees in her hands and looking down into her lap. Like a little girl.

'Laurie, please talk to me.'

You are the strong one and I am the smart one – that's what I'd once thought. Except that it had been that same strength that made her so vulnerable. The toughest girl in school, the tomboy, strong enough to tear a hardback in half, the girl even the boys wanted to fight. Who wanted to fight everyone else.

'I don't care that you didn't pull me through the line,' she said. 'That doesn't make a difference to me. I don't even care that you let me think you did.'

I'd prepared myself for this moment for so many years, through all our disappointments and regrets, and now it was here I had nothing to say. I looked again at the clouds above our heads, slashed with black sky. All the damage that wore away at us – Laurie and I and the rest of them. All the bruising and the scars.

She went on: 'All I wanted was for you to be there for me. Not then, whatever happened – I don't care. I just wanted you to be there when I needed you.'

I crouched down and put my arm around her and she flinched when I pulled her into me but she didn't stop me.

'I'm such a coward,' she said.

I held her in my grip, I wanted to shake it out of her. 'What do you mean?'

'Rojava. Syria, I mean. I still could have gone. I got in touch with them and I was speaking to some people but then after the arrest…' Her voice was broken now, laid bare. 'I'm such a coward.'

'It's alright,' I said, but that was all I had.

I wanted to tell her that just because everything had gone to shit it didn't mean life was over. There were new challenges now, new stuff to take on. Even if the next decade might be worse than the last, or if indeed everything we knew was about to go to shit, which maybe it was. I thought of Alejandra and her baby and the dining room all full of pictures of Antonio, the best moments of his life. Maybe I'd had the best of mine already and maybe Laurie had had hers. It didn't matter. None of it was over.

'I'm here for you,' I said, and I held her there beside the broken branch while she held her knees in her hands and a sound came from her – a low sound choked with phlegm. The sound of my sister crying.

'Laurie…' I gripped her by the jacket and she held on to me before the sobbing started. Her pain sounded physical, something in her chest or stomach, like a disease working its way out. I just held her there and realised that for whatever reason I wasn't crying. No, I was just holding her.

'Listen to me.' I took her face in my hands and saw the red blotches around her eyes and the long curve of her scar in the dim light. The smooth skin shining like a medal. 'I know I'm not the person you thought I was. I'm not the person I thought I was either. Whatever I've done, I'm here for you now.'

A loud breath left her like the life leaving her body. 'Forget about it, George,' though I couldn't tell whether the words were bitter or resigned or accepting or at peace.

'Laurie—'

'Alright.'

She sniffed and muttered *Fuck it* and clambered to her feet. I wanted to grab her but she was already walking off, off again down the darkness of the country lane while the Sussex night closed in and the clouds bore down on us. Lit by the light of her torch that cut through the blackness for me to follow. I caught her up and we walked on, matching steps, and by the time we reached the conifers my teeth were chattering and there was still so much left to say.

'Come back to the house,' I said. 'We'll have a drink.'

She shook her head.

'Fine.' I shivered, stood firm. 'Then I'll walk with you until you're ready to go back.'

'No, George.'

'Laurie, let me—'

'I said no.'

I felt desperate then, like something awful was happening that I couldn't prevent, but still the right words wouldn't come. She turned to walk off. I felt like I was watching Antonio walking into the sea with his clothes folded up on the shoreline. I felt like time was slipping away.

'Laurie—' And then I was thinking of the hospital at Whitechapel, though now it was as if that whole thing had happened to two completely different people. 'Laurie, I *am* sorry.'

She stopped and turned back. She came up to my face and she was huge and dark and belonged completely to the village. She put both hands on my shoulders and looked down at me. Her strength was back and I wondered how I could break it down again. I would have to learn how, just like other men learn how to shoot or fight or chop wood.

'I know,' she said.

I thought that was it. I really thought that was the end of it. But then she put both arms around me and squeezed me, and I looked over her shoulder where the wind had blown the clouds to pieces, and where the hills now cut their hunched, painful silhouette against the stars. I looked up at the millions of stars separated by their millions of light years, swimming in a shimmering blur with the water in my eyes, and I felt the love wash over me in a cool, black wave. The feeling rising through my body like bubbles. The weight of my heart sinking into the depths of it. And the stars slowly blurring into one.

She let a hand linger on my neck as she turned, and then walked away and said over her shoulder: 'We can talk about your moving to London later. Maybe I'll come and crash on your floor one night.'

I could have followed her to wherever she was going, and at the time I wanted to follow her but my legs just didn't move. When she walked off I felt one more wave of love, strong enough that it felt like it might wash the countryside away, before the feeling was drowned by my tiredness and by the sense that yes, this is how it's supposed to be, how it was always going to be. Like the West Pier off Brighton whose charred skeleton Antonio and I had sat admiring for so long, jutting out of the sea in all its hollowed pride, like the whole city and its grandeur and grubby underbelly. As if yes, that was all natural and good – so I told myself – and yes, I had time to reach out to my sister, though how much time I couldn't say. Plenty of time, our whole long, difficult lifetimes. Or maybe less time than I thought.

'Wake me up when you get in,' I shouted, and she lifted a hand in the air but didn't answer.

I could have followed her, but instead I stood there by the conifers, with the wind rushing gently around me like the sound of the sea at Brighton, and watched her walk down the country lane with the stars shining statically above her, led by the light from her torch, which slowly faded and disappeared.

Between 1936 and 1938, around 2,500 British and Irish volunteers joined the International Brigades to fight against the Francoist invasion of Republican Spain. These men and women, many of whom gave their lives, entered willingly into what was ostensibly the first conflict in the European fight against fascism. Returning home, many were branded as 'premature anti-Fascists', and later broadly discouraged by the UK government from fighting in the Second World War.

Since the beginning of the Syrian civil war in 2011, dozens of British volunteers have joined the YPG and YPJ in defence of the autonomous democratic region of Rojava. Among these was Anna Campbell, a twenty-six-year-old woman from Lewes who lost her life in the Turkish invasion of Afrin on 15 March 2018. Two months after her death, a mural by the artist Agent Petrusconi went up over Morley Street in Brighton. The inscription reads: *I want change. I want a revolution.*

ACKNOWLEDGEMENTS

For their early feedback, I'd like to thank Fraser Bryant, Yuemeng Ge, George Green, Chris Hollands, Sam Jordison, Nick Joslin, Georgie Kett, Graham Mort, Kelsey Pinna, Catryn Thomas, Deborah Thwaites and Fabian Wagner. For research help, translations, advice and encouragement, thank you to Alice Ash, Richard Baxell, Rose Campbell, Melanie Damret, Kit de Waal, Rónán Hession, Emily King, Agent Petrusconi and Anna Vaught. For practical help, a huge thank you to staff members and administrators at Felixstowe Library, Lancaster Central Library, Lancaster University and Arts Council England. For their faith in my work, I'd like to thank Robert Harries and Richard Lewis Davies at Parthian Books, alongside Emily Courdelle for her wonderful front cover and all those who read and endorsed the novel in the run-up to publication. For their enduring support, thank you to Mum, Dad, Adam, Emily, Margot and my extended family. And finally, for sharing their lives with me, thank you to Sandra Cardenas, Francesca Pridham, Javier Rodriguez Jimenez and the people of Brighton and Hove.

PARTHIAN

Fiction

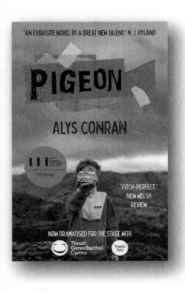

Pigeon
Alys Conran
ISBN 978-1-910901-23-6
£8.99 • Paperback

**Shortlisted for the
Dylan Thomas Prize**

'An exquisite novel by
a great new talent'
M. J. Hyland

Ironopolis
Glen James Brown
ISBN 978-1-914595-60-8
£10.99 • Paperback

**Shortlisted for
the Portico Prize and
the Orwell Prize for
Political Fiction**

'A triumph'
The Guardian

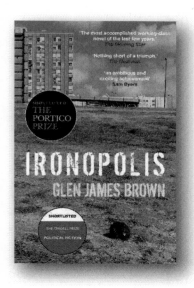

PARTHIAN Fiction

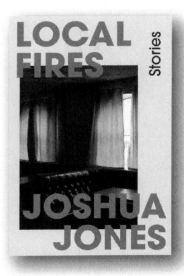

Local Fires
Joshua Jones
ISBN 978-1-913640-59-0
£10 • Paperback w/flaps

In this stunning series of
interconnected tales, fires both
literal and metaphorical, local and
all-encompassing, blaze together
to herald the emergence of a
singular new Welsh literary voice.

Published 7 September 2023

The Half-life of Snails
Philippa Holloway
ISBN 978-1-914595-52-3
£9.99 • Paperback w/flaps

**Longlisted for
the RSL Ondaatje Prize**

'suspenseful and delicate'
Jenn Ashworth

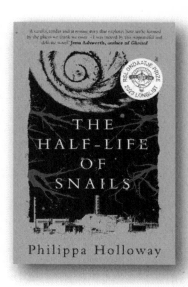

PARTHIAN   A Carnival of Voices

Parthian started publishing with a loan from the Prince's Youth Business Trust in 1993, a business start-up course provided by the Enterprise Allowance Scheme and one book – *Work, Sex and Rugby* by Lewis Davies, who was also one of the founding partners. The other partners were Ravi Pawar and Gillian Griffiths. Parthian's first novel became a Welsh bestseller and eventually a modern Welsh classic. Our second book was a selection of winning stories in the Rhys Davies short story competition. Working with support from the Rhys Davies Trust and first the Arts Council of Wales and then the Books Council of Wales Parthian has developed into a leading independent publisher of fiction, narratives of the culture and society of Wales as well as fiction in translation from many European languages into English and occasionally Welsh.

We aim to work collaboratively and to develop new initiatives.

We aim to give new writers as much development support as we can. Our recent successes include writers such as Richard Owain Roberts (Not the Booker Prize winner 2020), Alys Conran (Wales Book of the Year winner 2017), Tristan Hughes (Edward Stanford Travel Writing Award – Fiction with a Sense of Place winner 2018), Lloyd Markham (Betty Trask Award winner 2018), Glen James Brown (Orwell and Portico Prize shortlists 2019), Auguste Corteau and Bianca Bellova (EBRD prize 2022 & 2023), and Philippa Holloway (Ondaatje Award long-list 2023).

An engagement with the culture of Wales through our Library of Wales series has reached fifty titles of classic writing. The series has been a fifteen-year publishing project with support from the Welsh Government which has seen a significant investment in the literary and educational culture of Wales, with sales of over 100,000 copies across print and digital formats. It was edited first by Professor Dai Smith and now by Professor Kirsti Bohata. It has changed the perception of Welsh writing.

The Modern Wales series, a collaboration with The Rhys Davies Trust, also edited by Dai Smith, takes a look at the recent history and culture of Wales. While a growing poetry list, edited by Susie Wild, continues to offer fresh perspectives on creativity.

Over the years we have developed good translation links throughout Europe and beyond, and our books have appeared in over fifty foreign-language editions.

We aim to produce attractive and readable books in our areas of interest: new writing, the heart of Welsh culture and a view to the wider world through our Parthian Carnival.

Please get in touch:
Richard Lewis Davies, Gill Griffiths, Susie Wild, Carly Holmes,
Ela Griffiths, Gina Rathbone, Rob Harries